PRAISE FOR THE NOVELS OF
VIRGINIA KANTRA

continued . . .

Carolina Home

VIRGINIA KANTRA

BERKLEY SENSATION, NEW YORK

THE BERKLEY PUBLISHING GROUP
Published by the Penguin Group
Penguin Group (USA) Inc.
375 Hudson Street, New York, New York 10014, USA

Penguin Group (Canada), 90 Eglinton Avenue East, Suite 700, Toronto, Ontario M4P 2Y3, Canada
(a division of Pearson Penguin Canada Inc.) • Penguin Books Ltd., 80 Strand, London WC2R 0RL,
England • Penguin Group Ireland, 25 St. Stephen's Green, Dublin 2, Ireland (a division of Penguin
Books Ltd.) • Penguin Group (Australia), 250 Camberwell Road, Camberwell, Victoria 3124, Australia
(a division of Pearson Australia Group Pty. Ltd.) • Penguin Books India Pvt. Ltd., 11 Community
Centre, Panchsheel Park, New Delhi—110 017, India • Penguin Group (NZ), 67 Apollo Drive,
Rosedale, Auckland 0632, New Zealand (a division of Pearson New Zealand Ltd.) • Penguin Books
(South Africa) (Pty.) Ltd., 24 Sturdee Avenue, Rosebank, Johannesburg 2196, South Africa

Penguin Books Ltd., Registered Offices: 80 Strand, London WC2R 0RL, England

This is a work of fiction. Names, characters, places, and incidents either are the product of the author's
imagination or are used fictitiously, and any resemblance to actual persons, living or dead, business
establishments, events, or locales is entirely coincidental. The publisher does not have any control over
and does not assume any responsibility for author or third-party websites or their content.

CAROLINA HOME

A Berkley Sensation Book / published by arrangement with the author

PUBLISHING HISTORY
Berkley Sensation mass-market edition / July 2012

Copyright © 2012 by Virginia Kantra.
Excerpt from *Carolina Girl* by Virginia Kantra copyright © 2013 by Virginia Kantra.
Cover art by Tony Mauro.
Cover design by Rita Frangie.

ISBN: 978-0-425-25093-8

BERKLEY SENSATION®
Berkley Sensation Books are published by The Berkley Publishing Group,
a division of Penguin Group (USA) Inc.,
375 Hudson Street, New York, New York 10014.
BERKLEY SENSATION® is a registered trademark of Penguin Group (USA) Inc.
The "B" design is a trademark of Penguin Group (USA) Inc.

PRINTED IN THE UNITED STATES OF AMERICA

10   9   8   7   6   5   4

ALWAYS LEARNING   PEARSON

To Michael.
You are my home.

ACKNOWLEDGMENTS

Dare Island exists nowhere and everywhere along the North Carolina coast. You can find pieces of it, as I did, from Manteo to Hatteras, Ocracoke to Swan Quarter, in Emerald Isle, Topsail Beach, Fort Fisher, and Southport. To the many residents who shared their love of the Outer Banks and inner islands with me, thank you.

Like an island, a book requires a community to bring it to life. Special thanks to Francis Castiller, M.D., and Angela R. Narron for their expertise and patience with my questions; to Robin Rue and Beth Miller of Writers House for their wonderful suggestions; to Cindy Hwang (Best Editor Ever) and Leis Pederson at Berkley for their hard work and constant support; to Rita Frangie and Tony Mauro for another fabulous cover; and to Carolyn Martin and Mike Ritchey, who read every word and critiqued every scene. Sometimes twice.

One

Matt Fletcher didn't go looking for trouble. Most times, it just found him.

His life was changing around him, slipping away like the sand of the Carolina coastline, and there wasn't a damn thing he or God or the Army Corps of Engineers could do about it. But a day working on the water gave him something to hold on to. Sweat and salt cured everything in time.

The smell of fish and fuel, mud and marsh grass thickened the air as he turned the *Sea Lady II* toward home. The September heat pressed down, flattening the inlet like glass. The twin engines chugged. Water churned, attracting a flock of greedy gulls that cried and hovered in his wake.

He navigated the fifty-three-foot *Lady* past bobbing boats and narrow slips, heading for the wharf and weathered shack that served as office for his tiny charter fleet. With Joshua back in school and unable to crew, Matt had been forced to leave the original *Sea Lady* in dock and bring his father,

Tom, along as mate. It hurt leaving a boat behind, losing business this late in the season.

But his passengers, doctors from Raleigh, wanted the kind of amenities the *Lady II* could provide. They hadn't balked at the full-day offshore rate, and they'd pay to have their catch cleaned, too, three big yellowfin, two dozen dorado, a cooler full of steely-faced wahoo.

A good day all around.

Satisfied, Matt revved the diesels, swinging the *Lady II* around in a tight arc. Fishermen learned to accept what the sea gave and the sea took away. A captain pitted his boat and equipment, his experience and skill, against the whims of the ocean, the season, the weather. Sometimes you did everything you could do and still came home empty-handed.

Which was why Matt was grateful for good days. Like today.

He backed into the slip. Fezzik, his rough-coated shepherd-Lab mix, lurched from the shadow of the cabin and barked. A pelican launched from the wharf, settling expectantly in the water.

Matt's father secured the lines. At six-two and sixty-four, Tom Fletcher resembled one of the pilings that lined the wharf, gray, tall, and spare. He wore a United States Marine Corps baseball cap, the red bill faded with sun and age.

"I was a Navy corpsman," one of the doctors offered as he jumped onto the dock.

"Nothing against the Navy." Tom grinned as he handed up the man's backpack, jacket, cooler. "The Marines need bus drivers."

A brief pause before the offended doctor decided to laugh.

Matt rubbed his jaw, feeling the scrape of a day's stubble, hiding his own smile. It was customary to tip the mate on a charter fishing boat. But twenty-five years as a career sergeant major hadn't taught the old man the value of keeping his mouth shut. Dad wouldn't get a tip from *that* ex-Navy man.

Along the waterfront, gawkers had gathered to compare the day's take from the different boats, couples strolling hand in hand, excited family groups with sunburns and ice cream. Tourists. Matt didn't mind them. Okay, they crowded the roads and the stores until it seemed a man couldn't talk with his neighbors until after Labor Day. But the tourist tide in summer kept the island economy afloat the rest of the year.

He scanned the small crowd, trying to pick the potential customers from the merely curious.

His gaze snagged. Caught.

A young woman stood at the end of his dock, her long blond hair bundled into some kind of ponytail, a *V* of pink skin at her throat, a flutter of skirt at her knee. Nice legs. Too young. And as tall, cool, and appealing as an ice-cold longneck.

For a moment his mouth went dry.

Matt shook his head, amused by his reaction. He wasn't about to break his long dry spell with a pretty young thing dressed like a model in a J. Crew catalogue.

No harm in looking, though. He studied her from the bridge. She wasn't a native. He'd have recognized her. Or the average tourist on vacation. She looked more put together somehow, like a real estate agent or his ex-wife's lawyer or somebody attached to one of the doctors. A daughter, maybe, or a trophy wife, although Matt didn't spot any big chunks of jewelry on her. No ring.

His father opened the fish box in the stern and began tossing up the catch. Fish flew in a rainbow arc, blue, gold, glittering silver, all their angry energy transformed by death to pale, stiff beauty.

But the girl wasn't watching the show. Her deep brown

eyes fixed on his father. Her chin lifted. Her soft mouth firmed.

Matt recognized the determination in her gaze and felt a tightening in his gut, tension gathering at the back of his neck like a storm blowing in.

Trouble.

ALLISON CARTER DIDN'T believe in hanging around waiting for her ship to come in. She was more likely to rush out and book passage to . . . well, anywhere. She had a trust fund. More importantly, and recently, she had a job. But here she was, standing under the weathered FLETCHER'S QUAY sign, watching as a big white boat slid through a thicket of masts and fishing rods to tie up at the dock.

It backed without a bump into the slip. A large black dog of indeterminate breed—she really didn't know much about dogs—stood in the stern. *Sea Lady II*, Allison read. At least she was in the right place.

In more ways than one, she hoped.

She'd fallen in love with the island at first sight, rising like a whale's back from the sea as she approached on the ferry. She loved its jumbled mix of old and new, weathered cottages side by side with bright tourist shops, gnarled oaks adjoining sunny summer gardens. She liked the mix of people, too, sturdy native islanders and enthusiastic transplants.

She wanted to be one of them, to put down roots here.

Of course her parents had other ideas.

This wasn't the first time, as her mother frequently pointed out, that she'd changed direction or location in hope of finding herself. Surely she could do her soul-searching closer to home? Especially as she was all they had left.

"I've lost one child already," Marilyn Carter had said

with practiced pathos after Allison had been there a week. "I can't bear to lose you, too."

"You haven't lost me, Mom." Allison had kept her tone determinedly cheerful. "You know where I am. You have my phone number on speed dial."

"Not that you ever answer."

Familiar guilt pounded in Allison's temples. "I told you I can't take calls during class."

"You can't take time to talk to your mother? I didn't complain when you spent all summer away from me building houses for the poor. Or when you turned down spring break in Paris to teach English on some reservation. But I thought when you finished that Peace Corps nonsense—"

"Teach for America," Allison corrected for the hundredth time.

Marilyn was too well-bred to sniff, but her tiny pause spoke volumes. "Whatever. You're not in college anymore, Allison. You had two years to get all that out of your system. I thought when you left Mississippi you'd come home where you belong. To Philadelphia. It's not like you need to work."

"I like to teach." She'd learned that much about herself. "I need to keep busy."

"You could keep busy here."

Running her mother's errands, serving on her mother's committees, a dull satellite in her mother's glittering social orbit.

No more.

"I'm lucky to have been offered a job at all," Allison had said. "With the recent budget cuts—"

"But you're so far away!"

Allison didn't tell her mother that the distance had been part of the offer's appeal. "Actually, Dare Island is ten hours closer," she had pointed out patiently. "Half the distance. In a better school district. Higher pay. Smaller class sizes."

Same damn heat.

Water slapped the pier. A bead of sweat ran between Allison's breasts to soak into her bra.

She shifted her weight in her ballet flats, wishing she could peel off her tissue-thin sweater and shove it into her purse. But she didn't. It was too easy for her to be mistaken for one of her students, dismissed because of her age. If she wanted to be taken seriously, she had to present a professional appearance.

Especially when she was meeting with a parent.

Not, she thought, one of the four men standing on the dock arguing over who took home the tuna. Men like her father, with gym-toned waists and salon-cut hair and a subtle air of entitlement.

She squinted into the sun sinking toward Pamlico Sound. Maybe the one on the bridge?

Her gaze skated over him. From a purely female, personal perspective, he was certainly worth looking at. Hard muscle packed into a faded T-shirt and jeans. Sweat-dampened hair jammed under a baseball cap. A lean, watchful face with a hint of pirate stubble.

Her breath escaped. Instant melt. Instant tingle. This one definitely didn't look like any high school father she'd ever seen.

She dragged her gaze away. She would not let a momentary appreciation for the, ah, scenery get in the way of doing her job. She had other fish—*ha ha*—to fry.

An older man was tossing fish into a large plastic garbage can. Now *he* looked the way she imagined a boat captain should look. Like Ahab in *Moby Dick*, all "compacted aged robustness." Minus the scar and the peg leg, of course.

She lifted her chin. "Mr. Fletcher?"

He spared her a quick glance from faded blue eyes before hauling the garbage can over to a long metal table under the shade of a wooden roof. "Yep."

She followed him. So did a dozen gulls, hopping, hovering, swooping, lighting on the roof and in the water.

"I'm Miss Carter." She had to raise her voice to be heard over the squawking birds. "Joshua's Language Arts teacher. I have to tell you how much I'm looking forward to working with your son."

Captain Ahab Fletcher flipped the dead fish out on the table, smooth as a blackjack dealer in Vegas. Out came a knife. *Cut, cut, cut,* down the row of heads. *Cut, cut, cut,* along the spines and bellies. "No, you don't."

Allison straightened to her full five feet, ten inches. She'd shoveled mud from flood-ravaged homes in Louisiana, provided child care in a domestic violence shelter in South Dakota. She had motivated, coaxed, and bullied 127 underachieving students in the Mississippi Delta into scoring at a Basic or Proficient level on the English II graduation exit exam. She could not be deterred by a little thing like dead fish or a bad attitude.

"Actually, I make it a point to talk to all my students' parents at the beginning of the school year."

"Then you want his dad." He winked at her before calling over her shoulder. "Matt! Josh's teacher is here to see you."

Her stomach sank at her mistake. She fixed a smile on her face and turned, determined to remain pleasant. Professional.

And came face-to-face with the solid chest and melt-inducing shoulders of the man from the boat. Of course. Because nothing beat getting off on the wrong foot with a parent like embarrassing yourself in front of a really hot guy.

She cleared her throat. "Mr. Fletcher?"

"Call him 'Captain,'" the older man suggested.

"Dad." The quiet tone held warning. Blue eyes, dark and level, met hers from under the brim of his cap. "I'm Matt Fletcher. What can I do for you?"

"I . . . *Oh.*"

Another jolt, right between her thighs. She looked down. The dog.

Her face flamed as she pushed its head from her crotch.

"Fezz. Quit." The same warning tone, laced with amusement.

The dog panted amiably and dropped its weight on her foot, its thick tail sweeping the dock.

"Allison Carter. Joshua is in my Language Arts class." She edged her foot from under the dog, aware of the crowded wharf around them. "Is there someplace we can talk privately?"

The senior Mr. Fletcher snorted.

She felt her flush deepen. As if she were her students' age and had invited him into the closet for Seven Minutes in Heaven.

"We're kind of busy right now," Matt Fletcher said politely enough. "Is Josh all right?"

She got a grip on herself and her teacher persona. At least the man cared about his son. That put them on the same side as far as she was concerned. "He's fine," she said. "Have you spoken with him today?"

Matt tugged off his cap, wiping his forehead with the back of his arm. His hair was the color of oiled oak, streaks of brown and gold darkened by sweat. He smelled, rather pleasantly, of salt and the sea. "We've been out on the water since five this morning. What did he do?"

"Nothing." And that, of course, was the problem. "I was actually hoping to talk to you about Joshua's progress. We've been in class now for almost three weeks and he has yet to open his mouth. Or, as far as I can tell, a book."

He regarded her without expression. "He's not giving you any trouble, is he?"

"He's very respectful," she assured him. If a total lack of interest in her subject matter could be called respect. "But

I am *troubled* because he's a bright boy who's obviously not living up to his potential."

The older Fletcher chuckled. "We've heard that one before."

Matt sighed. "Look, I appreciate you coming by, but I can't do this now. I've got customers to deal with and a boat to hose down. I need a shower and I want a beer."

"Of course," she said stiffly. She tried really hard not to get personally involved. If you cared too much for your students, you could burn out. You could break your heart. But Matt Fletcher was Joshua's *father*. It was his job to care. "I'm sorry to have bothered you at work. But when I called the number on file, your wife said I should come down to the harbor to talk to you."

"I'm not married."

Oh. *Good.*

She pulled herself together. *Not good.*

Things were awkward enough already. She had no business prying. And no interest in Joshua Fletcher's hunky dad, married or not.

"Josh's mother is out of the picture," Fletcher Senior said. "That was my Tess you talked to. Josh's grandmother. You want that boy straightened out, you should let her know."

"Josh is my son," Matt said. "I'll talk to him."

Allison had met parents struggling simply to survive, so overwhelmed by the effort of feeding their families they couldn't focus on their children's education. And parents like her own, who wanted perfect trophy children on display in the background of their own well-ordered lives, parents for whom a child's degree from Harvard or Princeton or MIT was simply another way of keeping score.

Too soon to tell which category Matt Fletcher fell into.

"It's important to begin the school year on the right foot," she said earnestly. "That's why I have all my students and their parents sign a contract. As I emphasized in the syllabus, communication is key to Joshua's future success."

Matt Fletcher looked at her as if she were speaking a foreign language or maybe had sprouted an extra head. "I said I'll talk to him. Tonight."

"After your beer?"

She'd meant it—hadn't she?—as a sort of a joke. An acknowledgment of his long day, an attempt to smooth things over.

He gave her a long, unreadable look. "That's right," he said. "Now, unless you're buying, you'll have to excuse me."

"THAT WAS A good-looking girl," Tom remarked, turning the key in the ignition. Fezzik jumped into the back of the pickup as the engine rumbled to life.

Matt glanced warily at his dad. Something about riding shotgun made him feel fourteen again. Maybe because while he and his dad had always been close, they'd never been chatty. Every major conversation when Matt was growing up had taken place right here in this truck, where they'd been trapped side by side, unable to make eye contact.

Matt massaged the back of his neck with one hand. Maybe he should take Josh for a drive.

"That girl is Josh's teacher," he said.

Tom winked. "You used to have an eye for teachers."

Matt grunted noncommittally.

Josh's mother was a teacher. A psychology professor at Chapel Hill. Of course, back when Matt first met her, she was just another student. They'd both been students.

"Long time ago," he said. "I'm older now."

And wiser. He wasn't like his poor dumb dog, sticking his nose where it wasn't wanted.

"You're not dead yet," Tom said. "You need to get out. Live a little. Christ, boy, when I was your age . . ."

"You were married with three kids. And don't spin me some yarn about liberty in the Marines," Matt added with a smile. "Because I won't believe you. Mom would have killed you if you'd cheated."

"Yeah, she would." Tom grinned with pride. "Besides, I knew what I had waiting at home. Hell of a woman, your mother."

Matt managed not to squirm. Bad enough his aging parents were getting more action than he was this summer. He could admire the rock solid nature of their thirty-eight-year marriage without needing to hear the details. Unless, of course, the change of subject got his dad off the topic of Matt's own love life.

"So you gave up your time ashore for love," Matt said dryly. "Touching, Dad."

"Hell, no, I'd go on liberty with everybody else. Somebody had to keep their dumb asses out of trouble."

"Then how did you . . ." Matt said and shut up. He didn't want to know.

"I'd go into a bar," his father said. "And pick out the homeliest-looking working woman there. And I'd buy her a drink."

Okay, he really didn't need to hear this. "Look, it's none of my business."

"Nice women, mostly," Tom continued. "They were glad for the attention and the booze. And they kept the other women away."

Matt grinned. "Sneaky."

"There was never anybody for me after your mother," Tom said. "That doesn't mean I'm blind."

"I'm not blind," Matt said.

Or celibate.

There had been women after Kimberly. Nice women, passing through on their way to someplace else. Temporary women, looking for comfort or diversion, to scratch an itch or enjoy a fling. Women who didn't want more than Matt had left to give.

Nobody like Allison Carter, with her big, brown, earnest eyes and long, smooth legs the color of honey.

A prickle of sweat, a rush of heat, washed over Matt. He needed that beer.

But first he had to talk to Josh.

Josh was a good kid. No drama, no trauma, no simmering resentment at being abandoned by his mother or any crap like that. Thank God.

But Matt could see how his son's it's-all-good attitude might not work so well in school. He couldn't force the boy to open his mouth in class, but he could make damn sure he was doing his homework.

"I just don't need that kind of distraction," Matt said. "Josh comes first."

Always had, from the moment the nurse first handed him to Matt in the hospital. Young and panicked and punchy from lack of sleep, Matt had cradled the baby's slight weight, dumbfounded by a sudden rush of love for the damp, squashy bundle in his arms.

His son.

His joy.

It had always saddened him that Kimberly never felt the same. Or maybe it was Matt she'd never loved.

She was gone from their lives before Joshua's first birthday, a casualty of what Matt now figured was postpartum depression. He didn't blame her anymore for listening to her parents and abandoning their hasty marriage. But he didn't understand how she could abandon their son.

He stared out the truck window at scrub oak and salt pine. His own parents had never questioned his decision to raise Joshua. In their eyes, in their lives, a man did what a man had to do.

Matt figured he was lucky to have Josh. Luckier to have had his parents' support.

But now Tom said, "You can't live for the boy forever. Or through him. He'll be off to school in another year."

"Not if he flunks English," Matt said, only half joking.

Another faded blue glance. "Maybe you should set up a, what do you call it, parent-teacher conference."

There was an idea. *Hello, Miss Carter, I'm here to discuss my son's classroom performance. Why don't you take off your clothes while we talk?*

Matt shook his head. He didn't mess with women on the island. There was too much talk that could get back to Josh. Too much awkwardness when Saturday night's date turned into Monday's encounter at the checkout line in the grocery store.

Reluctantly, he let go of the image of a naked Allison Carter lying back against her desk. "I was thinking more along the lines of knocking Josh's head in."

Tom chuckled. "Worked for you. Not so much for your brother."

Matt rubbed his stubble with one hand, remembering the battles that had raged at home before his brother's abrupt departure for the Marines. Josh wasn't a hothead like Luke. He was kind and even-tempered, easy to get along with. He kept up with his chores, at least with his grandmother's eye on him. But the boy had developed a tendency to let things slide, a plate on the floor, the lock on the door, the volume on the TV. His homework.

His curfew.

Generally Matt let it go, trusting Josh would learn responsibility in time. He was a good kid. A smart boy.

Allison Carter's accusing brown eyes stabbed him. *A bright boy who's not living up to his potential.*

Matt set his jaw, a headache still throbbing at the back of his neck. So, fine. This time they'd talk. *Dammit.*

The low-hipped roof of the Pirates' Rest rose from the shelter of the surrounding trees, the generous eaves accented by white and green trim. As a teenager, Matt and his buddy Sam Grady had scraped and repainted every one of those windows. Matt's parents had restored and added to the two-and-a-half story Craftsman, transforming it into a successful bed-and-breakfast. But to Matt the century-old house, with its views of the sound and the sea, had always felt like home.

Oyster shells crunched under their tires. Tom parked the truck in back. At this hour, most of the inn's guests were out to dinner, but there were still a few vehicles pulled up to the white picket fence.

Fezzik sniffed the tires of a late model Toyota that hadn't been there this morning.

"New guests?" Matt asked.

Tom hefted the cooler from the back of the pickup. "Must be."

"That's good midweek this late in the season."

Tom shrugged. "You want some of this fish?"

Matt appreciated the implicit invitation, the promise of dinner, the offer of support. He was almost tempted into asking his dad's advice about Josh. But that had never been their way. Tess was the one they all confided in, the one who prodded and pried and talked things out.

He shook his head. "We're good. Josh and I will grab a pizza or something." Nothing to be gained by yelling on an empty stomach. And maybe the pizza would help the conversation go down easier.

Tom nodded, accepting the limits Matt set. "Right. We'll see you tomorrow, then."

Matt could never repay his parents for everything they'd done. It couldn't be easy, having your twenty-year-old son and his baby show up on your doorstep. He was determined not to burden them anymore, financially or otherwise. Which was why, as soon as Josh could be trusted not to set himself or the house on fire, Matt had insisted on renting one of the guest cottages behind the inn.

He opened the door to the bachelor quarters he shared with his son. "Josh, I'm home."

Fezzik's toenails clicked across the hardwood floors.

No answer.

Tess must have put Josh to work at the inn, turning rooms for the new guests. Which meant the kid was safe from Matt and out of trouble for at least another half hour.

Matt snagged a cold beer on his way to the shower.

By the time he strode up the path to the inn's back entrance, his mood had improved considerably.

Chocolate chip.

The smell—and the memories—reached out to envelop him at the kitchen door. Some things didn't change. Like his mother baking cookies to set out for the inn's guests at bedtime.

As Matt swung open the screen door, she turned from the oven, baking sheet in hand, a slim woman with short, gray-streaked dark hair, her eyes creased by smiles and the sun.

Matt grinned, reaching. "Those for me?"

She swatted at him with a spatula. "Wash your hands first."

"I'll arm wrestle you for them," another voice offered.

Stunned, Matt turned toward the kitchen table, where his father sat cradling a cup of coffee. And beyond him . . .

"Luke!"

His baby brother. The Marine.

Luke's chair scraped back as he stood.

Matt grabbed him hard in a one-armed hug as they pounded on each other's backs. They were almost the same height, eight years apart in age.

His brother had lost weight, Matt thought as he drew back to search his clear blue eyes. His frame was as tense as coiled steel.

"I thought you were in Afghanistan," Matt said.

"I should be." Luke's usually cocky grin was strained.

Matt gripped his brother's shoulder. "You all right?" he asked, as if he'd just hauled him out of another childhood scrape.

"Fine. I'm on leave."

"He goes back day after tomorrow," Tom said.

Matt's brow knotted. Flying to Kandahar on military transport could take days. Why would his brother come home only to turn around again?

He glanced toward their father, seeking an explanation, and for the first time noticed the kid hunched in the chair beside him. A skinny boy—girl?—maybe nine or ten years old, wearing an oversized T-shirt and a Kinston Indians cap. A guest's kid, maybe. Matt had never seen him—*her*—before in his life.

She raised her head. Familiar blue eyes stared at him from a sulky face.

Matt sucked in his breath. "Who's that?"

But he knew. In his gut, in the back of his neck. *Trouble.*

"This is Taylor," their mother said brightly.

Matt switched his gaze back to his brother. "What's she doing here?"

"She's come to stay with us awhile," Tess said.

"Why?"

"Luke was just telling us." Tess set a plate of cookies in front of the girl, who ignored them. "Her mother died a month ago. She named Luke as Taylor's guardian."

"Her guardian," Matt repeated slowly. *No shit. No way.* "You mean . . . her father."

Luke's gaze collided with his. A corner of his mouth lifted in a humorless smile. "Spare me the sermon, bro. I'm just following in your footsteps."

Two

THEY WERE TALKING about her like she wasn't even there.

Fine. Taylor stared at the plate of cookies until they blurred. Her throat ached. It's not like she wanted to be here anyway. She wanted to be home in her little blue bedroom in the house she shared with Mom.

But she couldn't think about her mother without crying. She swallowed hard.

"Taylor." Luke—she wasn't going to call him Dad, no matter what the letter said—touched her shoulder. "Say hi to your Uncle Matt."

Uncle.

The word thumped into her like a fist. She already had an uncle. She didn't want another one.

"Hi, Taylor." He had a nice voice, deep and kind of quiet.

She shot him a look from under her cap brim. He was wider and older than her . . . than Luke, with darker hair and eyes and big hands. Taylor looked at the jagged white scar running across his knuckles and felt kind of sick and out of breath, like she'd had the wind knocked out of her on the playground.

She didn't say anything.

He regarded her silently a moment. "I can see a resemblance."

Tess nodded. "She has Luke's eyes."

"I was thinking she had his attitude," he drawled.

Stung, Taylor jerked her gaze up. Her Uncle Matt smiled at her crookedly. Her stomach cramped. She ducked her head.

She didn't want him smiling at her.

She hunched her shoulders, slumping deeper in the chair. She didn't want him noticing her at all.

THE KID WAS scared, Matt realized.

Not just nervous at meeting her new family or grieving at losing her mother but as angry and anxious as one of the island's feral cats and as determined not to show it. Poor kid.

Matt looked at Luke. "Where's she been the last four weeks?" *The last ten years.* "Who takes care of her?"

White lines bracketed his brother's mouth. "I do now. She's been staying with her mother's parents. Until the will was probated."

"You remember the Simpsons, Matt," Tess said. "Ernie and Jolene?"

Dare Island had a year-round population of fifteen hundred souls. Matt knew most of them. Ernie Simpson had worked at the fish house until it shut down, eight years back, and he moved off island with the rest of his family. The son, Kevin, was a few years younger than Matt and a real tool. The daughter . . .

"You dated Dawn Simpson," he said to Luke. "Back in high school."

Dated being the nicest word Matt could think of for *screwed every chance you got.*

"Did you know about . . ." Matt's gaze cut to the kid in the chair.

Luke shook his head, still looking grim around the mouth. "Not until the lawyer contacted me in Kandahar a month ago."

Well, that was something. The situation still sucked, but at least his brother was taking responsibility. The way Matt remembered, Luke had been pretty broken up when Dawn dumped him their senior year and started banging Bo Meekins.

Matt wondered if his brother had demanded a paternity test.

Not a question he could ask in front of the kid. Anyway, she looked like him, same clear blue eyes, same kiss-my-ass chin.

Luke, a father.

Matt could hardly believe it.

"Where's Josh?" he asked.

Tess set another plate of cookies on the counter. "I sent him to turn the rooms. I'm putting you in Calico Jack's room," she said to Luke. "And Taylor in Anne Bonney." The rooms at the inn were all named after pirates of the North Carolina coast.

"Has Josh met . . ." Matt indicated Taylor with a jerk of his head.

"Not yet," Tess said.

"Right." Matt rubbed his face with his hand. So it was up to him to explain to Josh that he'd somehow acquired a cousin. And maybe deliver another lecture on the importance of always, always using a condom.

"I'll help him finish up, and then we'll get out of your hair."

"I thought we'd have dinner as a family tonight." Tess's eyes dared him to object. "To welcome Luke and Taylor home."

Luke looked like he'd rather go unarmed into a known terrorist hideout than face a family dinner. Matt felt a twinge of sympathy.

"I don't want to butt in," he said. "You all have a lot to talk about."

"After dinner," Tess said.

"Nothing to talk about." Tom locked his gaze on Luke. "You get her an ID card yet?"

A muscle twitched in Luke's jaw. "Yeah. I drove her down to the base yesterday, set her up for benefits. Tomorrow I'll go to the bank, open an account you can draw on for expenses."

"We don't need your pay," Tom said.

Tess squeezed his shoulder. He patted her hand, volumes of communication in a simple touch. Seeing his parents like that—united, rock steady—brought a lump to Matt's throat.

"You'll take it anyway," Luke said. "And Taylor's got some money from her mother."

Matt raised his brows. The Simpsons hadn't exactly been rolling in dough back when they lived on the island. Not that it mattered. What mattered was what the girl needed now.

"You should enroll her in school," he said. He had a vision of Allison Carter standing on the dock, tall and cool and complicated, and shook it away. "As long as she's staying."

"Who's staying?" Josh asked.

The teen sauntered into the kitchen, drawn, as Matt had been, by the smell of baking. He scored a cookie from the counter.

"Hands off," Tess said. "Those are for the guests."

Josh flashed her a grin, shoving the cookie in his mouth. "What about poor, starving hotel workers?" he asked around the crumbs.

"On the table." Tess smiled. "Don't spoil your appetite."

Josh turned obediently toward the table. His blue eyes widened. "Unc Luke!"

Matt watched them hug, their two heads close together, his brother's short bleached cut against his son's sandy mop, and something in his chest expanded and contracted painfully.

"You're taller," Luke observed, holding Josh at arm's length.

Josh straightened proudly. "Some."

"Still ugly, though."

Josh's eyes gleamed. "Dad says I take after you."

Luke snorted. "Maybe. If you lost the Justin Bieber hair and weren't so scrawny."

"They don't feed me enough," Josh said, reaching over Taylor's head for the cookie plate.

The girl scrunched lower in the chair, glaring as his hand brushed the top of her head.

Josh smiled down at her cheerfully as he grabbed a handful. "Dibs."

She shot him a look of disdain from under the brim of the baseball cap. Very deliberately, she extended her arm and selected one cookie. With her gaze fixed on Josh, she took a small, precise bite. Her first. Matt could almost hear her thinking, *Bite this.*

He swallowed a grin. "Josh, meet your cousin Taylor."

Josh's jaw dropped. "My . . . ?"

"Cousin." Blandly, Matt met his stunned look. "Taylor."

"She's going to live with us when your Uncle Luke goes back to Afghanistan," Tess said.

"Are you shitting me?"

Matt cuffed him lightly, aware the girl had stopped nibbling on her cookie and was watching them with wide, blue eyes. "Watch your mouth."

"But . . ."

"We'll talk about it later," Matt said.

They had lots to talk about. Like the dangers of high school sex and the consequences of not using protection.

Spare me the sermon, bro. I'm just following in your footsteps.

Not an easy road, Matt thought. For any of them.

He'd been barely twenty when he'd stumbled home after pulling double shifts at the Food Lion to find Kimberly waiting at the door of their rat-hole apartment, Joshua crying in his crib and a suitcase packed at her feet.

But at least he'd had a couple of months to get used to the idea of being a father. He'd had the advantage of knowing and loving his child from birth, the help and support of his parents.

They'd taken in him and Josh without question. The family had stood by him then. *Back to back to back.*

The family would take care of Luke's child, too.

TESS LIVED BY The List.

Planning had served her through countless moves in her married life, had saved her through deployments and redeployments with three children in tow. Organization ensured the running of the inn and the functioning of her family.

With her arms full of dirty linens, she descended the front staircase, every tread and spindle painstakingly restored when she and Tom had purchased the inn more than twenty years ago. The flowers in the front hall needed replacing. She put that on The List for tomorrow. New guests were coming in, the Martins from New Jersey, she had to figure out someplace else to put them now. *Tomorrow.*

She bumped through the double doors into the silent kitchen, stopping to stuff the sheets and towels into the laundry room. A tiny light glowed over the stove. Mentally, she reviewed The List, dishwasher running, rolls rising, service laid out for tomorrow's breakfast, *check*, *check*, *check*, everything under control.

Almost.

She tested the back door—*locked*—and set the coffee to brew for the morning. Should she go with Luke to enroll Taylor in school tomorrow?

Better not, she judged. Her son had to forge his own relationship with his daughter in the little time they had.

Luke, leaving. *Don't think about that now.* Dawn, gone. That poor little girl upstairs . . .

Tess wiped down the counter by the sink, focusing on the familiar routines to distract herself from grief. The child needed new clothes. Shoes. Supplies. Too soon to take her shopping, perhaps. The girl wasn't comfortable with her yet. With any of them. Maybe by next weekend . . .

Tess opened the door to the master suite, part of the addition Tom and Matt had built with young Sam Grady, and heard water running in the bathroom. Tom was shaving, as he had every night before bed all the years they were married.

The sight of him standing before the sink, long and lean and shirtless, steadied her. His chest hair was gray now, his boxers drooping on his narrow hips, but his shoulders were still broad, his face still handsome and infinitely dear.

She waited until he lifted the razor from his chin before she slipped behind him and slid her arms around his waist.

"Where have you been?" he asked.

The smell of his skin, the scent of his shaving cream, spicy and familiar, enveloped her. She pressed a kiss between his shoulder blades.

"Helping Luke make up his bed."

Tom frowned at his reflection. "You think after ten years in the Marines, the boy can make his own bed?"

She smiled at his grumpy tone. "I don't mind. It's nice to have some time with him alone."

"You work too hard," Tom said. "He takes advantage of you."

Tess knew her man. She'd loved him for almost forty years, since he was a cocky Leatherneck on leave in Chicago, sauntering into her family's restaurant in Little Italy, trying to pick her up before she could write down his order.

"You're not upset about the bed," she said.

Tom didn't answer. He didn't talk about his feelings. He never had.

She twisted around him, keeping her arms loosely linked around his waist, until they were front to front. "It'll be all right," she said softly. "Luke needs us. Taylor needs us. She's our granddaughter."

Tom grunted. "What happened to her mother? You get that out of Luke while you were making his bed?"

"Dawn's lawyer told Luke it was some kind of brain bleed from a congenital condition. No prior symptoms, no warning." Tess shivered. "It was all very sudden and horrible."

Tom stroked her back, instinctively giving comfort. "Christ. Was Taylor with her?"

"No, Dawn was at work when it happened. Apparently she was a receptionist at the law office. The lawyer said they got her to the hospital right away, but it was already too late."

They stood a moment in silence. What if it had been her daughter, her baby, struck down like that in the prime of life? Tess wondered. She couldn't stand it.

"How's Luke?" Tom asked.

He had always counted on her to keep up with the details of their children's lives, to tell him as much—or as little—as he needed to know.

"He doesn't say." And in that, Tess thought, their younger son was very like his father. "But you can see he's affected by her dying like that. He's not heartbroken, he was over Dawn a long time ago, but he still feels it. And now this business with Taylor . . . It's just so much for him to deal with right now, in the middle of a deployment. Did you see how thin he is?"

"He'll be all right as soon as he gets back to his squadron."

She bit her lip. "It's still a distraction."

"Not as much as you think." He rubbed her neck, his strong hand reaching under her hair. "Men compartmentalize better than women."

They were still pressed together, front to front.

Tess grinned suddenly, realizing her husband's focus had shifted. "Is that what you call this? Compartmentalizing?"

His fingers found the knot at the base of her skull. "That's one word for it."

She sighed in pleasure, letting her head drop forward as he kneaded the ache away. "I just worry about them, Tom, no matter how old they are. Matt's not happy, and Meg's living with that man who's never going to marry her, and now Luke—"

"You can't live their lives for them, babe."

"I'd do a better job," she mumbled.

His laugh rumbled in his chest. "You did a good job already. It's their turn now."

"But I want them to have what we have."

"I'd be happy if they'd just stop dumping what they have on you."

She raised her head. "Tom!"

"We're not getting any younger, Tess. It would be nice to have the house to ourselves before we're too old to enjoy it."

"*Mm*. You, me, and an inn full of guests. Very romantic."

She settled her weight more firmly against him, enjoying the feel of him hot and potent against her stomach.

He patted her butt affectionately. "You don't want me going soft in my old age, now, do you?"

She laughed at him. "I can feel just how soft you are."

He smiled down at her, the old gleam in his eyes, the one that still made her breath come faster after all these years. "Why don't you come to bed and I'll show you?"

Three

THE PERIOD BELL buzzed. Released from their seats, Allison's students rose like a flock of gulls, more interested in flight than the consequences of Hester Prynne's doomed passion for that weed, Dimmesdale.

At sixteen, they were still blind to the connections between their own struggles with conformity and identity and poor Hester's fate.

It was Allison's job to help them see.

"Make sure you get those permission slips signed by Friday," she called as they jostled past her desk. "Anyone who doesn't have a signed form for *Easy A* will spend both periods next week in the library."

Her students grunted and shuffled by. Most of them had turned in their slips days ago. There were only a few holdouts.

She spotted one of them making his way through the rows of desks to the front of the classroom. "Joshua, can you stay after class a few minutes?"

He regarded her without expression, a tall boy with broad shoulders and steady blue eyes. His father's son. "It's my lunch period."

"After class or after school," Allison said firmly.

He shifted the three-ring notebook on his hip—the only book she'd ever seen him carry—and glanced toward the hall. "I guess I have a minute."

Lindsey Gordon stood in the doorway, twirling a strand of hair around her finger.

"Save me a seat," Joshua said to her. "I'll be right there."

Allison waited until the girl left for the cafeteria before she spoke. "You were awfully quiet in class today."

Joshua shrugged, giving her non-news the non-response it deserved. He was quiet every day, and they both knew it. What she didn't know was why. She'd seen his transcript. His test scores. She'd talked with his other teachers. Everyone agreed he was a bright boy. All of them acknowledged he was falling behind.

And not one of them appeared particularly concerned about it.

"You have to understand it's still the beginning of the school year," Gail Peele, who taught geometry and trig, had said this morning in the faculty lounge. "And the end of tourist season. Most families around here depend on the season to get by. These kids won't have their heads back in their books until October."

Allison wasn't convinced. Her other students were at least turning in their work. October could be too late for Joshua.

She handed him a dog-eared paperback. "Here."

Something flickered behind his eyes. "What's this?"

"*The Scarlet Letter* by Nathaniel Hawthorne. I want you to read it by Monday."

He made no move to take the book. "I mean, why are you giving it to me?"

"Last year's students had the option of donating their

used books and supplies to the school. Since you apparently don't own a copy, I'm giving you this one."

A red flush crept under his tan. "I've got a book."

"Then you should be doing the reading."

He lowered his head, shuffling his feet like a bull tormented by a matador.

Like Miles.

The memory of her brother caught Allison in the chest, a sharp and unexpected pang. She couldn't afford to hang her heart on the success of every student. But there was no way she was leaving this ring without a fight.

"I've been busy," Joshua said. "Working."

Well, Gail had warned her. He probably needed the money. Or his family did. How much did a fisherman make in a year?

"Do you think that's the wisest investment of your time?" she asked.

"Not really. My grandmother pays me in cookies." He offered her a smile, quick and crooked as lightning. "I'll do a lot for chocolate chip, but I can make more money going out with my dad."

The image of this lanky teenager toiling for cookies was unexpectedly charming, his humor even more so.

But his words confirmed Allison's fears. "You work for your father."

"When I can. Now that I'm stuck in school all day, I'm cleaning toilets at the Pirates' Rest. That's my grandparents' place," he explained.

The bed-and-breakfast overlooking the harbor. Allison had seen it on one of her exploratory bike rides. Not the kind of place she'd spent her vacations as a child. Richard and Marilyn Carter preferred luxury hotels with heated pools, well-stocked bars, and private balconies. But Allison had admired the Rest's weathered charm, the neatly painted trim, the blooming garden.

The upkeep on an old place like that must be tremendous.

She drummed her fingers on her desk. "You work there every day?"

"Just about." His grin transformed his sullen expression. Allison blinked. No wonder Lindsey was hanging around waiting to walk with him to the cafeteria. "My dad says it keeps me out of trouble."

His dad.

Allison's mind flashed back to the dock, to Matt Fletcher's hard-packed abs and sweat-dampened hair. She flushed. Thank goodness she wasn't like Lindsey, sixteen and susceptible. She couldn't be dazzled anymore by a handsome face and a pair of broad shoulders. Okay, maybe dazzled, but not distracted.

"Did he talk to you last night?"

Joshua stared at her blankly.

Allison sighed. "Your father. About your schoolwork."

The boy shook his head. "Like I said, we were busy."

Ridiculous to feel disappointed. Parents didn't always follow through on their promises. Why should Matt Fletcher be any different?

She folded her hands in front of her. "I don't know what you've been getting away with in your other classes. But you've got to do the work to get a passing grade from me."

"I don't really care about grades."

"Colleges will," she pointed out.

"I'm not going to college."

She'd heard that before. She worked damn hard to convince her students they didn't have to be defined by their parents' example. By their expectations.

Or the lack of them.

"A college degree can help you get a better job."

Joshua shrugged. "I'm going to captain a fishing boat. Don't need a degree for that."

"You might feel differently in a couple of years," Allison

suggested. "A college education could broaden your interests. Your horizons. You need to experience what's out there before you can decide what's right for you."

"I don't think so." He looked at her from under his shock of hair. "Are we done? Can I go now?"

She expelled her breath. "Yes, you can go."

He left.

But the problem of what to do about him stayed with her for the rest of the day, a niggling frustration, a hovering sense of failure. When she first went down to the Mississippi Delta, she'd still been floundering to find herself. During her brief internship in her father's office, she'd barely been trusted to change the paper in the copy machine. What made her think she could change lives?

But Allison had discovered she loved to teach. Despite the struggles with discipline and lesson plans, the lack of hope and supplies, she'd watched her students learn, bloom, and grow. She truly believed she'd found her profession, if not her place.

Now she wondered if she'd been right to leave.

She'd always felt like an outsider in the Mississippi community where she had lived and taught. But in the school, at least, she'd been needed and appreciated, part of a team.

She liked her fellow teachers at Virginia Dare Island School. Gail Peele was already a friend. Before Allison signed her contract, she'd been assured that teacher burnout and turnover were low. The school's ties to the community were strong.

But the other teachers didn't really accept her yet as one of them. She didn't have the roots, the ties, the accent, that peculiar island brogue that slipped out when they thought no one was listening.

Allison had read up on the Outer Banks before she came. Despite the welcome she'd received, she knew outsiders were generally regarded with stoic tolerance. For generations, the island had endured government experts from the Park Service, Marine Fisheries, Coastal Management Division, all full of education and good intentions, all convinced they could solve the problems of the community here. They made their recommendations and their rules, and then they went away again and nothing changed. Or things got worse.

For Allison to be truly effective, she had to convince them she was different.

She had to stay.

She wanted to make a difference in her students' lives, to offer them new ideas, a fresh perspective, a future beyond the one laid out for them by their parents and their environment.

Her after-school meeting with the staff of the *Dare Island Beacon* was a step in the right direction.

"A blog?" Behind her dark-framed glasses, Thalia Hamilton's eyes sharpened with excitement. "Do you think we could?"

Allison smiled. Thalia's parents had been among the first to welcome her to Dare Island, showing up at the door of her rental cottage with smiles and a sack of vine-ripened tomatoes from their organic garden.

"We've reserved the use of the computers anyway," Allison pointed out. "Of course you'd need to come up with a design. Links. Content."

Nia Jackson shook her head. "I can't come up with a new column every day."

"You could if you divided the responsibility." As their new faculty advisor, Allison could only suggest. She couldn't make them follow her suggestions. "There are three of you now. If you each took one day . . ."

"We could add more people," Thalia said. "Maybe guest bloggers? Then we'd each only have to post once a week."

Nia nodded slowly. "It would be good to report stuff as it happens. Instead of putting it out once a semester."

"I'm all in favor of putting out," stuck in Brandon Scott.

Nia kicked him under the desk.

He grinned. "Ow."

"A blog won't replace the print paper," Allison cautioned. "But it would give you a platform to respond immediately to school events."

And the practice would sharpen their writing skills.

"Oates won't like it," Nia predicted. "He'll say we're in conflict with the official school website."

"Let me talk to Principal Oates," Allison said. "It's not your job to speak for the administration."

In the boil of conversation and ideas (*Who knew computer code? How much lead time would be required for approval?*), the meeting ran late. By the time Allison got on her bike, the shadows were lengthening under the pines.

As she pedaled, her mind circled back to the problem of Joshua Fletcher.

She couldn't afford to get personally involved in the lives of her students. But there must be some way she could motivate him, something he cared about.

She just hadn't found it yet.

Her rear tire hit a bump, almost unseating her. She gripped the handlebars, her messenger bag bouncing on her back as she fought to stay on the pavement. The bike dragged. Slowed. She pedaled harder, but it was clear she had a problem. A puncture? She glanced behind her.

A flat.

Wobbling to a stop in the soft sand at the side of the road, she got off to inspect the damage.

Damn. She bit her lip. There was a bike pump on the frame. She'd never used one before, but surely she could figure it out?

Ignoring the cars whooshing by, the hot breeze lifting her skirt, she dropped her bag and squatted in the weeds and sand. As she wrestled the pump from its bracket, her cell phone rang. Automatically, she lifted her head to count. One, two, three rings and silence.

Her mother.

Allison expelled her breath. Marilyn Carter didn't believe in voice mail. She would call again and again until her daughter picked up.

"Sorry, Mom," Allison muttered and twisted the cap from the tire.

She jammed the pump over the nozzle.

One, two, three and . . .

Somewhere behind her, a car coasted to a stop. A door slammed.

"Need a hand?" drawled a masculine voice.

She almost fell on her butt. And wouldn't that have been just perfect?

Matt Fletcher descended from the cab of his pickup, the sun at his back, his face in shadow, looking very big and broad against the slanting golden light.

"No, I'm . . ." Was that her voice, high and breathless? She frowned and cleared her throat. "I'm fine. Thanks."

He sauntered closer, thumbs hooked in the pockets of his jeans. "You've got a flat."

"I know." Frustration with herself, with the situation, sharpened her voice. She didn't like being at a disadvantage with this man. Again. "I'm trying to get enough air in the tire to make it home."

He watched as she pumped. And pumped. She appreciated—didn't she?—that he didn't shoulder her aside and take over.

Sweat beaded on her upper lip and between her breasts. Air hissed out as fast as she could pump it in.

"You need a new tube," Matt said. "Bill over at the bike rental can fix you up."

She pushed the hair out of her eyes. "Thanks."

He grasped the frame and hefted the bike.

"What are you doing?" she asked.

He lifted the bike into the back of the truck. His big black dog scrambled over to make room. "Taking you there."

"Oh."

Well.

Returning, he offered his hand. He had nice hands, she thought as he helped her to her feet, warm and work-hardened. A tingle went up her arm.

She swung her bag onto her shoulder and wiped her palm on her skirt. "You don't have to do that."

The corners of his eyes creased. "You think I should just drive off and let you push your bike two miles?"

Put like that . . .

An answering smile curved her lips. "Thank you for stopping."

"No problem." He opened the passenger door for her.

See? A gentleman after all, noted the part of her brain that had been raised to appreciate such things.

She climbed into the cab, tugging on the hem of her skirt to cover her knees.

Maybe it was fate, Allison told herself, stowing her messenger bag and the pump at her feet. Maybe she should take this opportunity to talk to him about Joshua.

She snuck a glance at Matt's strong, tanned profile as he swung in beside her. And maybe not. Hard to berate him about his son's classroom performance while he was doing her a favor.

They drove in silence. She racked her brain for something to say. She was usually good at making conversation. In her parents' house, small talk plastered over a multitude of cracks and silences.

But his closeness seemed to have tied her tongue. She was uncomfortably aware of him, his hands on the wheel, the faint stubble on his jaw, his thigh jutting into her space. His scent.

She cleared her throat. "Lucky for me you came along."

"Somebody would have stopped eventually."

"But not everybody has a truck."

He glanced at her sideways, a dry look out of dark blue eyes. "Around these parts they do."

She seized gratefully on the topic of conversation. "Why is that? The island is only a couple of miles across. The most efficient way to get around is on foot. Or by bicycle."

He smiled, a crook at the corner of his mouth that did funny things to her insides. "You read that in a guidebook?"

She raised her chin. "As a matter of fact, yes."

"It's true enough for visitors," he conceded, surprising her. "Roads are crowded. Fuel's expensive. The more tourists ride bikes, the less impact on the island. But you can't haul nets or tools or goods from the mainland on a bicycle. It's not practical."

"So as a native of these parts, you don't have a bike."

"I didn't say that. I have a 1947 Knucklehead Bobber. Vintage Harley," he explained in response to her blank look. "I like to tinker."

"Oh, very practical," she teased.

His grin spread. "Keeps me out of trouble."

Joshua's words, she remembered abruptly even as attraction crackled and snapped between them. He was Joshua's *dad*.

She didn't want to think of the parent of her problem pupil as a motorbike-riding bad boy. She shouldn't think of him in a personal way at all.

She shifted forward to peer through the windshield. "There's the bike place."

He pulled into the almost empty parking lot under a blue and yellow sign.

Her gaze went to the red sign on the door. "It's closed."

"Let's see." Matt opened his door.

"It's after five. Maybe I could leave the bike locked up somewhere. If I call tomorrow . . ."

But he had already lifted the bike from the back and was carrying it away around the side of the building.

Leaving her alone in the truck with the Hound of the Baskervilles.

She heard nails clatter in the truck bed before a large black doggy head stuck through the sliding glass window at the rear of the cab. Hot breath. Pink tongue. Sharp white teeth.

"Um . . . Nice dog," Allison said.

Big dog. Its panting filled the cab.

"I'll be right back," she told it, easing open her door. "Er . . . Stay."

She felt its eyes between her shoulder blades as she crunched down the gravel walk.

A side door stood open to the shop. Matt was already inside, talking to a short, spry man behind the counter.

". . . hardly your speed," the man—*Bill, presumably*—was saying.

"Funny," Matt answered. "You got a tube for it?"

"Sure." Bill slapped a box onto the counter. "You gonna fix it yourself?"

"I need you to check out the rim first."

Allison pushed the screen door open.

Bill looked up at the creak. "Sorry, ma'am. We're closed."

"It's her bike," Matt said.

"In that case . . . You need a new wheel."

Allison swallowed her dismay as she surveyed the dented back rim. "Can't you repair it?"

"Not worth fixing," Bill said. "New one will run you about seventy-five dollars."

"Or he can pull a used one from the back," Matt said. "That way you'd only have to pay for labor."

A glance passed between the two men.

"This is Allison Carter," Matt introduced her. "New teacher up at the school."

"Well, why didn't you say so?" Bill straightened, wiping his hands on a rag. "Yeah, sure, we can work something out."

"That would be wonderful," Allison said. She felt like Dorothy being welcomed into the Emerald City: *"That's a horse of a different color."* She smiled at both men. "Thank you."

A flush crept over Bill's narrow face. "No big deal. I'll have it ready for you tomorrow."

Tomorrow?

"I can wait," Allison said. "If you want to do it now."

Bill shook his head. "You could if it was the front tire. But I've got to take off your gear cassette, transfer it to the new wheel. That'll take a little more time."

"Of course," Allison said. "I appreciate it."

"I'll run you home," Matt said.

"Thank you," she said again.

She owed him already for the rim and the rescue. Surely tapping him for another ride wouldn't tip the scales that much more?

Besides, she rationalized as she followed him to the parking lot, she really needed to talk to him about Joshua.

"Where to?" Matt asked when they were seated in the truck.

"214 Pelican Way. But first . . ." She pleated her fingers together.

She couldn't invite him into her house for a parent-teacher conference. She might not be part of the island grapevine, but she knew that single female teachers did not entertain hunky dads in their living rooms.

And if they went to his house, there was a good chance Joshua could interrupt them.

She raised her gaze to his, her heart tripping in her chest. Matt had blurred the lines when he'd stopped to help her. But she was about to cross one.

She moistened her lips. "Can I buy you that beer?"

Four

ALLISON CARTER PINNED him with those big brown eyes, those just-licked lips, and every hormone in Matt's body jumped to attention. "Can I buy you that beer?"

He ought to say no, he thought, regarding her fresh, flushed face.

Correction. He ought to say *Hell no*.

He liked to keep things simple. Allison Carter was a distraction he didn't want, a complication he didn't need.

Whatever she was looking for, he was damn sure he wasn't it.

But her scent filled the cab of the truck, fresh and sweet, soap and woman and something else, vanilla with a hint of spice.

Matt rubbed his jaw, aware he hadn't shaved since the day before yesterday. "You sure you're old enough to have a drink with me?"

She narrowed those gorgeous eyes at him. "What does my age have to do with anything?"

Straight-faced, he explained, "You have to be twenty-one to purchase alcohol in this state."

Suspicion dissolved into a smile. "I'm twenty-five."

So, okay, she was older than she looked.

Still too young for him.

But it was only a beer, he told himself. Only an hour on his way home. She was new to the island. No harm in being friendly.

Right.

Matt's friends tended to gather at Evans Tackle Store. He couldn't see pretty Allison Carter gulping coffee and griping about bluefish quotas. He'd have to take her someplace else. Still casual, still public, but . . . nice, he decided, with a glance at her skirt and her little flat shoes.

With a shrug, he drove to the Fish House.

When he got there, luxury cars and SUVs with out-of-state plates crowded the parking lot. Matt whistled Fezzik from the back of the pickup and gestured for Allison to precede them up the new wooden steps to the outdoor eating area overlooking the bay.

The afternoon sun flooded the marina, yellow and hot, sparkling on the water. Gulls wheeled and dipped and cried against the blue. The deck was shaded by long green awnings, protected from the birds by almost invisible wires strung above the railing.

A fresh breeze fluttered the napkins on the tables. Beach music—*Hey, he-ey, baby*—sounded from the speakers, floating over the flap of the canvas, the lap of the water.

"Okay if we sit out here?" he asked Allison. "They don't like dogs in the bar."

"This is perfect," she responded promptly. "I love the view."

He did, too. Against the backdrop of sea and sky, she looked long stemmed, pink cheeked, gently curved. Like one of Tess's tulips. He wanted to lean over and sniff her neck, her ankles, and everywhere in between.

Since he had slightly more finesse than Fezzik, he refrained.

"Welcome to the Fish House." A dark-haired waitress with a mermaid tattoo twining around her arm bustled over. Cynthie Lodge, recovering from asshole husband number one and on the lookout for number two. "Hey, Matt. Draft?"

"Thanks, Cynthie. Carolina Pale Ale." He looked at Allison. "Two?"

She was young enough to like those fruity drinks that masked the taste of alcohol. Classy enough to order wine.

"Beer is fine, thank you."

"I'll have to see some ID," Cynthie said, flashing a look at Matt. A *she's-too-young-for-you, she's-not-one-of-us* kind of look.

Allison flushed as she dug among the books and papers in her bag for her wallet.

"Do you come here often?" she asked when Cynthie had left with their order.

Matt rubbed Fezzik's head under the table. Only a beer, he reminded himself. Only an hour on the way home. The dog sighed and settled at his feet. "I used to. Back when it was a real fish house."

"Excuse me?"

He should have kept his mouth shut. *Keep it light, keep it simple.* "When I started with my grandda, fifteen, twenty years ago, there must have been a hundred boats bringing their catch here. Now it's mostly vacation boats and armchair fishermen."

He waited for her eyes to glaze over.

She leaned forward, interested. Or giving a damn good impression, anyway. "Armchair fishermen?"

He shifted uncomfortably. But since he'd already waded in, he might as well plow ahead. "They want to fish, but they really want to be comfortable. Flat screen TVs in the boat lounge, full-size showers. Boats like the old *Sea Lady*, running charters May through September, commercial fishing in the off-season, are going the way of the dinosaurs."

He felt like a dinosaur himself droning on about the old days.

"A vanishing way of life," she observed softly. "No wonder you want your son to follow in your footsteps."

Surprised, Matt met her gaze. "I don't."

"But . . . Joshua said he was going to be a fishing boat captain."

Matt wasn't sure what he'd expected from her, but her warm interest, her determination to understand, stirred him in ways he wasn't ready to think about.

"If that's what he wants. I want him to go to college first. Let him get his feet wet in something besides bilge water."

She blinked. "Have you told him that?"

"He knows."

They didn't talk a lot. But Josh had to understand that much.

Cynthie returned with their beers. Matt watched Allison take a small sip before setting her wet glass down precisely in the center of her napkin, every gesture smooth. Careful. The same way she picked her words, he reckoned.

What was the matter with him, that her neat, controlled movements made him want to see her ruffled?

She licked the foam from her upper lip. "Perhaps you should talk to him anyway."

So that's what this was all about. Matt shook his head, amused by his own disappointment. Allison Carter wasn't putting the moves on him. She was following up on his conversation with Josh.

"I'll do that," he said.

No point in explaining that his brother's sudden appearance, kid in tow, had shoved every other topic off the table.

Last night Matt had been too busy drumming the birds and the bees into Josh's head to talk about his schoolwork.

A cell phone rang in Allison's bag. She ignored it. "Joshua told me he works at your parents' inn. I think it's wonderful that your family is so"—*ring, ring* before the call went to voice mail—"close. But it might help Joshua focus academically if he did something else after school."

"Like his homework," Matt said dryly.

"I was thinking more along the lines of an extracurricular activity. What are his interests?"

"Girls. Food." The boy was sixteen, at the mercy of his hormones and appetite. "Basketball. Fishing."

She smiled and arched her eyebrows. "That's hardly enough to impress a college admissions committee."

Probably not. It sure as hell hadn't impressed Joshua's mother. Not in the long run.

Water under the bridge, Matt reminded himself.

Allison's phone rang again.

He glanced at her bag. "You need to get that?" he asked politely.

"What? Oh, no. Just let me . . . There." She reached into a side pocket; fumbled with the phone. "I didn't mean to criticize. I'm trying to help."

"I appreciate that." He did. She was a nice girl. *Woman*, he corrected himself. He hated to be the one to scrape the gloss off all that shiny new idealism. He took a swig of beer. "What I'm trying to say is you're still new here. You can't tackle everything in the first couple of weeks. You might want to take some time, get to know the situation, before you start making changes. Or judgments."

She lifted her chin. "I can't understand the situation if no one will talk to me."

She didn't give up. Hard not to admire that.

"We're on an island," he said. "Everybody knows everybody's business. Make it through the first winter, ride out the next hurricane, and you'll hear more secrets than you'd ever want to know."

Her brow pleated in frustration. "And what am I supposed to do in the meantime? Sit on my hands until winter is over and your son's flunked out of school?"

MATT FLETCHER LEANED back in his chair regarding her, an unreadable glint in his eyes. "You're really set on this."

Her heart beat faster. Was he finally taking her seriously? "Yes."

"How long have you been a teacher?"

Classic student diversionary tactic, answering a question with another question.

Allison shook her head. "You don't want to hear about me."

"I might." He surveyed her over his beer glass. "My son's in your class. It might be a good idea to get to know you before . . ."

"You make any judgments?" she offered.

His mouth quirked. "Something like that."

Her nerves sparked. She felt breathless. It had been a long time since she'd let herself respond to that look in a man's eyes.

Too long.

Attraction thrummed between them, palpable, almost visible. She glanced at the tables around them. No one she recognized was looking their way, but she'd met so many people in the past month that names and faces were beginning to blur. As a teacher, she had to be careful.

She cleared her throat. "I spent the past two years in the Mississippi Delta with Teach for America."

"That's quite a commitment."

She flushed. "Yes, it was."

The biggest commitment of her life. Because if she'd failed, if she'd quit, she wouldn't only be letting herself down, or her parents. She'd be letting down her kids.

"I enjoyed it," she said.

"Why leave?"

She was not getting into a discussion of the emotional boundaries, the physical distance, she was negotiating with her parents. She shrugged. "I guess I'm looking for something . . ."

"More."

"Different. The Delta never felt truly like home to me."

He nodded thoughtfully. "It's not easy for a community to trust outsiders."

Were they still talking about her years in the Delta?

"Reagan used to say that the scariest words in the English language are 'I'm from the government and I'm here to help.'" Her smile flickered. "But that's why I went down there. I wanted—I want—to make a difference in people's lives."

She winced. Great. Now she sounded like a Miss America wannabe. All she needed to ensure he never, ever took her seriously was to throw in a sash and a reference to world peace.

She folded her napkin, determined to get this conversation back on track. "About Joshua . . ."

"I'll talk to him. I can't promise better than that until I hear what he has to say."

"That's fair."

He shrugged. "He's sixteen. I can't promise he'll listen."

"But you're willing to listen to him." She leaned earnestly across the table. "He's lucky. Not every child can count on his parents' support."

"Sounds like you're speaking from personal experience."

"Well, I . . . Of course as a teacher I see all kinds of . . ."

"Or didn't your parents ever get called to spring you from the principal's office?"

The image made her smile. She shook her head, more used to asking questions than answering them. "Oh, no. I was the good daughter," she said, proud of her ability to speak lightly. "I was too busy throwing myself into activities to rebel. Cross-country, choir, tennis, student council . . ."

"Let me guess. Oldest child?"

"Now who's speaking from experience?" she asked and was absurdly pleased when he laughed. "No, I have an older brother." Whom she never talked about. Her smile faded. "I learned from watching Miles that it was generally easier to meet my parents' expectations than to rebel."

"That would depend on what they expected, wouldn't it?"

She looked at Matt with surprise and respect. "Yes, it would. It did. They despaired of me in college. I kept changing majors, trying new things, hoping to discover something I could be passionate about, something I was good at. And when I did, of course, it turned out to be something completely different from what my parents wanted for me." She swallowed. "They still think teaching is something unpleasant I'll get over eventually. Like the flu."

Matt started to say something. Tossed back his beer instead.

"What?"

He set down his empty glass. "You didn't run off and join the circus. Or a cult. You didn't get busted or pregnant. You're a teacher, for God's sake. Seems to me your parents should be proud of you."

She hadn't expected him to take her side. Ridiculous that his sticking up for her choices—even after the fact—could make her flush with pleasure. "Well," she said, trying to be fair. "They were very disappointed in my brother. I suppose they count on me to provide them with bragging rights."

"And grandchildren," Matt said dryly.

She laughed. "Those, too. They really always just wanted to see me excel."

"And what did you want?"

"What every child wants, I suppose."

To be accepted. Loved.

Matt nodded. "To get away."

Allison blinked. Not the answer she was expecting from him. *More personal experience?*

"Is that what you wanted?" she asked.

"Maybe. Once. But I always knew I'd be back." He turned his head to look out over the water, beautiful in profile, his eyes the same deep blue as the sea. "I'm a Marine brat. We moved around a lot, living in military housing. Spent some time with my mom's folks in Chicago while my dad was overseas. He'd bring us here on vacations sometimes to visit my grandfather. This island was the first place, the only place, that felt like home to me. Guess you could say it's in my blood."

A wave of wistfulness hit her. She'd never felt that kind of connection anywhere with anyone. Maybe that's what she'd come to Dare Island to find.

A place to belong.

And maybe the alcohol on an empty stomach was making her stupid.

"How old were you when you moved here?"

"Fifteen."

"Almost Joshua's age," she observed.

He smiled wryly. "A long time ago."

He was hardly ancient. Midthirties? Not that she was speculating about his age. Exactly.

"You said I should get to know the island. Why don't you tell me about it?"

He regarded her for a long moment, while her heart pounded and the Shirelles sang "Mama Said" over the speakers.

Heat rose in her cheeks. The curse of the born blonde.

Matt smiled slowly. "Why don't I show you instead?"

Before she could respond, their waitress reappeared. "Another beer?" she asked Matt.

He looked at Allison.

"Not for me," she said.

"Just the check, thanks, Cynthie."

"Sure. If you want anything, anything at all . . ." She scrawled on her pad and smiled. "You know where to find me."

"All set?" Matt asked.

Allison collected her bag and her thoughts. "Yes. I've got that." She reached for the bill.

And saw that the waitress had written her phone number beside the total.

"No." He put his hand on the check.

"You can have her number," Allison said when she was sure the waitress had moved out of earshot. "But I invited you. I pay."

"Not when you're with me."

"This isn't a date. Dating rules don't apply."

"Guy Rules," Matt said. Standing, he anchored some bills under the saltshaker.

"The guys I know go Dutch."

He met her gaze, that lazy smile in his eyes. "Maybe you know the wrong guys."

He looked so good, solid and strong in the sunlight, that her breath evaporated.

Too much sun, she thought dizzily, and pushed back her chair.

"Well." She took a deep breath and stuck out her hand. "Thank you. I appreciate your time and the beer."

"I'm taking you home."

"It's not that far," she said. "I can walk."

"Sure you can," he said patiently. "But I brought you here. I'll take you home."

She tilted her head. "Another Guy Rule?"

"Yep."

The dog lurched from under the table. Matt stood back to let Allison go ahead. She threaded her way through the tables, aware of him warm and close behind her.

"Matt!"

A man—tall, with unruly dark hair and a killer smile—made his way toward them from the direction of the bar. "Cynthie told me you came in. Good to see you."

"Sam." Matt's voice warmed with pleasure. "Heard you were back."

The two men moved together into a one-armed, two-pat guy hug before stepping apart.

"How's your dad?" Matt asked.

"Still making life hell for his nurses."

"His heart?"

"Black as ever. But at least it's beating." The man stooped to scratch the dog behind its ears; straightened and aimed the smile at Allison. "Sam Grady."

"Allison Carter." Politely, she offered her hand.

He held it an instant too long, his grip smooth and strong. The part of her that had been raised to notice such things observed that his teeth were white, his watch a TAG Heuer, his black polo shirt from Brooks Brothers. Money there somewhere.

"I haven't seen you before," he said.

"She's with me," Matt said.

Sam winked. "At least for now."

Were they serious? Should she be offended? Or flattered?

She was a little of both, she decided, and cleared her throat. "I just moved here. At the beginning of the school year."

Sam snapped his fingers. "Carter. You're the new schoolteacher. On Pelican Way, right?"

She was a little taken aback that he knew where she lived. But she had come to Dare Island to be friendly, she reminded herself. To be part of the community. Maybe she should feel encouraged that the parents were talking about her. "That's right. Do you have a child at the school?"

"Nope." He flashed another smile. "I'm single and unattached."

"Then how did you know . . ."

"I'm your landlord," Sam said. "Grady Realty and Construction."

"Small world," Matt said.

Small town, Allison thought.

"Then I should thank you," she said. "I really appreciate the special discount."

Matt narrowed his eyes. "Special discount?"

"For teachers," she explained. "I was a little taken aback when I started looking for a place to live. I should have realized that the demand for vacation rentals would drive up rents on the island. But then the realty office told me there had been a mistake. They have a special rate for teachers."

"All teachers?" Matt drawled. "Or just the pretty ones?"

"All of them," Sam said. "But especially the pretty ones."

"First I've heard of it."

"New policy," Sam said. "Local businesses have a responsibility to give back to the community."

"Your old man know about this?"

"He will when he gets out of the hospital."

A long look passed between the two men.

"I'd give something to hear that conversation," Matt said.

"Maybe I'll tell you about it. If I'm still around afterward." Another sharp smile. "Buy you a drink? On the house."

Allison's gaze darted from Sam to Matt. There were undercurrents here she did not understand. Was he asking her? Or both of them?

"Thanks, but we were just leaving," Matt said.

Sam nodded. "Another time, then. Anytime."

"Great to see you, Sam."

"Nice meeting you," Allison said.

Matt steered her toward the stairs, his hand warm at the small of her back. A tingle radiated up her spine.

She glanced over her shoulder at Sam Grady standing at the rail of the deck, his dark hair ruffled by the ocean breeze, classic nose, square jaw, master of all he surveyed.

She cleared her throat. "He seems friendly."

Not merely friendly. *Single and unattached*, he'd told her. *Eligible*, her mother would have said with that when-I-was-your-age-I-was-already-married-to-your-father gleam in her eye. No strings, no complications, no sixteen-year-old son in Allison's class.

Allison sighed. Too bad she didn't feel any zings and tingles when she looked at him.

"Sam's a good guy," Matt said.

She waited for him to fill in details the way a woman would. When he didn't, she prompted, "Have you known each other long?"

Matt opened her door. "Since ninth grade. We used to raise hell together in high school."

The dog jumped into the back. She heard its nails on the truck bed and then Matt slid in beside her.

She arched her eyebrows. "Used to?"

In the close confines of the cab, she could smell the ocean on him, sweat and salt and man. His shoulder was hard and warm, capped with muscle. She wanted to turn her head and bite him like an apple.

Allison jerked her gaze up, shocked at the direction of her own thoughts. He was watching her, that little quirk at the corner of his mouth, his eyes so blue . . .

"He left the island eight years ago," Matt said.

They were talking about Sam, she reminded herself. His friend, Sam Grady.

"I thought he owned the realty company."

Matt turned the key in the ignition. "His family does. His old man was always pushing Sam to come into the business. But they never saw eye to eye. When the old man turned the fish house into a restaurant, that was the last straw for Sam."

She forced herself to focus. "Why would Sam's father do that?"

"Old Grady makes more money feeding tourists than he could processing fish." The truck lurched as Matt pulled out of the parking lot. "So the fishermen lost out, and Sam took off to start up his own construction company."

"Then that remark about local businesses giving back to the community . . ."

"Was a line." He glanced at her sideways. "Sam's good at lines."

"I thought you were friends."

"We are." Matt smiled. She felt the pull of attraction deep in her stomach. "That doesn't mean I'd let him date my sister."

The man had strings, she reminded herself. Connections, complications, a warm, involved family who lived and worked together on the island.

Which sounded lovely, except Allison had come to the island to escape her family.

"Wouldn't that be up to your sister? Unless you don't trust her judgment."

"I trust her fine. Meg's the smart one in the family. It's Sam I don't trust."

She raised her brows. "How old is your sister?"

Matt grinned, acknowledging her point. "Thirty-four."

"Where does she live?"

"New York City. She's vice president of marketing for Franklin Insurance."

Allison blinked. Okay, so the Fletcher family didn't all live on the island. Maybe Matt was right. Maybe she really did need to get to know the situation before rushing to judgment.

"But you know how it is," he said, interrupting her thoughts. "You have a brother. Miles, right?"

He remembered her brother's name. He actually listened. That was something different for her.

She twisted her fingers together, slightly uncomfortable at being the focus of his attention. "My brother isn't . . ." She had to clear her throat. "It's not like that for us."

"He didn't look out for you?"

"Never." That sounded harsh. Unfair. All through her childhood, Miles had been the one who encouraged her to go her own way, to take risks, to experience life. To collect moments, instead of things the way their parents did. "I can take care of myself."

"He didn't beat up your boyfriends? Protect you on the playground?"

The thought made her smile. "No. Well . . ." She stopped, caught by a memory. "Sometimes at night . . . I had nightmares as a kid. Our parents said I had to get over them. But Miles . . . Sometimes he'd let me climb into bed with him."

"There you go," Matt said. They pulled into her driveway, under the shadow of the porch. "Doesn't matter how old or far apart you are. He'll always be your big brother."

"He left," she said, the words jerked out of her. "When I was twelve. I haven't seen him in thirteen years."

"I'm sorry," Matt said quietly.

To her horror, she felt tears sting her eyes. She stared at her knees, willing the tears not to fall. "It's all right. It's not like he died or anything. He just . . ."

Packed a bag and ran away.

Broke my heart.

Abandoned me.

"Left," she repeated. Leaving her as the only target of their father's anger and their mother's dissatisfaction.

"Sometimes that's worse," Matt said.

"How would you know?" she asked and remembered, too late, that he was divorced with a sixteen-year-old son.

"Because most of the time leaving is a choice." He turned off the engine. "Death isn't."

"I didn't mean to be rude," she said into the silence. "I don't usually overshare like this."

She didn't usually talk about herself at all.

He was a very good listener.

He shifted slightly, facing her. His cheeks creased in a smile. "Not ever? Or not on a first date?"

She picked at the hem of her skirt. "We're not dating."

"I picked you up, I bought you a drink, I brought you home." The creases deepened. "What am I missing?"

Those lazy blue eyes missed very little, she thought. Despite his easy manner, he must see, he must know, that she was attracted to him.

"We didn't eat," she said.

"Next time," he promised. "When I show you my island."

"We didn't . . ." Her gaze fell to his mouth. Her pulse clamored. *Shut up, shut up, shut up, Allison.*

His eyes darkened. "I can take care of that now."

He stretched his arm across the back of her seat, giving her time to stop him, giving her space to move away. She did neither. Her pulse went wild with anticipation as his fingers caught a strand of her hair, stroking it behind her ear.

He leaned in, warm and close. She inhaled and closed her eyes, need pooling in the pit of her stomach and lower, between her thighs. He kissed her hot cheek, making her shiver, pressed his lips to her forehead and made her sigh. Cupping her face with his free hand, he laid his mouth on hers.

His lips were warm, firm, parted. Like his touch, his kiss teased and tempted, a promise of heat, a whisper of excitement along her nerves, surging in her blood. Without thinking—*Don't think*—she opened her mouth, inviting him in.

He deepened the kiss immediately, nudging inside her, licking inside her while his hand tightened on the back of her neck. Heat flared, blanketing her brain. She fisted her hand to pull him closer, wanting more. More heat, more contact, more tongue. He gave it to her, swamping her with sensations, the softness of his shirt, the roughness of his stubble, the taste and textures of his mouth.

His hand stroked from jaw to shoulder, brushing the outside curve of her breast, sliding from hip to thigh, rousing and soothing at the same time. Her skin tingled in the wake of his touch. She made a sound in her throat and strained forward, her knee bumping the gearshift.

"Let's take this inside," he said against her mouth. Another kiss, deep and drugging. "I want to come inside with you. Let me come."

Oh, yes. Inside me. Come.

Oh, no.

Allison broke the kiss, banging her head on the back of the seat.

"Easy." He gathered her closer, his thumb stroking the sensitive skin of her neck.

His eyes were dark and dilated, his lips wet and close. She almost lunged for them again. *No, no, no.*

"I don't do this," she said. *Not anymore.*

His body tensed. Stilled. "Okay."

"I can't do this." She struggled to remember the reasons why. "Your son is in my class."

The inside of the cab was sweltering. Her breathing rasped in the quiet.

Matt eased back, his gaze on her face. "My son doesn't have anything to do with this."

Maybe not.

She swallowed, feeling hot and dorky and embarrassed.

It wasn't like she was a virgin or anything. In college, she'd had her share of drunken fumblings and awkward couplings. But she was trying so desperately now to be an adult, to only say yes when she meant yes. When it meant something. She didn't need a commitment, but . . .

"I don't know you. I don't jump into . . ." Bed, she thought. "Things with someone I don't know."

"I understand," he said.

She stared. "You do?"

"Sure. You don't do one-night stands." He took a deep breath; released it slowly. "You got a way to get to school tomorrow?"

"What?"

"Without your bike."

"Oh. I . . . Yes." Her blood was still warm, her face hot. "I do have a car. In the garage."

He nodded. "Okay." His eyes met hers. "Call me if you get a flat."

Five

THAT NIGHT, MATT spent the hour after dinner fixing a leaky valve on the Harley. Classic bikes were best, everything simple, stripped down, easy to service. He didn't have the time or inclination to go poking around with some complicated new fancy equipment. Low maintenance, that's what he wanted.

But even as he repaired the worn valve guide and installed new plugs, his mind kept sliding to Allison, remembering the flush on her face, the warm interest in her eyes.

The way her hand had fisted in his shirt.

He stepped out of the work shed, rolling his neck to ease the muscles there. His body felt restless. Needy.

Cicadas whirred and chirred their mating cries, a rising, falling call that worked its way under his skin and into his blood. Hell, even the bugs were getting more action than he was. There had been the usual influx of tourists this summer, but no woman who really caught his eye. Maybe he'd been too busy. Maybe he was getting too particular.

Matt made a face. Or too old.

Whatever the reason, he hadn't been with a woman in a really long time. Four months, he realized.

Jesus. After four months, a man was bound to get a little edgy and off his game.

Which didn't excuse him moving on his son's new teacher like she was a woman he'd picked up in a bar.

His brain replayed the scene in the truck in 3-D with sound effects, all that warmth, all that heat, that sound she'd made deep in her throat.

Matt shook his head to clear it. Allison Carter didn't do one-night stands.

And he didn't do anything else.

He'd always had a ban on dating island women. On dating any woman who would expect more than he had left to give. Promises. A ring. A life.

The trees in the garden, all fragrance and shadow, blocked the moon and the lights from the inn, leaving him alone in the dark.

On the other hand, Allison Carter didn't really fit the island profile, Matt decided. She looked like a woman who came from money. She talked like a person who had places to go. *I kept changing majors, trying new things, hoping to discover something I could be passionate about.*

He could give her passion, he thought. But he didn't expect her to stick around.

Lots of people moved here, drawn by the idea of island life, seduced by the summers, only to discover when the last tourist left and the first hurricane blew in that they couldn't put down roots in sand. When the school year was over, maybe sooner, Allison would move on. He could show her around, show her a good time, without anyone thinking he was auditioning another mother for Josh.

Simple.

But first he had to square things with his son.

Matt crossed the strip of yard to his porch feeling almost cheerful.

Inside the cottage, Josh sprawled on the living room couch, eating cereal from the box, the dog at his feet and his gaze locked on ESPN.

Matt closed the door behind him, shutting out the incessant grind of the cicadas. "Done your homework?" he inquired.

Josh sank lower into the couch. "Pretty much."

Another time that would have been enough.

Allison's face rose in Matt's mind. Her voice echoed in his head. *Perhaps you should talk to him anyway.*

He walked into the open kitchen to pour a glass of water from the fridge. Fezzik's tail thumped the carpet as he passed.

"Saw your new teacher today," he remarked.

Josh snorted. "The DB."

Dingbatter. The island epithet for newcomers, uplanders, and Yankees.

"Miss Carter to you," Matt said mildly.

Josh shrugged one shoulder. "Yeah, whatever."

Matt took a long drink of cold water. *Keep it light.* "She mentioned something I was supposed to sign."

"Permission slip. We're watching some lame movie in class next week."

Matt thought back to yesterday's conversation on the dock. He didn't remember a movie. "This was some kind of contract," he said. "On the syllabus."

"Oh, yeah." Josh returned his gaze to the TV. "I took care of it."

That figured.

Matt rubbed his face with his hand. The truth was, he was out on the water ten, sometimes twelve hours a day. God knew he tried to keep track of the important stuff, doctor's appointments, basketball games. Tess, bless her, filled in where she could. But over the years they'd all learned to make accommodations for him being a single parent.

He strolled back into the living room, blocking Josh's view of the discussion of Carolina's starting lineup. "You sign my name?"

Josh eyed him cautiously. "Maybe."

Matt nodded. "You still have trouble forging the *h*?"

Josh relaxed. "No, I'm good." A corner of his mouth kicked up in a smile. "Good enough to get away with it, anyway."

"I'll be the judge of that," Matt said. "Pull it out and let's have a look."

"Can't it wait until after *Sports Center*?"

Matt had a feeling he'd already waited long enough. *We've been in class now for almost three weeks and he has yet to open his mouth. Or, as far as I can tell, a book.*

Matt hit the MUTE button. "Syllabus," he said. "Let's see it."

Josh heaved an exaggerated sigh before lurching from the couch. He retrieved his backpack from beside the door and dumped it on the couch, pawing through its contents like Fezzik digging for a bone. Eventually he unearthed a slim paperback and several crumpled sheets stapled together. He flipped over the top two pages before handing them to Matt.

Matt thumbed back to the beginning—course outline, homework policy, letter to parents, promises to students. Phrases leaped out at him until he could almost hear Allison's earnest voice. *"Excited about working with your child . . . welcome your concerns . . ."*

"You don't have to read it," Josh said.

Matt raised his brows. "That signature says I did. Let's not make a liar out of us both."

Josh flushed and fell silent.

Matt read. "*Scarlet Letter*. They still make you read that, huh?"

Josh shifted. "Well . . ."

A rap sounded on the front door. Josh wriggled like a fish on the line, preparing to slip away.

"Stay put," Matt said and went to open the door.

Luke stood on the stoop, his face in shadow. "Got a minute?"

Matt glanced over his shoulder at Josh. "Now?"

Luke held up a six-pack. "I brought beer. I thought we could go out on the boat."

"Cool," said Josh.

"Not you," Matt said. "Can we do this later?" he asked Luke.

Luke grinned. "If you don't mind warm beer."

Despite his brother's cocky smile, his voice was strained. Luke never had been any damn good at asking for help. Tromping across the yard, six-pack in hand, was as close as he could come to a distress call.

Tension knotted Matt's neck.

"I'll get my keys." He cocked a finger at Josh. "You stay here. TV stays off."

"So what do I do while you're gone?" Josh asked, aggrieved.

"Find that permission slip I'm supposed to sign." Picking up the paperback, Matt tossed it to his son. "And catch up on your reading."

THE NIGHT BREEZE ruffled the silver bay as the old *Sea Lady* rocked at anchor. Water lapped the side of the boat.

Luke tipped his head back against the seat. The moonlight bleached his fair hair, emphasizing the bones of his skull and the shadows under his eyes. His face, pale and skeletal, motionless under the moon, dug at Matt's chest like a hook biting hard.

Luke had lost a lot of weight in Afghanistan. He looked gaunt. Older.

Shit.

Matt popped open another beer and stared at the sky until the burning in his eyes went away.

That haze around the moon meant dust in the air. A high pressure system. That should keep the clouds away.

"Another clear day tomorrow," Luke said.

Matt glanced at his brother, surprised by the echo of his own thoughts.

But despite their differences in age and temperament, they were brothers, bound by blood and memory, by a thousand inside jokes and shared experiences. You couldn't escape family.

How many nights had they gone out together with their father, grandfather, and watched the moon?

Matt set down his beer, untasted. "You didn't drag me out here your last night home to talk about the weather."

"No."

Matt waited. He wasn't comfortable putting his emotions into words. But at least he had some experience dealing with feelings, some practice at being a parent. Luke didn't.

The silence stretched.

"You get the kid settled down all right?" Matt asked at last.

"I said good night." Luke's tone was defensive. "She's a little old for bedtime stories."

Maybe so. Matt couldn't remember at what age he'd stopped reading to Josh. But he remembered the wriggly warm weight against his arm, the tousled head against his shoulder.

Luke had missed all that with his daughter.

Why? Why hadn't Dawn told him about the child they'd supposedly made together? Sure, they broke up in high school, but why hadn't she come after Luke for child support? The Simpsons had never had any money.

"We had to move her," Luke said abruptly. "Mom needed the room for some guests coming in late tonight. She made up a bed for Taylor in the old sewing room." The small room at the top of the stairs off the kitchen. "The kid looked at me like I was making her sleep in the crawl space."

"You could have given up your room," Matt said.

Luke shook his head. "The sewing room is right above Mom and Dad. I didn't want to leave her alone in a guest room next to a bunch of strangers."

"Isn't that what you're doing anyway?" Matt asked quietly. "In her eyes, we're strangers, too."

Luke's jaw set in a mulish expression Matt recognized. "We're her family."

Matt held his brother's gaze. "You sure about that?"

Luke expelled his breath. "I had a paternity test done first thing. There's a place in Texas that'll get the results back in twenty-four hours if you pay them enough."

"What did you do?" Matt asked dryly. "Hold her down and draw blood?"

"I didn't have to. Dawn's lawyer made sure I was appointed Taylor's interim guardian until the court determines final custody. That gives me the right to take her to a doctor on base."

"Jesus. No wonder she's hostile."

"Hey, I didn't tell her why," Luke said. "I picked her up, told her she needed a physical before school started. Which she does. Anyway, while he was at it, the doctor did a . . ." Luke waggled his finger next to his cheek.

"Swab," Matt guessed.

"Yeah. Then I checked us into a motel and waited for the DNA results. I wasn't bringing her here until I knew."

Matt tried to picture it, his brother holed up overnight with a scared, snotty ten-year-old, waiting to find out if he was a dad. What a nightmare. For both of them.

"Why the hell didn't you just take her back to Dawn's parents?"

Luke dug in his front shirt pocket. "The lawyer said it might not be so easy to pick her up the second time. The Simpsons want to keep her."

O-kay.

Matt sympathized with Luke's situation. To find out you were a father after ten years, to be given a chance to reconnect with a child you never knew you had . . .

But the child's interests trumped a father's feelings. Not to mention what *she* must feel.

"Maybe you should think about that," Matt said. "The kid just lost her mother."

Luke tapped a cigarette from the pack. "And I'm her father."

"You're also deployed, for Christ's sake. At least she knows Dawn's folks."

Luke flipped his lighter without speaking. A flame jumped against the dark.

"I thought you quit," Matt said as Luke cupped his hand around the cigarette.

"I did." Luke inhaled slowly, closing his eyes.

Their dad had smoked, too, Matt remembered, every time he went on active duty, in Lebanon and Libya and the Gulf, no matter how much Tess nagged him about it. Cigarettes were a way to cope with boredom, sleep deprivation, and the stress of combat.

Not to mention the shock of coming home. *Congratulations, it's a girl.*

Luke blew a long stream of smoke out over the water, light against the dark. "Dawn left a letter," he said at last. "With the will."

"A letter," Matt repeated carefully.

"She wanted me to raise the kid. Not her parents."

Matt raised his brows. "But our parents raising the girl is okay?"

"Don't bust my chops. You never minded accepting their help with Josh."

He'd minded, Matt thought. But he hadn't seen a choice.

"They were sixteen years younger then. And so was I. Anyway, I didn't dump a baby on their doorstep and run."

Instead, he'd come home from college, where his future had once stretched as bright and unbounded as the ocean.

"Taylor's not a baby," Luke said. "She's ten. Hell, she'll be in school half the time."

"The bigger they get, the bigger their problems. You should be here."

"Not an option," Luke said.

"Bullshit," Matt said. "You could get hardship leave."

"I have a responsibility to my men."

"I hate to break it to you, bro, but you're replaceable to the Marines. Your men can find another squad leader. Your daughter can't find another dad."

"I know what I'm doing over there. I don't have the first clue how to be a parent."

Matt shrugged. "So you learn on the job like everybody else. You can't do that in Afghanistan."

Luke ground out his cigarette on top of his can. "The kid will be fine without me. She doesn't know me. Doesn't need me. Hell, she doesn't even like me."

"Maybe you should work on changing that."

"If something happens over there, she's better off not knowing. This way she won't miss me."

"If you believe that, you're an idiot."

Luke reached for another beer. "I can take better care of her by doing my job. At least she'll be provided for." He smiled crookedly. "Hell, I'll be home in another three months. Plenty of downtime between deployments for us to get to know each other."

"Provided you live that long," Matt said quietly.

"Yeah." Luke tipped back his beer, his throat muscles working in the moonlight. He lowered the can. "That's what I want to talk to you about. If anything happens, I need to know you'll be here."

"We all will. You know that."

"Yeah. But you said yourself Mom and Dad aren't getting any younger. You done good with Josh. This kid . . . If the shit hits the fan, I'm counting on you, bro."

Matt's chest hurt. He cleared his throat. "I'll be here."

Luke met his gaze and smiled. "Back to back?"

"To back," Matt promised solemnly.

It was the rallying cry of their childhood. Growing up in a military family, moving from base to base, the three Fletcher siblings had always stood by each other. *Back to back to back.*

There was no question Matt's life was about to get more complicated.

And no help for it.

"Does Meg know yet?" Matt asked. "About Taylor?"

"I called her." Luke rolled his eyes. "She asked if I updated my will."

"And?"

"Well . . . She told me to buy more life insurance."

Matt swallowed a laugh.

"I HEAR YOU'RE seeing Matt Fletcher," Gail Peele remarked the next morning as she rinsed her coffee mug in the teacher's lounge.

Allison froze, her tea bag suspended over hot water. "Who told you that?"

"Suzy Warner told me Pam Gordon saw you two together at the Fish House last night."

Allison's thoughts scrambled like students at the end-of-day bell. Suzy Warner, Social Studies, the biggest mouth in school. Pam Gordon, mother of Lindsey. Her daughter was in Allison's fourth period class with Joshua Fletcher.

Her stomach sank. Lightly, she said, "Well, we were there. But we're not seeing each other. He gave me a ride home, that's all."

And flushed at the memory of Matt smiling at her, saying, *I picked you up, I bought you a drink, I brought you home. What am I missing?*

"*Mm.*" Gail gave a little hum of acknowledgment or interest. "Bill at the bike shop said you had a flat."

"Er . . . yes." Allison dunked her tea bag up and down. Was it only yesterday she was complaining about not being part of the island grapevine? "Matt stopped to help me."

Gail turned from the sink. "And you just happened to wind up at the Fish House."

Her hand in his shirt, his tongue in her mouth, the sound of her breathing loud in the stillness . . .

Allison's face heated. She liked Gail, a comfortably upholstered woman with a sharp brain and an easygoing disposition. But they'd known each other less than a month. Not really long enough to confide the details of that hot, groping kiss in the front of Matt's pickup.

"Is that a problem?" she asked.

"Not for me." Gail filled her mug—MATH TEACHERS KNOW ALL THE ANGLES—from the staff coffeepot. "You're both grown-ups. Unattached. But . . ." She looked around the lounge, as if the two teachers deep in conversation on the other side of the room could hear.

Allison nodded. *But.*

"It's not a good idea for a teacher to date the parent of a student," Allison finished for her.

Gail tipped in milk. "I'd say that depends on the teacher and the parent. This is a small island. You can't avoid personal connections with the students in your classroom. If they're not your kids, then they're your neighbor's or your cousin's or your mechanic's. It's not against school policy for you to have a social life as long as you're impartial in the classroom."

"So it's not an issue if I date a parent."

"Not unless you make it one. It's just . . ." Gail's round, pleasant face creased.

"What?"

"Like I said, there's been talk. The Fletchers are a hot topic around here. Well, especially now, with Luke showing up like that yesterday with his little girl."

"Who?"

"Luke, Matt's brother. He didn't tell you about that?"

Dumbly, Allison shook her head. "We just had one beer." *One kiss.*

"So you don't really know him very well."

Allison stuffed away the memory of her own voice stammering, *I don't know you. I don't jump into things with someone I don't know.* Her pride was pricked . . . along with her curiosity.

"You're not going to tell me he keeps the bodies of six ex-wives in the attic, are you?"

Gail laughed. "Ha. No. Not that he didn't have the girls lining up. Both the Fletcher boys always were hot as sin, plus Matt's got that whole still-waters-run-deep thing going on. Even I was tempted when he came home from Raleigh, and I was already with Jimmy back then. There's not a woman on the island who hasn't, you know, thought about him."

Including the waitress, Allison thought. What's Her Name. Cindy? *Cynthie.*

She arched her brows. "Are you suggesting I take a number?"

Gail grinned and shook her head. "If Matt Fletcher took you to the Fish House, I'd say he's already moved you to the front of the line. Our Matt doesn't date locals. Even his ex-wife . . . He met her in college, you know."

"I didn't know. We didn't really talk about it." Carefully, Allison squeezed out her tea bag and set it beside her mug. There were a lot of things Matt hadn't talked about, she thought, a hollow feeling in her stomach. He certainly hadn't mentioned college. "What was she like?"

"Kimberly? Smart. Rich. Blond," Gail said, apparently unaware she could be describing Allison. "Not that we saw much of her. Just that one time she was visiting for Thanksgiving, and less than a year later Matt had dropped out and came home with the baby. And no Kimberly."

Allison took a hasty sip of tea and burnt her tongue. "What happened?"

Gail shrugged. "He doesn't talk about it."

"Imagine," Allison murmured.

Gail smiled wryly. "Doesn't stop the rest of us. Not much to do here in the winters but talk." She hesitated and then added, "Nobody blames him. He's a good guy, Matt."

"I'm sure," Allison said, because Gail so obviously needed reassurance and Allison felt guilty gossiping about Matt behind his back.

"The thing is . . ." Gail wavered, clearly torn between island loyalty and female solidarity.

Allison waited.

"In all these years, I've never known him to date a woman longer than a couple of weeks," Gail confided. "A couple of months, if she's here for the summer."

"Maybe he isn't over his ex-wife," Allison suggested.

"He was over Kimberly the day she walked out on him and their baby," Gail said frankly. "But he hasn't been in a relationship since. Nothing serious. Nothing long-term."

"And you're telling me this because Lindsey Gordon's mother saw us together at the Fish House?"

"Word gets around." Gail met her gaze, concern warm in her eyes. "I just thought you should know."

Allison's throat constricted. She swallowed, thinking back to that scene in her driveway.

You don't do one-night stands, Matt had said to her in that deep, attractive drawl.

At the time, she'd appreciated his respect for her boundaries. She'd actually been grateful for his restraint. His understanding.

And afterward, he couldn't drive away fast enough.

She felt slightly sick to her stomach. It was one thing to be the subject of gossip. It was much worse, she was discovering, to be an object of pity.

"Thanks. But you don't have anything to worry about. I'm sure he's a nice guy, but I'm still finding my feet here. I'm not looking to get carried away."

Gail nodded, unconvinced.

Allison tried again. "I've done the whole hookup scene before. I didn't find it particularly satisfying or exciting. Next time I get involved, it has to mean something. I want an honest, adult relationship with a man who appreciates me. Who needs me, not just a warm body in bed."

"Matt's plenty adult," Gail said. "By the time he was your age, he was already divorced with a five-year-old child. Which probably explains why he's not looking for a commitment now."

"Don't worry." Allison smiled. "I'm really not interested in being known as 'that girl Matt Fletcher used to date.'"

"There you go." Gail patted her arm. "I told Suzy you were a smart one."

He was leaving.

Taylor sat huddled at the kitchen table, glaring from under the rim of her baseball cap at the three men standing at the door, the old guy Tom and Uncle Matt and her . . . and Luke in camouflage and boots.

He wasn't as tall as Uncle Matt, but the uniform made him look wider and scary, like Master Chief in Halo, like nobody would mess with him, and in the week she'd been with him nobody had messed with her, either.

She had never had a dad. She didn't need a dad. But he was all she had left, and he was leaving.

First she lost Mom. Then she'd lost their house and her little blue bedroom with the crepe myrtle growing outside her window. And then she lost Snowball, because Grandma Jolene was allergic to cats. She had to switch schools and she missed her friends and she missed her life and she really, really missed her mom.

Her chest ached and her eyes hurt, and she felt tired and stiff from sleeping on the floor behind her bed. Her face was stiff, too, like it would crack if she tried to say anything.

"Taylor." Tess spoke, her voice kind. "They're leaving for the airport now. It's time to say good-bye."

Like she couldn't figure that out by herself.

That's why they'd kept her home from school today. To say good-bye.

Her eyes burned and she opened them very wide so she wouldn't cry. School hadn't started yet when they buried her mama, but this felt horribly the same, all the grown-ups standing around looking serious and saying stupid stuff like, *Are you all right?* and *You're such a brave little girl* when she wasn't brave and things were never going to be all right again.

She didn't like it here. She didn't have her own room, and nobody talked about her mom, and they didn't want her really. But at least nobody rubbed up against her when she wasn't looking. Nobody was creeping around at night, trying to touch her with hard, damp hands.

Taylor gritted her teeth together so that the howl that was building in her chest wouldn't sneak out.

Uncle Matt nudged Luke. His shoulders stiffened and then he crossed the kitchen, his big tan boots clomping on the wooden floor, and squatted in front of her chair. His knees stuck out on either side of her legs and his face was level with hers so that she had to look at him. His hat was pulled down low just like hers, but she could still see his eyes, blue and bright.

She swallowed hard.

"Well." A muscle jumped in his jaw. "Take care of yourself, kid."

She would have to, wouldn't she? Since he was leaving.

"You listen to Grandma and Grandpa," he continued. "Do good in school. I'll be back as soon as I can."

She scowled at him without saying anything.

Luke pulled off his cap and ran a hand over his short bleached hair. Mad and miserable, she waited for him to get up, to go, but he didn't move away. Not yet.

He dropped the cap in her lap. It was still warm from his head and it smelled like him, like Luke and tobacco, and her chest got all tight and tears burned the back of her eyes.

"I've got to go now," he said and laid a hand briefly on her knee.

"I don't care if you go." The words burst out of her, shocking them both. "I don't need you. I don't care if you never come back."

"Oh, sweetie . . ." Tess moved closer, but Luke held her back with one raised hand.

"It's all right," he said. To which one of them, Taylor wasn't sure. His eyes met hers. "You may not like it, but you're stuck with me, kid, whether you need me or not. Stuck with all of us, Grandma Tess and Grandpa Tom, Matt and Josh. They're all going to be here for you until I get back."

He lowered his head so that his face was close to hers. "I'm coming back," he said, low and sure.

Her hands clenched on the cap in her lap.

Don't go, she wanted to beg. But nothing she said would make any difference. Ever made any difference.

Memory crashed over her, cold metal rails and beeping, breathing machines, and her mom's hand, cold and thin, unmoving under hers. *Don't go, Mommy, don't leave me . . .*

Taylor's jaw wobbled. Her eyes burned. If she opened her mouth, she was going to start bawling.

So she didn't.

After a minute, he straightened.

Don't cry, don't cry, don't cry . . .

"The kid should come," Matt said unexpectedly from over by the door.

Luke turned his head. "What?"

"The kid should come with us to the airport."

"You never did," Tom said.

"We had a hell of a sight more to hold onto when you'd gone," Matt replied. "It's an hour-and-a-half drive to the airport. Even if they say good-bye on the curb, that's another hour and a half she has with her dad."

"Truck only holds three."

"We can take my car," Tess said.

Luke rolled his eyes. "So now we're all going?"

"I'd say that's up to Taylor." Matt's gaze sought hers, steady, blue. "What do you want, kid?"

Her heart pounded in her chest. It didn't make any difference. Luke was still leaving.

Even if they say good-bye on the curb, that's another hour and a half she has with her dad.

Wordlessly, she slid from her chair.

Luke cleared his throat. "Right. You can ride shotgun with me."

"I'm not sitting in back," Matt said like he was Josh's age.

Luke grinned at him, and something inside Taylor loosened. "This was your idea, bro."

"You yahoos can ride together," Tom growled. "Your mother's in front with me."

So that's how they drove to the airport, with Taylor squashed into the backseat between her . . . between Luke and Uncle Matt and Tess turning around every few minutes with a wink or a pat or a smile.

She was surrounded by Fletchers.

Their legs stuck out on either side of her like the arms of some really big chair, their shoulders warm and close, but for once she didn't feel trapped. The backseat was wide and comfortable, the vibration of the car soothing. Taylor clutched the field cap in her lap and let her head tip back, her shoulders relaxing against the smooth leather as their voices washed over her.

Six

MATT RUMBLED INTO the school parking lot on his Harley like Stallone in *The Lords of Flatbush*.

Not exactly the image of a responsible guardian for a ten-year-old girl.

But he had no choice. He was already on the boat, prepping for an afternoon run, when the call came in on his cell phone.

"Matt Fletcher?"

He set down the oil, juggled the phone. "Yeah."

"This is Karen Nelson."

He searched his mind. There were over a dozen Nelsons on the island, descended, they claimed, from one of Blackbeard's crew. Like having a murdering pirate in the family tree was something to be proud of. Didn't Dick Nelson have an older sister named Karen?

"Vice principal for the primary grades at Dare Island School," she added smoothly. "I'm calling about your niece Taylor."

The back of Matt's neck tightened. "Is she sick? Hurt?"

"Taylor is fine. However, it is our policy to notify the parent or guardian when we have to remove a student temporarily from the classroom. I'm afraid Taylor became belligerent with her teacher this morning."

He cupped the phone, trying to cut the interference from the wind. "What do you mean, belligerent? The kid never opens her mouth."

"Apparently she found her voice today," Nelson said dryly. "Perhaps it would be best if I spoke with Taylor's grandmother. Is Tess at home?"

"She's on the mainland." Picking up supplies for the weekend. And Tom was God knew where with the truck, hunting a replacement part for the inn's generator.

Which left Matt. *If anything happens, I need to know you'll be here.*

He eased the hatch into place, covering the twin diesels. "What do you need?"

"We'll be sending home a Problem Report with Taylor. The next step is a parent meeting. Taylor needs to understand what constitutes appropriate dress and language at this school."

The Nelsons always were tight asses. After two hundred years, the family had gone respectable.

Matt thought of several possible responses, none of which could be considered appropriate language.

"You want a meeting, I'm there." He wiped his hands on an engine rag. "Give me fifteen minutes."

It was closer to twenty by the time he parked the bike and headed up the stairs. The administration offices occupied the original school building between the new elementary wing and the middle and high school. Since Matt's school days, an attempt had been made to update the building with new lights and new carpet. But the scarred woodwork was the same, and the smell, a compound of bubble gum, dust, and sneakers.

It took him back. Simpler times. Good times, mostly. Not that he was in any mood to feel nostalgic.

This wasn't his first trip to the school since he'd graduated. He'd made it to all of Josh's open houses, to most of his basketball games. But Tess was the one who usually handled calls during the day. Matt couldn't turn a charter trip around every time Josh threw up or got into a fight on the playground.

It was pure luck Matt wasn't already out on the water this morning.

Through the glass doors, he could see Taylor slumped in the short row of chairs in front of the reception desk, shoulders hunched, small, miserable, and defiant as a kitten in the rain. His heartstrings twinged.

He pulled open the door. "Hey, kiddo. What's going on?"

Her head jerked up. Her chin wobbled before she yanked her scowl back into place.

"Matthew Fletcher!" The school secretary greeted him from behind the high counter, pleasure warm in her raspy voice.

Lois Howell had survived two husbands, five principals, and a pack-a-day habit. She must be nearing seventy now, Matt thought, her orange hair a cloud around her weathered face, but she still had a smile that burst like sunshine over even the hardest case students.

He grinned at her. "Hey, Mrs. Howell."

"You go right in, dear," she said. "I told Karen not to keep you waiting. Third door, next to the copy room."

"Thanks." He dropped a hand on Taylor's bony shoulder, pretending not to notice when the girl flinched under his touch. "Let's get this straightened out."

Vice Principal Karen Nelson looked up from her computer as he stopped in the doorway. She was all beige, her hair, her lips, her sweater. "Mr. Fletcher."

He recognized her now. She used to teach second grade, a thin, nervous woman with a fondness for rules and worksheets.

"Karen. What's up?"

She pokered up at his use of her first name. "Won't you sit down?"

There were two chairs in the office. He lowered himself into one, nudged Taylor toward the other.

"Taylor and I have already spoken. She doesn't need to be here."

Matt rubbed his jaw. "I'd agree with you. So why isn't she in class?"

Nelson straightened in her chair. "I'm afraid there are discipline issues which need to be addressed before Taylor can return to a learning environment."

"Issues," Matt repeated.

"Her attire, to begin with. She's in violation of the dress code."

Matt regarded Taylor, wearing jeans and a Kinston baseball jersey, Luke's field cap pulled low over her eyes. Unless it was against school policy for a girl to dress as a boy, he didn't see the problem.

He turned back to the vice principal, his irritation in check. *Keep it light.* "You got something against the Indians?"

"Her hat, Mr. Fletcher. It's against the rules to wear a hat inside the school buildings."

"You pulled her out of class—you pulled me off my boat—over a damn hat?"

Red crept into her beige face. "Of course not. But when Mrs. Williams attempted to deal with the situation, Taylor became blatantly defiant."

At least two people in the room were taking this situation

seriously. Which meant Matt had to, too. Suppressing his grin, he looked at Taylor. "What did you do? Punch the teacher?"

Taylor stuck out her chin. Christ, she looked like Luke. "She tried to take my hat."

Matt's amusement died. He swung on Nelson, keeping his tone even. "That true?"

"After Taylor refused to store her hat in her cubby, Mrs. Williams attempted to confiscate it, yes. Taylor was rude and disruptive."

"I called her stupid," Taylor said, her expression torn between defiance and satisfaction.

"Well, it's a stupid rule," Matt said. Karen's mouth clamped shut like a bonefish biting on bait. He collected himself. "But you can't call your teacher names."

"Headgear, including hats or bandanas of any kind that could display gang affiliation, is strictly forbidden in school buildings," Karen said.

"Gang affiliation? On Dare." He didn't bother keeping his voice down this time. "Are you kidding me?"

Nelson drew herself up, a fearful, stubborn woman with wide eyes and a tiny mouth. "The island is changing. Our population is changing. A sixth of our students speak English as a second language."

"I'm going to pretend I didn't hear that," Matt said. "Or I'll have to think you're racist as well as insensitive. You know damn well those aren't gang colors. That's a U.S. Marine cap given to Taylor by her father, my brother, who left yesterday to serve our country in Afghanistan. I can't believe you have a problem with that."

MATT'S RAISED VOICE penetrated the hallway.

Allison stood in the copy room with Monday's quiz, her heart banging uncomfortably against her ribs.

She wasn't trying to eavesdrop. She definitely wasn't going to get involved. Matt's presence at school was none of her business. The little girl—his niece?—wasn't her student. As a new teacher, Allison was trying hard to be a valued member of the team. To fit in. The last thing she needed was more talk.

Or a reprimand.

But the door was open, and she couldn't help but overhear Matt's angry words. Couldn't help, either, the sympathetic lurch of her heart.

My brother, who left yesterday to serve our country in Afghanistan . . .

The copy machine glowed and clacked and hummed as phrases escaped into the hall. *New home, new school . . . Just lost her mother . . . Doesn't need this kind of grief . . .*

Poor baby, Allison thought.

A deployed parent had a profound effect on a child's behavior in and out of the classroom. The girl's teacher should know better than to . . .

Unless she hadn't been informed.

Allison retrieved her copies from the tray. *She* hadn't been informed, and the deployed Marine was Joshua's uncle.

Of course, it didn't surprise her that Joshua hadn't said anything. A student who barely answered roll call was unlikely to volunteer personal family information.

But Matt could have told her. If not over beer at the Fish House, then later, when he was driving her home. Or parked in her driveway.

You really don't know him very well, Gail had said.

Her mind slid to the front seat of the truck, the soft cotton of his shirt, the roughness of his stubble, the taste and textures of his mouth . . .

She dragged her thoughts back to hear Karen Nelson say,

"I'm sorry, but we can't make exceptions to the rules because of one student's circumstances."

"Karen, it's a damn hat."

"Matt, it's school policy."

"You always were a stick, Karen. Lighten up. It's not going to kill anybody if she wears a hat to class."

Allison winced. Matt was doing the right thing—her heart warmed at the way he was standing up for that little girl—but he was going about it all wrong. She knew school administrators like Karen. The harder he pushed, the deeper the vice principal would dig in behind her wall of regulations.

Not her business, Allison reminded herself.

Not her problem.

Gail had warned her against taking too personal an interest in Matt Fletcher. Tangling with the VP over a discipline problem was no way to quiet the school gossips.

Chest tight, Allison slipped the original test paper from the glass.

And rapped on the vice principal's doorjamb. "Hi, Karen. I just overheard . . . I wonder if I could help?"

All three people in the room looked at her as if she'd lost her mind.

And maybe she had.

Allison gripped her test copies until the paper trembled. Okay, she could fix this. She was good at fixing things. Growing up she had been the one to keep the peace, to smooth over heated words and icy silences.

"I don't know what you think you can do, Miss Carter," Karen said coldly from behind her desk. "I have the situation under control."

It was important that the vice principal go on believing that. Any solution would be as much about saving face as following the rules.

"Of course." Allison edged into the office. After that one brief glance, she hadn't dared look at Matt. "I already heard you tell . . ."

Oh, crap. She glued her smile in place while she tried desperately to recall the child's name.

"Taylor," Matt supplied. "My niece."

Gratefully, she grabbed the lifeline he'd tossed her. "*Taylor* that it would be all right for her to keep the hat in her cubby."

Maybe Karen hadn't used those words, exactly. But close enough, Allison hoped.

Karen frowned. "I don't see—"

"So the issue isn't whether Taylor has the hat in her possession," Allison said hurriedly. "She just can't wear it in class."

"Well, obviously," Karen said.

"So she could keep it in her book bag," Allison continued.

Taylor scowled. "I don't *want*—"

"Hold on," Matt said quietly, his eyes on Allison's face.

"I suppose," Karen said.

"Or even *on* her book bag," Allison suggested. "Like, pinned to it or something."

"I fail to see the point," Karen said.

"But it's not against school policy," Allison said.

"Well, no."

"And there's no rule against her keeping her book bag with her at her desk."

"It would be very inconvenient if all the students' book bags were at their desks, cluttering the aisles. Someone could trip."

"I know you're concerned about the students' safety," Allison said. "It's so important for the school to maintain a sense of order and stability and . . . and security. Especially for a student like Taylor, who's going through a tough time."

A pause, which Allison counted in heartbeats, while Karen considered the child in front of her.

"We certainly don't want to make things more difficult for any of our students," the vice principal said at last.

Allison beamed at her. "Exactly."

"Anything we can do to support our servicemen . . ."

"I appreciate that, Karen," Matt said.

"As long as Taylor understands that we do not wear our hats inside, there's no reason she can't keep her father's hat with her," the vice principal concluded.

Matt stuck his thumbs in his pockets. "It's not a bad offer," he said to the girl.

"It's a good compromise," Allison said.

Matt kept his gaze on Taylor. "You okay with it?"

The girl put her head to one side, her blue eyes wide and doubtful in her thin face. Someone, sometime, had done something to destroy that child's trust, Allison thought.

Slowly, Taylor reached up and dragged off the hat.

"Right." Matt turned back to the VP. "We'll take the deal. But she's not going back in that classroom until you square things with her teacher."

Karen rose from behind her desk. "If you'd like to wait here, I can certainly discuss the situation with Mrs. Williams."

"You do that," Matt said. "I'm taking Taylor home for the day. She can come back on Monday."

Karen pursed her lips. "Perhaps a fresh start would be best for everyone. Thank you for coming in, Matt."

He nodded. "Thanks for calling me."

Problem solved, Allison thought, relieved and gratified. Now she just needed to make her escape before Karen started questioning why the new high school Language Arts teacher was negotiating disciplinary consequences in her office.

"Well," Allison said brightly, backing toward the door, "I should get back to my planning period."

"We'll walk out with you," Matt said.

Taylor raised her head.

Karen looked from Matt to Allison, speculation in her eyes.

Allison bit her lip. "It's not necessary."

"We're going the same way."

"I don't want to intrude."

A corner of Matt's mouth kicked up in a smile, the warmth in his eyes raising the room temperature by about twenty degrees. "Too late for that now."

SHE LOOKED SO damn cute, Matt thought as they walked down the hall, her blond hair in a long, straight tail, her cheeks pink with victory and embarrassment. Taylor scuffed ahead of them, her sneakers squeaking on the linoleum tile.

"I appreciate what you did in there," Matt said quietly.

Allison's chin firmed. "I would have done the same for any child."

Something had put a chill in her voice since their last meeting, a reservation in those big, brown eyes.

Which made it even more remarkable that she'd gone to bat for Taylor.

"Maybe so," Matt acknowledged. "But most people wouldn't have done anything at all."

Nobody but family had ever stepped up for him, stepped in like she had. Not even his wife. It took compassion to take on somebody else's problems. It took guts.

"Maybe you know the wrong people," Allison said.

Matt grinned in acknowledgment. He'd used almost the same words to her two days ago. "Maybe. Anyway, thanks. I owe you."

"You stopped to help me." A brief smile. "I stopped to help you. I'd say we're even."

With another woman he would have shrugged and let it go. But something about Allison Carter got under his skin, tugged at his gut.

"I didn't know we were keeping score," he drawled.

He watched her quick color with satisfaction. Why should he be the only one getting hot and bothered?

But her voice was cool as she said, "Now isn't the time for this discussion. You need to get Taylor home."

The kid was waiting up ahead by the heavy wooden double doors.

He nodded. "Fine. What are you doing tomorrow night?"

"Tomorrow?"

"Saturday. Come out with me."

"I barely know you."

He held her gaze. "We can change that."

The echo of her words reverberated in the space between them. *I don't jump into things with someone I don't know.*

"Take a chance," he said, his voice husky. "Take a leap."

"I'll think about it."

A tall black girl, one of the Jackson kids, bustled out of the high school wing. Running an errand to the office, Matt guessed. She slowed as she passed, throwing a greeting at Allison and a curious glance at Matt.

"Hi, Miss Carter."

Allison smiled. "Nia." She turned back to Matt, drawing a deep breath that did nice things for her blouse. "I'm going back to my classroom now. Before the entire school starts speculating what we're doing together."

He could think of all kinds of things he'd like to do with her, to her, on her, but not with people watching. Not in front of Taylor and whatever students happened to wander by.

"I'll call you," he said, like he was Josh's age again, trying to make it with some pretty girl after school.

He'd never had to try this hard, he remembered as he

strode to the exit. There had always been girls dropping by the Pirates' Rest to watch him mow the grass or tinker on his bike or play one-on-one with Sam.

You think they'd have more sense. Or pride, his sister Meg used to snap on her way out the door to the library or to one of her jobs, waiting tables, scrubbing bathrooms, handing out towels at the club. Always moving, Meggie, always working, always going somewhere. *Sam Grady is the biggest hound in school.*

But not all of the girls had gone for Sam.

He turned his head to watch Allison walk away, the swing of her hair, her long, honey-colored legs under the little blue skirt she wore, and felt that buzz, that healthy jolt of lust and anticipation that belonged to his past, to memories of summer nights around a bonfire and double dates in the backseat of Sam's daddy's car.

"Is she your girlfriend?" a voice piped up.

Startled, Matt looked down into Taylor's face. He pushed the door, holding it open for her. "No."

The minute they were outside in the sunlight, she jammed the hat back on her head, tugging the brim down low. "Why not?"

Because despite his recent crush on Teacher, he wasn't in high school anymore. He was too old for girlfriends. He had sex, relationships that began without commitment and ended without drama.

None of which he could explain to Luke's ten-year-old daughter.

"I don't need a girlfriend," he said carefully. "I have Josh and Grandma Tess and Grandpa Tom. And you."

That was enough commitment for anybody.

Taylor sighed, a forlorn sound that rippled through him like wind over water. "That's what my mom used to say. As long as we had each other, we didn't need anybody else."

Is that why she never bothered to get in touch with your

dad? Matt wanted to ask, but it didn't feel right to lay that question on the kid after the crappy day she'd had.

"Well, you've got me now," he said. "Come on, I'll take you home."

Taylor tensed.

"What?" Matt asked.

"He said I could stay." Her voice was pitched too high, her face pinched and white.

"Who?"

"Luke. My . . . my dad. He said I was staying with Grandma Tess now."

"Yeah, that's where we're going. Home."

And then it occurred to Matt that "home" probably meant something else to her. The kid had been shuttled around too damn often in the past couple of months to take anything for granted.

He squatted down so he could look her square in the eyes and asked, "Okay?"

He watched her think about it—*Nobody's fool, this kid*—before she nodded.

But when they got to his bike, she balked.

"Are we riding on that?"

He lifted his helmet from the back. "Yep."

"Where do I sit?"

He patted the custom seat. "Here. Behind me."

"I'll fall off."

"Not if you hold on," he said patiently.

He waited with the helmet on his hip while she looked from the bike to him and back again, suspicious as a fish testing artificial bait.

"Fine," she growled at last.

He grinned at her, tapping a finger on the bill of her cap. "You have to stow this. No riding without a helmet."

"Yeah? What about you?"

"I'm the grown-up," he told her. "I get to do what I want."

Which was a lie. North Carolina law required helmets, and being an adult meant taking on all kind of responsibilities you didn't necessarily want. But at ten, she didn't need to know that yet.

She snorted and dragged off Luke's Marine cap, stuffing it in her book bag, standing at attention while Matt fit the helmet over her blond head and adjusted the chin strap. Her bones were sharp and light as a bird's, the skin under her jaw baby fine and smooth. His gut clenched. She was so much younger than Josh, smaller, female, vulnerable. He gave the helmet an extra tug at the back, making sure it was secure, making sure she was safe.

His brother's child.

He hadn't expected this sense of responsibility to grip his chest so suddenly, so tight, another claim, another complication he hadn't been looking for in his life. But there was no way he would wish her away now.

TAYLOR FLINCHED AS he jumped on some kind of kickstand thing and the motor choked and roared to life.

She stood, her feet superglued to the ground, her heart banging as loud as the engine, while he twisted the handlebars and swung one long leg over the rattling frame.

Turning his head, he smiled at her. "You step up on the footrest there. Don't touch the exhaust pipes. They're hot."

He looked really big, straddling the big, noisy bike, and the seat was so small.

She didn't—couldn't—move.

"It's okay," Uncle Matt said gently. "I'm holding her steady. You won't fall."

He thought she was afraid of the motorcycle.

Pride and scorn and desperation propelled her forward. Jerkily, she climbed up on the narrow seat behind him, clutching his arm and then his shirt. His arm was warm and steady. His back was hard and wide, a living wall.

Taylor swallowed.

"You've got to really hold on," he shouted over the rumble of the bike. "Around my waist."

She tensed, greasy panic balling in her stomach. She didn't want to get that close to him. She didn't want to get that close to anybody.

At least he took her side. In Nelson's office. He'd showed up in the middle of the day, mad and solid, and stood up for her.

Taylor relaxed a little, remembering how he yelled at the vice principal. Even when the pretty blond teacher had fixed things, he hadn't expected Taylor to shut up and go along the way everybody else did, just because she was a kid. Like what she thought, how she felt, didn't matter. He *asked* her what she wanted.

You've got me now, he'd said.

Slowly, slowly, her arms crept around him and clung.

Seven

TAKE A CHANCE, Matt had invited in his deep, husky voice. *Take a leap.*

And just for a moment, Allison's heart had wanted to tumble right off a cliff. Except she no longer jumped from one thing, one man, one enthusiasm, to another.

She was an English teacher now. Literature was full of cautionary tales about women who took foolish chances and crashed. Look at sweet, suicidal Juliet. Or poor, crazy Miss Havisham. Or . . .

"Hester Prynne," Allison said to her fourth period class, "is publicly shamed and socially ostracized because she sleeps with the wrong guy and gets pregnant. Could that happen in today's society?"

She sat back, delighted, as her sixteen-year-olds waded in on both sides of the argument, jumbling together references to Puritan Massachusetts and *16 and Pregnant*. What was the difference, really, between a slut and a reality star? What were Dimmesdale's responsibilities as a Baby Daddy?

Did having children out of wedlock still pose a threat to the social order? Occasionally Allison interjected a question to encourage an insight or lead them back gently to the text. This was her favorite part of teaching, when the stories she loved and the students she cared about came alive.

Most of the students, anyway.

Her gaze flickered to the back of the classroom where Joshua Fletcher sprawled at his desk, arms across his chest, legs in the aisle. If he cared at all about the discussion crackling around the room, he certainly didn't show it.

Allison suppressed a sigh. She had to remain impartial in the classroom. But she was disappointed by her failure to reach Josh. She would have been disappointed by her failure to reach any student.

The period bell shattered the discussion. Even a debate about sex couldn't compete with lunch. The room erupted with scraping chairs and slamming books.

Allison raised her voice over the noise. "Don't forget! Five hundred words on one character's social and sexual identities. Due Monday," she called to a chorus of groans.

"Bye, Miss Carter."

"See ya, Miss Carter."

"Have a nice weekend."

"Miss Carter." Thalia Hamilton stopped by her desk, eyes sharp behind her thick black frames. "Are you going to be in the computer lab after school? I want to show you the banner for the blog. I think I can finish the layout tonight."

"Tonight? It's Friday. I'm happy to look at it, Thalia, but it can wait until the next newspaper meeting."

"It's not like I have anything better to do," Thalia said.

Allison smiled. "I guess there aren't a lot of places to hang out on the island." Not for Thalia's age group. No mall, Allison thought. And only one movie screen.

"Not unless I want to hang out under the pier drinking Gatorade and Everclear," Thalia said.

Allison winced slightly.

Joshua sauntered between the rows of desks, one arm around Lindsey Gordon, the other holding his binder on his hip.

"Joshua." Allison was *not* singling him out for attention. She was offering a friendly reminder, that was all. "You still need to turn in your permission form."

"Oh, yeah." He shifted his grip, exposing the battered paperback wedged on top of the notebook. *The Scarlet Letter.*

Well. A sliver of hope opened inside her. At least he'd brought the book to class.

He fished a wrinkled slip of paper from between the pages. "Here."

She glanced at the signature—Matt Fletcher, large, upright, dark, the *T* a stab, the *R* a scrawl—as she smoothed the note. "Thank you." Ripping a strip from the page, she handed it back to Josh.

"What's that for?"

"To keep your place."

He shook his head. "Naw, I'm good. Thanks."

She wondered if he was actually doing the reading or if he'd stuck the form in the book at random. "Which character are you writing about this weekend?"

"I dunno."

"Well, who do you like?"

He shrugged. "They're all kind of lame."

"Why do you say that?"

He shifted uncomfortably. "You know, the way the girl and the preacher guy let Chillingsworth pull the strings. I don't get why they don't just leave."

"They *want* to leave," Thalia said. "I mean, when Hester

and Dimmesdale meet in the forest, they plan to go to Europe."

His gaze switched to her. "I guess I didn't get to that part yet."

Lindsey tugged her hair. "Speaking of leaving . . ."

"Yeah, okay." Josh nodded at Thalia and Allison. "See you around."

"Are you going to the pier tonight?" Thalia asked.

His eyes rested on her briefly. "Maybe. I've got to be up early in the morning to crew for my dad."

Lindsey leaned against his side, her breast pressing his arm as they left.

Thalia watched them go.

Allison raised her eyebrows. "I thought you didn't like hanging out at the pier."

The girl turned red. "I don't. I just thought . . . that was probably the most he's talked to me since seventh grade."

Allison felt a twinge of sympathy. It was certainly the most he'd said in class. "And you want him to say more."

"I want him to notice me," Thalia said frankly. "He's the hottest guy in school, and he doesn't even see me."

Allison looked at Thalia, pretty, round, and animated with a flag of dark red hair and smart girl glasses. Different. Her heart ached for her.

"I'm sure he sees you. You're in most of the same classes."

"Since kindergarten. And as far as he's concerned, I'll always be the brainy girl with the crunchy granola parents and the weird first name."

Another example of how we're still shaped by social roles and expectations, Allison thought, but the girl needed reassurance from her, not another lesson derived from *The Scarlet Letter*.

"You have a beautiful name," she said instead. "Thalia was one of the Greek muses."

"Yeah, the muse of comedy." Thalia rolled her eyes. "Like that will get me dates."

Allison smiled. "It could be worse. Your parents could have named you Terpsichore."

Thalia laughed and then sobered. "It's not just my name, Miss Carter. It's this school. This island. It's hard to get romantic about somebody who watched you eat paste. I think that's why Josh doesn't have a girlfriend."

"I thought he and Lindsey . . ."

Shut up, Allison. She was a teacher, for crying out loud. She had no business gossiping about her students' love lives.

"Lindsey wishes," Thalia said. "But they're not exclusive or anything. Josh dates summer girls. That way when he wants a change, he doesn't have to go through the drama of breaking up with them."

Allison's throat went dry. *Our Matt doesn't date locals,* Gail had said, sympathy in her voice. *In all these years, I've never known him to date a woman longer than a couple of weeks. A couple of months, if she's here for the summer.*

Apparently this was a case of like father, like son.

"Don't you think you and Lindsey deserve better?" Allison asked.

"In the long run? Sure." Thalia grinned, sharp and quick. "But I'm not looking for commitment. I just want a date before I die. Preferably before I go to college."

"Do I sense a double standard here? Are you crushing on him just because he's . . ." Allison hesitated, casting for an appropriate word to describe a student, to apply to Matt's son.

"Incredibly hot?" Thalia asked. "Heck yeah. I mean, that's part of it. But he's also a nice guy. Sometimes that's enough."

WHEN ALLISON ARRIVED home at the end of the day, she found her repaired bicycle propped against the front steps of the cottage. She loved living in a community where bike theft wasn't an issue. She was touched by the neighborliness of the gesture, encouraged by this sign of acceptance. As soon as she unloaded her car—she'd stopped by the garden center on her way home—she called Bill at the bike rental place to thank him.

"Really nice of you," she said. "I wanted to pick up the bike after school, but there was no way I could fit it in my car. I didn't expect you to make a special delivery to my house."

"Wasn't me," Bill said. "That was Matt. He didn't want you to have to walk out here."

"Oh." Allison regrouped. "Well, that was very thoughtful of him. I'll drop by tomorrow with the check."

"All taken care of."

"You have to let me pay," Allison protested.

"Matt already did. Guess you can settle up with him when you see him." Bill chuckled, making it clear what kind of payment he thought Matt could expect.

Heat washed Allison's face. *Wonderful.* That would certainly give the faculty break room something to talk about on Monday.

"I'll do that," she promised and thanked Bill again before disconnecting.

Slowly, she lowered her cell phone.

Maybe she shouldn't read too much into what was basically a friendly gesture, she thought as she changed into jeans. Maybe this was simply Matt's way of saying thank you because she'd intervened on behalf of his niece this afternoon.

You stopped to help me. I stopped to help you. I'd say we're even, she'd said to him mere hours ago.

The look in his eyes made her pulse pound. *I didn't know we were keeping score.*

Allison took a deep breath as she went back out to her car. She was not playing games with Matt Fletcher. She was pretty sure she'd lose.

Yes, he was nice. And thoughtful. And, to use Thalia's criteria, incredibly hot.

But Allison wasn't sixteen anymore. Once upon a time, she'd believed sex was an okay trade-off to feel close, to feel warm, to feel accepted. No longer.

She wasn't her mother, either. She didn't see every relationship as "marriage track" or weigh the worth of a man in carats. She truly believed that in love, as in life, the journey mattered as much as the destination.

That didn't mean she had to hop every bus that came along.

She dragged her garden supplies up onto the deck, two large, square planters and a load of potting soil.

She admired Matt. But no matter how nice he was, how interested he seemed to be, he was as reluctant to volunteer things as his son. He hadn't confided in her about anything that really mattered. No insights about Joshua that could help her in the classroom. Not a word about Matt's brother or his niece. Nothing Allison couldn't and hadn't heard from a casual acquaintance.

She required more these days than zings and tingles, than sexual buzz. She wanted a guy who was the opposite of her father, someone who would share himself with her, who was emotionally available.

She climbed the steps again with a flat of mixed pansies and some two-inch pots of herbs, plants the woman at The Secret Garden had promised would winter well.

Allison wasn't foolish enough to expect intimacy after only one date. Not even a date, she reminded herself. She knew from teaching how hard it was to be a single parent. Maybe Matt gave so much to his family he didn't have anything left to invest in a relationship.

But she needed more. She deserved better. And since "better" hadn't presented itself, she was better off alone.

When her phone rang, she was prepared to tell him so.

She brushed the dirt from her hands and hit TALK. "Hello?"

"It's after seven."

Oh, God. Allison shifted the phone to her ear. "Hi, Mom."

That would teach her to not check caller ID.

"You should have called hours ago," Marilyn continued, ignoring her daughter's greeting. She was adept at hearing only what she wanted to hear.

A pulse throbbed in Allison's temples. Sweat beaded on her upper lip and between her breasts. "Sorry. It's Friday. I thought you'd be at . . ." She racked her brain, staring at the bright, blank faces of the pansies. What was Friday? Book club? Symphony? "Going to dinner with the Pearsons."

"We're meeting them at Bec Fin in an hour. That's why I called."

Allison tried and failed to find a connection. "You want directions?" she hazarded, only half joking.

"Guess who's joining us," Marilyn said.

"I have no idea."

"You remember Walter and Claudia's son, John?"

Allison sighed and swiped at the sweat, leaving a tickle of dirt on her face. "Is he the investment banker or the lawyer?"

"Johnny is an anesthesiologist. At Temple. And," Marilyn added triumphantly, brandishing the reason for her call like a magician pulling a rabbit from a hat, "he's left his wife."

"That's too bad."

"What?"

"Are there children?"

"A little girl, I think. The point is, Allison, this would be a perfect time for you to come home for a visit."

The throbbing became a twitch. Every time her mother called, it was the same. Some acquaintance at the club had a daughter who had just gotten married, a son who'd recently been divorced. Marilyn wouldn't be happy until Allison's wedding announcement—two columns with accompanying photo above the fold—appeared in the Sunday *Inquirer.*

"Mom, you know I can't do that." Allison climbed to her feet, her back aching, her shoulders tight. "I'm teaching five classes. I have papers to grade and a unit test to prepare."

"It's the weekend."

"You want me to drive to Philadelphia for the weekend?"

"You keep telling me how close you are."

"Nine hours."

"You could be here by lunchtime tomorrow."

"If I started at three in the morning."

"Your room's all ready. You can take a nap before you meet Johnny for cocktails. The Pearsons are free for brunch on Sunday. Or we can go shopping. Make a real weekend of it. You deserve a little treat. And I need some time with my daughter."

Allison rubbed her forehead, massaging away her guilt and frustration. Marilyn, the social butterfly, loved the idea of a daughter—dressing her up, taking her out, showing her off—much more than she enjoyed the socially conscious bookworm she'd produced. But saying so would only prompt tears and accusations.

"Mom, I have to be back on Monday."

"I'm sure you could arrange one day off to be with your family."

"Sure I could." Probably she could. "If somebody died."

Her mother's breath hissed, followed by a deep, offended silence.

"Sorry, Mom," Allison said.

"I suppose you think that's funny."

"No, I—"

"How could you . . . After Miles . . ."

"I'm *sorry.*" Her brother wasn't dead. He was just gone,

leaving Allison as the sole target of their father's hopes and their mother's disappointment.

The pansies listed, limp in the heat.

"There's no need to take that tone with me," Marilyn said. "I'm only thinking of you. Your happiness. Your future."

"Mom, I am happy. I wish you could be happy for me."

But as usual, Marilyn could not hear her. "How can I be happy with my little girl so far away?"

The pulsing was a full-fledged headache now, pounding in Allison's temples.

"A minute ago you said I was close enough to drive up for the weekend," she pointed out unwisely.

"And you begrudge me even that much. We haven't had any girl time in ages. But apparently I'm not a priority for you."

Guilt hammered at Allison. She knew her parents' marriage lacked any real emotional intimacy. Marilyn would not dream of unloading on her husband, could no longer dump on their son. She would never tarnish the Christmas card perfection of her image by venting to her friends. But with Allison, all her pent up grievances escaped like an evil genie from a bottle.

"Mom, I love you. But I have to work."

"Oh, please. Your father has to work. He has a career," Marilyn said. "You're just going through a phase. Like that time you stopped eating meat. Or when you went to Wyoming."

"South Dakota."

"Whatever. Just because you think you've found some new way to save the world doesn't entitle you to neglect your real responsibilities. When I volunteered at the Junior League, I never neglected you."

Allison swallowed the ache and anger of a hundred remembered brush-offs, *don't mess my hair, don't bore my friends, can't we talk about this later?* It was useless to remonstrate. It always had been.

"I'm not neglecting anything, Mom."

"You're neglecting yourself. When was the last time you had a manicure? Or a date?"

Allison glanced at the black crescents of dirt beneath her nails before shoving her left hand in a pocket. "I have a date," she heard herself say.

She bit her tongue. Too late.

"Really?" Marilyn's voice wavered between pleasure and suspicion. Allison closed her eyes. Her mother wanted her only daughter to attract and keep a man. The Right Man, which in the world according to Marilyn meant a potential son-in-law with the genes and job description to give her bragging rights at the club. "Well, why didn't you say so?"

Because he's a fisherman with a teenage son.

Because he rides a motorcycle.

Because you'd hate him.

She opened her eyes. "I have to go now. He'll be here any minute. Have a nice dinner."

"Wait! What does he do? He's not another teacher, is he? Is his family . . ."

"Bye, Mom. Love you!" She punched the END CALL button, breathless with rebellion.

Her phone rang again almost immediately.

Her heart pounded. *Don't answer, don't . . .*

She glanced at the display. Not her mother. No name at all, just an unfamiliar North Carolina number.

"Hello?" she answered cautiously.

"Allison, it's Matt."

It was karma. She was going to hell for lying to her mother.

"I'd like to take you out to dinner tomorrow night," he said in his low drawl.

"Tomorrow?"

"If you're free. How about seven?"

"How about tonight?"

A pause while her brain scrambled to catch up with her mouth. *Oh, God.* Maybe she'd shocked him. She'd certainly shocked herself.

"It doesn't have to be dinner," she added hurriedly. "I mean, if you've already eaten . . ."

"I can do dinner."

"Someplace quiet." Somewhere they wouldn't be seen. Not the Fish House. Not anywhere on the island. If she was going to revert to her reckless ways, she could do without an audience. "Jacksonville, maybe. Or the moon."

"I wouldn't call a military town on a Friday night quiet," Matt said, his voice deep and amused. "Are you all right?"

She was out of her mind.

"I'm fine." She was twenty-five years old, too old to let her mother make her crazy. "Look, maybe this is a bad idea. Joshua mentioned you have an early morning tomorrow. I shouldn't have suggested . . . You caught me at a bad time, that's all. Let's just . . ."

"I'll pick you up in an hour," Matt interrupted. "We'll go someplace quiet and talk."

WHEN MATT CAME out of his bedroom, Josh was on the couch, one eye on the Food Network and both thumbs on his phone, texting.

The teen glanced up, taking in Matt's freshly shaved face and clean jeans, and smirked. "Hot date?"

Matt set the small cooler on the counter that divided living room and kitchen. "Maybe."

Josh grinned. "You know we have an early start tomorrow, right?"

Matt opened the fridge. Not much there. Beer, ketchup,

mayonnaise, eggs, a half-empty gallon of milk, and a carton of orange juice. "There's more to life than work, son."

There hadn't been lately.

Maybe that was the reason an evening with pretty Allison Carter held so much appeal. She made him feel things, reminded him he was a man with a man's needs.

"So you don't care if I go out tonight," Josh said, testing.

A man's needs and a sixteen-year-old son, Matt thought wryly.

"Not as long as you stay out of trouble and get home at a reasonable hour."

"Cool."

A quick survey of the refrigerator drawers yielded a packet of lunch meat, two withered apples, and a bunch of grapes. Matt left the lunch meat, tested the grapes by popping one in his mouth. Not bad.

Josh wandered in, hands in his pockets, drawn by curiosity or the open refrigerator. "So who is she?"

Matt tossed the apples into the garbage and rinsed the grapes under the faucet. "Do I ask you about your love life?"

"No." Josh grabbed the orange juice and drank. Lowering the carton, he grinned before assuming a mock serious expression. "I don't need to warn you about the dangers of premarital sex, do I, Dad?"

"Wise ass." Matt tossed the grapes into the cooler and headed for the door.

Josh called after him. "Don't forget condoms!"

Eight

Talking with her mother didn't usually drive Allison to drink. But she reasoned a single glass of wine would settle her nerves and bolster her courage.

Setting down her empty glass, she tugged open the door.

Matt Fletcher stood on her front porch in a black T-shirt and jeans, thumbs hooked into his front pockets, a hint of a smile on his lips, totally at ease.

Without even trying, he made every gym-toned banker and golf-playing engineer her parents had ever pushed at her seem overdressed, insecure, and uninteresting. He was so entirely male, so completely comfortable in his own skin.

Her insides danced with a mix of lust, rebellion, and Chardonnay.

"You look pretty." His gaze brushed her bare shoulders before settling firmly, warmly, on her face. The tiny hairs on her upper arms tingled in awareness. "Might want to bring a sweater, though."

Allison flushed with heat and wine. She'd spent twenty

minutes digging in her closet for an outfit that didn't make her feel like Laura Ingalls Wilder, finally unearthing a halter top from spring break five years ago and a pair of skinny jeans. She had good arms. And decent legs.

But despite what Gail had said about Matt's reputation, he was obviously in no hurry to talk her out of her clothes. Maybe she should suggest that he keep her warm? But she needed more daring for that.

Or another glass of wine.

Wordlessly, she fetched a cardigan from her bedroom.

"Thank you for going out with me," she said when they got to the truck.

"My pleasure." He shifted gears with one hand, steering with the other. He had great hands, she noticed. Working hands, tanned and strong, with a thin line of white scar across his knuckles. "Thank you for saying yes."

"I asked you."

He glanced over in surprise.

"Tonight," she explained as he backed smoothly out of the driveway. "You asked me for tomorrow. I asked you tonight."

"Yeah, you did." Another sideways glance. "Why did you?"

To spite my mother didn't seem like a tactful reply.

Or even a very good reason.

She cleared her throat. "My mother called. I told her I had a date to get off the phone."

A corner of his mouth kicked up. "And you don't like to lie to your mother."

"Yes. No." Allison took a deep breath to still her jittery stomach.

If she wanted honesty from Matt, she owed him honesty in return. This wasn't about her mother. Allison was a grown-up, old enough to make up her own mind about what she wanted, what she needed.

And woman enough to change it.

"I wanted to go out. With you," she said, so there could be no doubt. "I'd like to get to know you better."

The echo of her previous words charged the air of the cabin. *I don't jump into things with someone I don't know.* She wiped damp palms on the thighs of her jeans. Did he remember?

"Most women from off island don't care about getting to know me. They're just looking for a good time."

"Which you no doubt provide." She meant to sound teasing, not wistful.

He slanted a smile at her. "I can."

The two words thumped softly in the pit of her stomach. The buzz was back, collecting on her skin like static before a storm. She had asked Matt out as a gesture of independence, a show of control over her life, her destiny. But she didn't feel in control of herself or the situation.

He sounded so sure of himself.

Of her.

But then, she thought crossly, she was practically throwing herself at him. He had every right to sound confident.

"So is this how you entertain your dates? By bringing them . . ." She leaned forward to peer out the windshield at empty road and shadowed, silent dunes. "Where are we, anyway?"

"I told you I'd show you my island. This is it."

Gnarled live oaks on one side; an uneven line of erosion fence on the other; marsh grass and sea oats everywhere.

"There's nothing here."

His teeth showed in a smile. "Give it a chance."

Their headlights jumped across the road. He turned left toward a gap in the line of pickets. She felt a bump as the pavement ended and their tires dropped onto sand. Shells crunched. The engine rumbled.

She gripped the door handle as the truck lurched, aware of leaving something behind, of venturing off the road she knew into the unknown.

And then the dunes fell away and the beach opened below, stretching away into the dusk on either side, gray sand and silver sea under a twilight sky.

Allison drew her breath in wonder.

Matt circled the truck to face the dunes, parking perpendicular to the water.

He cut the engine. Silence rushed in, cool and laced with the scent of the sea.

Allison craned her neck to look out the windows. "Wow. Just . . . Wow."

"Yeah."

The horizon ran with paint box colors, purple, red, and gold. Low breakers rolled toward shore, dissolving in a flurry of foam against the flat sand.

Matt came around to help her from the truck.

"Easy." He steadied her as her heels sank into sand.

"I'm okay." She was *not* drunk. "I wasn't expecting a walk on the beach."

"We're not going far."

She glanced down the shoreline at the glowing line of lights over the water. "Is that the pier?"

"Yep."

"What is it, like a mile?" She could walk a mile if she took off her shoes.

"We're not walking. We're parking." He went to the back of the truck.

The soft sea breeze was clearing her head. "I didn't know you could park on the beach at night," she said conversationally.

"Now, yeah. Not during the season."

"Because of tourists?"

He grinned and lowered the tailgate. "Because of turtles. Sea turtles lay their clutches in May. They hatch at night, follow the moon's reflection to the sea. Headlights confuse them. And they can get trapped in tire tracks. But this time of year, it's not a problem."

He grabbed a quilt from the back and spread it over the truck bed. "Up you go."

He boosted her onto the tailgate, his hands hard and strong. She caught her breath as he swung up beside her, the truck bouncing beneath his weight. His thigh brushed hers, his body warm and close. He stretched an arm behind her, making her heart beat faster.

Making his move, she thought.

He dragged a cooler forward from the back and began to unload it.

A picnic.

Her lips curved as he laid out grapes and cheese and wrapped sandwiches. She found the simple spread more appealing than her mother's themed and catered menus, more romantic than an overpriced meal in some fancy restaurant.

Matt lifted a bottle of wine from the cooler.

And far more seductive.

She watched as he lit a Coleman lantern, as he pulled a corkscrew from his pocket.

"Very nice," she said. "Do you come here often?"

"I used to. With my grandda, fifteen, twenty years ago." Expertly, he uncorked the wine. "It hasn't changed much."

"You don't like change?"

"I didn't say that. You can't live on an island without accepting change. Storms come, beaches erode, families die out or move away. Old houses are bulldozed to make way for a parking lot or a septic tank."

He poured wine into two plastic tumblers, handed her one. "You live with loss, you learn to appreciate the things that endure. The sea. The moon. The lighthouse."

"The things that endure," she repeated softly. "I like that."

Wasn't that what she'd come to Dare Island to find?

She wanted to build a life here, to make a permanent place for herself, something solid, something lasting.

She didn't want to be another in the long line of Women Who Had Dated Matt Fletcher, the summer girls who lasted a few days or weeks.

It was both tempting and dangerous to believe she could be more.

She sipped her wine. "Thank you. You're very good at this."

He paused, unwrapping a sandwich. "This?"

She flapped her hand, encompassing the scene. "The secluded beach, the private picnic, the bottle of wine. It's really nice," she said again. "You're awfully . . ." *Practiced.* "Prepared."

"Not me. My mom."

Allison blinked. "Your mother?"

"The inn keeps supplies on hand for the guests, wine and cheese, box lunches, that kind of thing. Those are my mother's cookies."

"Oh." She tried to imagine her mother's reaction to anyone casually helping themselves to the contents of her kitchen. Favors in the Carter household always came with strings attached. "How does your mother feel about you raiding her pantry?"

"She's okay with it. I'll replace the wine tomorrow, turn over part of my catch for dinner."

"That's . . . really sweet," Allison decided. "The way you all interact with each other."

"That's what families do."

She drank more wine. "Not mine."

"You talk with your parents. You said your mother called," he added when she looked at him, surprised.

"My mother and I don't talk. I say 'hello' and then I listen while she tells me how I've disappointed her again." Allison shook her head, impatient with herself. "That isn't fair. My mother wants a relationship with me. She wanted me to come for a visit. Drop everything, take a day off, meet her latest candidate for son-in-law."

"Candidate?"

"It doesn't matter. The point is, she's lonely."

"She has your father, right? They're still together."

"Yes."

There had been a time, after Miles left, when she'd thought her parents' marriage would not survive the strain. But a divorce was too expensive for her father, too embarrassing for her mother, to be pursued.

"My father's gone a lot, chasing projects, entertaining clients. He has more important things to do with his time than go shopping and out to lunch or listen to my mother talk about her flower arranging class." Allison stared at Matt, struck. "Oh, God, maybe I'm turning into my father."

He refilled her glass. "Not happening."

"How would you know?"

"I don't want to go out with your father. I definitely don't want to see him naked."

She snickered before she could stop herself. "Thanks. I feel so much better now."

"Well," he said mildly, "that was the idea."

She sipped her wine, aware she was talking too much. The goal was to get to know him, not to blurt out every pathetic detail of her family relationships. "They're not bad people, my parents. It's just that when I'm with them, I revert to this awkward, uninteresting twelve-year-old. I can't please them. And they can't accept that."

"Listen, it's none of my business, but maybe you're fishing with the wrong bait."

"Excuse me?"

He unwrapped another sandwich and laid it on the napkin by her knee. Somehow, without noticing, she'd eaten the other one. "I read that syllabus you sent home with Josh. It was great.

You lay it all out, what you expect from the kids, what they can expect from you. You're nice about it, but you let them know what your boundaries are, what your consequences are. You want your parents to see you as an adult, you need to treat them like you do your students. Set boundaries."

He was right.

Wine, or maybe frustration, made her say, "I don't see you setting boundaries with your parents. You live with them."

"Behind them, yeah. The rent helps in the off-season. They wouldn't accept money from me otherwise. That doesn't mean we're in each other's business all the time." He smiled a little. "They have boundaries, too."

She sighed. "You're lucky to have them."

"I know."

"And they're lucky to have you."

He shrugged. "They take care of me and Josh, I take care of them."

"I envy you. It's easier for me to blame my parents than to try to change them."

"You can't change them."

"Meaning, I'm the one who has to change?"

He moved his shoulders again, clearly uncomfortable with continuing the conversation, just as obviously committed to help. "Meaning all you can do is be straight with them."

"I'm afraid if I'm honest, I'll alienate them completely," Allison confessed. "The way my brother did. I won't have any relationship with them at all."

"Your brother was a kid. Eighteen when he left home, right? You're not the person he was."

"They still get to me."

"Because you love them. That's a good thing." He reached out and tucked a strand of hair behind her ear. His touch lingered. "Just don't let them use it against you."

Their eyes met.

He was so sane, strong, solid. A nice guy.

Sometimes that's enough, Thalia's voice whispered in her head.

Leaning in, she laid her lips on his.

HEAT. HUNGER.

She tasted salty sweet, like woman and wine, and when she licked his bottom lip, Matt angled his head, taking her in, taking control.

Her bare shoulders were driving him crazy. He ran his hands up her smooth, toned arms, jerking her forward, pushing her back, falling with her into the deep and the dark as he kissed the hell out of her.

As she kissed him back.

His head spun. His blood rushed in his ears like the sea. Her arms twined around his neck as she stretched beneath him, as she arched against him. He sank into her, taking the kiss deeper still, tongues tangling, desire rising fast and hot. He skimmed his hands along her sides and felt her tremble, nudged his thigh between her legs and heard her moan. She was taut and pliant, moving under him, her mouth eager under his. His hand brushed the side of her breast, and she gripped his wrist, guided his hand beneath her top. His mind blanked.

No bra. Only flesh, only Allison, soft and warm. He palmed her breast, scraped the delicate point with his thumb. Her breath hissed.

Too hard, he thought.

Too far, too fast.

He had to stop.

She had to stop him. They were—he was—rapidly reaching the point of no return.

Goddamn it. He didn't want this time to be like the others.

He raised his head. Jesus, she was beautiful, her hair spilled like moonlight over his arm, her mouth wet, ripe, swollen. She curled up to kiss him again, stealing his breath, robbing his reason, but his conscience was awake now, prodding, chafing.

She didn't do one-night stands, his conscience said. She was vulnerable. She'd been drinking. All reasons, good ones, not to take this where he wanted to go. He had more respect for her, more restraint, than to peel her out of those tight jeans and fuck her on a public beach on their first real date.

Didn't he?

Quickly, before his lust overcame his good intentions and his judgment, he rolled off her and onto his back, willing his body to cool, his erection to subside.

If she touched him, he was toast.

He heard her sigh and closed his eyes so he wouldn't turn his head, so he couldn't watch the rise and fall of her breasts under that flimsy excuse for a shirt she wore.

"You okay?" His voice was hoarse. Rough.

She emitted a choked sound. He thought . . . God, he hoped it was a laugh. "Yes. Thank you," she added.

He had no idea if she was expressing polite appreciation for his question or if she was grateful because he hadn't fucked her in the back of his truck.

Maybe he was better off not knowing.

The sounds of the night and the sea washed over them, the whisper of the wind, the rush and retreat of the waves.

She touched him, just the tips of her fingers to the back of his wrist, an almost-by-accident brush of hands.

Turning over his palm, he laced his fingers with hers and gripped hard.

She sighed again.

He could feel the tension leaching from her tight muscles as they lay side by side, as his blood hammered in his head and behind his fly. The stars swam overhead. He drifted, anchored only by the feel of her hand warm and delicate in his, wanting her so badly his balls ached.

"Come on." He jacked to a sitting position, tugging at their joined hands.

She sat up, blinking, mussed, and beautiful. "Where?"

"For a walk."

Before he did something they'd both regret.

THE FOAM RUSHED in, the foam rushed out, breaking and dissolving around Allison's ankles. She struggled for footing, her bare feet sinking in the sand.

Matt gripped her hand.

Swept away.

She'd never actually believed it could happen, that it would happen to her, that she'd be leaving her shoes and inhibitions behind on a moonlit beach.

But then, she'd never been with anyone like Matt before.

She snuck a look at him, his strong profile etched against the night sky, his thick hair tousled by the breeze. He'd rocked her world and seriously shaken her self-perception.

"You know, Gail Peele warned me about this," she said conversationally.

He slanted a smile at her, still holding her hand. "About . . . ?"

"About you and your amazing effect on women."

His face froze for a moment before he grinned. "I never touched her. Not since the fifth grade dance."

Despite her pounding heart, Allison smiled. "Your moves must have improved since then." She cleared her throat. "I should probably thank you."

He shot her another sideways look and she flushed. Because she *had* thanked him. Less than half an hour ago. Right after she'd put his hand on her breast and her tongue in his mouth and he'd still pulled away.

Why had he pulled away?

"You want to thank me," he repeated. "For what? Showing you my moves?"

"For not . . . you know. I don't usually get swept away like that," she continued. "I'm not a go-with-the-flow kind of girl."

"I get that. You want to establish expectations. Set boundaries. I respect that."

She turned, digging her heels in the sand. "Is that why you stopped?"

The pier loomed closer, its misty lights gleaming on the water, casting deep shadows on the beach.

Matt moved his shoulders uncomfortably. "We got carried away."

"I certainly did. That doesn't mean I expect you to be responsible for my behavior. My choices."

His jaw set in a way she was coming to recognize. "I figured we should take a breather, come up for air."

"That's very sweet," she decided. "And now?"

"Now . . ." Waves slapped and echoed against the pilings of the pier. "I think we should go back."

She blew out a frustrated breath. "I don't want to go back. I think if we just talk about this, we can find a way to move forward."

"To the truck, Allison. We should go back to the truck."

She opened her mouth to argue.

Light flashed at the corner of her vision. She caught a scramble of movement between the black pilings, voices floating on the fitful breeze.

"*Shit.* It's my dad."

"Who's he with?"

"Is that *Miss Carter*?"

Allison froze. *Busted.* The Dare Island teenagers were on the loose, hanging out under the pier on a Friday night.

"Now can we turn around?" Matt asked grimly.

Nine

MATT PUT HIS arm around Allison to get her out of there.

Too late.

As they turned, he heard, "Man, Miss Carter's hot. Think he tapped that?"

"Shut up, asshole." That was Josh.

Allison covered her face with her hands. "I'll never live this down."

Matt didn't blame her for being upset. He tightened his arm around her shaking shoulders as he led her away.

"But it's almost worth it." She lowered her hands, her face alight with laughter. "Their reactions were priceless." She dropped her voice in wicked mimicry. "'Think he tapped that?'"

"Little bastard," Matt said.

"Maybe they won't say anything," Allison said. "Outside of school, I mean. Maybe they don't want to have to explain to their parents what *they* were doing under the pier on a Friday night."

Their parents knew. Matt knew. He should never have taken her down that way.

"Josh won't say anything."

Not if he knows what's good for him.

"Oh, who am I kidding?" Allison said. "They're teens. They'll talk. Talking about a teacher is irresistible. I just hope they don't post pictures on Facebook."

"They didn't see anything. We were walking. We had our clothes on, for Christ's sake."

"Except for my shoes. But it doesn't matter. I'm new and I'm young and I've been spotted with you. They all talk about you anyway."

Gail Peele. Matt remembered. He frowned. "Being seen with me doesn't make you some kind of . . ."

"Island slut?" Allison supplied with forced cheerfulness. "I'm going to embroider a shirt to wear to school on Monday. With the letter *A*. If I have to face the gossip, I might as well look the part."

He admired her ability to joke about the situation, but he could hear the effort her humor cost her. If she was right, at least some of the gossip she would have to endure was because of him.

After Kimberly walked out on their marriage, he'd kept his life and his relationships as uncomplicated as possible. Keep things light, keep things simple, and nobody got hurt. He'd never considered his choices could create complications for a woman like Allison.

Not a go-with-the-flow kind of girl, she'd said.

Maybe that's why he admired her, because of her willingness to take a stand, to put herself out there for the things she believed in, the people she cared about. Her students. Josh. Taylor.

He could put himself out just a little for her.

Because she was different from the women who had

come before. He needed to prove that. Not to the island grapevine, but to Allison.

And maybe to himself, too.

"You could come to dinner," he said.

She shook her head. "You're not listening. Going out with you is what got me in trouble in the first place."

"Not out. In. Come to Sunday dinner with my family."

She looked at him in disbelief. "And you think inviting me home to meet your parents will stop people talking?"

"No," he said truthfully. "But it might change what they say."

"Why are we eating in the dining room?" Josh asked Tess on Sunday.

"Because your English teacher is coming to dinner." Tess coated the bottom of a rectangular pan with a ladle full of red sauce. No big deal, Matt had told her. Just a nice, family style dinner to welcome the new teacher to the island.

That didn't mean they had to eat in the kitchen, Tess thought, arranging a layer of flat noodles on top of her sauce. According to Lois Howell in the school office, Miss Carter came from money, some fancy Philadelphia family.

"Six place settings," she directed Josh. "Use the good plates in the china cupboard."

Josh shuffled his feet. "I was going to Ethan's house tonight. We have a big project due for science class next week."

Tess narrowed her eyes. She'd never known her grandson to turn down her lasagna to do homework before. "Josh, it's Sunday. You know the rule. It's the only night we can count on eating together as a family. Taylor, honey, can you fold these napkins?" She wiped her hands and grabbed the stack of pretty flowered napkins, checking the oven temperature with one eye. "Besides, your father only invited Miss Carter because of you."

"Yeah, right."

"What do you mean?"

Josh lifted a shoulder. "Ask him."

"I will. In half, sweetie, like this, see?" Tess demonstrated the fold for Taylor. "Right now I'm asking you."

"Is Miss Carter your teacher?" Taylor asked Josh.

"English teacher, yeah."

Taylor nodded and made a precise fold.

"Why?" Tess asked.

"Nothing." Taylor concentrated on the napkins. "She's nice."

"Good job," Tess said.

She laid down a layer of browned ground beef and sausage, her mind returning to The List.

The powder room was clean, the guest soaps out, the toilet seat down, at least for now. There were candles on the dining room table. No flowers. She still had time to cut some from her garden. *No fuss*, Matt had said, but, really, when was the last time he'd invited somebody to dinner?

Not in years.

She dolloped her ricotta mixture on top of the meat. "Taylor, when did you meet Miss Carter?"

"When Uncle Matt picked me up from school."

Tess hummed in her throat. *The hat incident.*

"She's not his girlfriend, though," Taylor added.

The oven dinged as it came up to temperature.

"Oh, really." Tess struggled to keep her tone casual. "How do you know?"

"I asked him." Taylor frowned at the salad bowl on the counter. "Why does the lettuce look funny?"

Tess reached for her patience. "Because it's not lettuce. It's a spring green mix."

"I don't like it."

Josh snorted.

Tess shot him a look. Her grandson grabbed a handful of silverware and bolted for the dining room.

The back door banged open. Her men, returned from the sea.

"Something smells great." Matt came in and set three bottles of wine on the counter. He'd already shaved, Tess noticed, *and* changed his shirt. "Thanks."

"Thank you." She looked at the wine, her suspicions now thoroughly aroused. "Are those to replace the bottles that went missing Friday night?"

"Yep. Plus a nice red to go with dinner."

"Excellent. Matt . . ."

Tom strode in with Fezzik panting at his heels, bringing muddy paws and the strong smell of wet dog into her kitchen.

"Hey, babe." He kissed the back of her neck on his way to the refrigerator.

"Hey, yourself." She smiled. Sniffed. "Okay, we've got company coming in half an hour. Somebody get that dog out of here. He smells like rotten fish."

Tom twisted the top off a beer, standing in the draft from the open refrigerator door to drink it.

"Must have rolled in bait again," Matt said. "I've got him."

"Not you. You're all clean." Tess raised her voice. "Josh, take Fezzik out back and hose him down. Matt, do you have a minute?"

Alerted by her tone, Tom gripped his beer and began to back away. "I'll just give the boy a hand."

God forbid her husband stick around for any discussion that might actually mention feelings, Tess thought, amused.

"You need to shower before our company comes. Taylor can help Josh. Go on, sweetie," she said when the girl gave her a wide-eyed, doubtful look. "I want to talk with your Uncle Matt."

"Some-one's in trou-ble," Josh sang.

Matt snapped a dish towel at him, locker-room style. Josh laughed and ducked out the door.

Boys, Tess thought.

Matt leaned against the counter and cocked an eyebrow. "Am I in trouble?"

She patted his cheek. "Of course not. I just want you to know I'm happy you invited Allison . . . That is her name? Allison?"

He looked at her warily. "Yeah."

"I'm very happy you invited her to dinner."

"Okay."

Tess smiled at her firstborn, her eyes misty. "It's been a long time."

"Not that long," he said. "I've only known her a week."

"Very funny." Tess turned back to the counter, topping the last layer of noodles with sauce, spreading it with the back of a spoon. "Your father knew after an hour that I was the one."

Matt bent down and kissed her cheek. "I'm not as lucky as Dad."

His compliment made her feel warm and a little sad. "Maybe your luck is changing."

"Mom." His blue eyes were steady, his voice kind. "Don't make too big a deal out of this. It's dinner, that's all."

"So I'm happy my son is bringing a nice girl home to dinner." She sprinkled a final handful of mozzarella on the lasagna, followed by some grated parmigiano-reggiano. "I'm not blind, you know. Or deaf. I hear what people say. I know there have been other women."

But nobody important enough to bring home, she thought, to introduce to family.

"I can't tell you how to live your life," she said. "You're too much like your father. You know what you know and you'll do what you think is right. But isn't it time you got over Kimberly?"

"I am over her."

Tess slid her lasagna into the oven and turned to face him. Her son, so grown up, so confident, so sure.

So wrong.

Tess had always felt sorry for Kimberly, knocked up at nineteen, saddled with a baby she didn't want, torn between parents who thought she'd thrown her life away and a husband who wasn't the rebel she'd imagined him to be.

Tess would always be grateful to the girl for giving them Josh. But she hated what their brief marriage had done to easy, openhearted Matt. Her older son was more sensitive than he let on.

And more wounded.

"If you were really over her, you'd stop blaming yourself that things didn't work out."

A muscle worked in Matt's jaw. "I don't blame anybody. That doesn't mean I'm eager to repeat my mistakes."

"It's okay to need somebody in your life, Matt," Tess said gently.

"Sure." He smiled without humor. "Until they're not there anymore."

SUNDAY DINNER AT the home of a man she had gone out with exactly once. Okay, maybe twice.

It wasn't a date, Allison thought as she parked behind the inn. Or a parent-teacher conference.

Which left her unsure what to wear and how to behave.

Her bedroom now looked as if a tornado had ripped through her closet, jumbling shoes and sweaters together, tangling belts and blouses, depositing jeans and purses on the bed. After wasting an hour in front of her mirror, she'd finally decided on a white denim skirt paired with a coral top and an attitude of polite friendliness.

She was grateful to Matt for trying to protect her from doing the walk of shame into her classroom on Monday. She had to be careful not to read too much into his invitation.

Play it cool, she ordered herself, reaching for the flowers in the backseat. Take it slow. Parents liked her. Especially guys' parents. It's not like she was meeting her future in-laws or anything.

Her heart hammered in her chest.

She was stalling, she realized.

Taking a deep breath, she got out of the car.

Pink blooming crepe myrtle screened her view of the yard, but she could hear water splashing and a child's high, excited laughter.

"Oh, crap. My shoes got wet."

"Watch it." Josh's voice, deeper, amused. "He's slippery."

Allison tightened her grip on her cellophane-wrapped bouquet, a flush creeping up her face. What did you say to a student who had seen you . . .

They didn't see anything, Matt had said. *We were walking. We had our clothes on, for Christ's sake.*

She had to face Josh sometime. Face them all.

Pasting a smile on her face, she swung open the gate and started up the walk.

A dog woofed.

"Look out!"

"Oh, shit."

Alarmed, Allison looked up as the big black Hound of the Baskervilles galloped across the sunlit yard, tongue lolling, teeth gleaming, water streaming from its sides.

Allison froze.

"Fezz! *Fezzik!*" Josh yelled. "Come!"

With a joyful—*menacing?*—bark, the dog launched itself

at Allison. She thrust out both hands to save herself, dropping her flowers to the ground.

Impact.

She staggered, grabbing the dog's front legs. They tottered together like dancers as it panted hotly, happily, in her face.

God, she hoped it was happy and not hungry.

"Sorry." Josh hauled the dog off by its collar. It dropped to all fours and shook vigorously, sending fur and water flying in all directions. "He's usually better behaved with strangers."

"That's all right," Allison said weakly. Her skirt was ruined, two big muddy paw prints smearing the white denim. Her blouse was wet and covered with hair and reeked of dog.

The dog collapsed on her foot, pressing against her leg. Its tail swept the grass. A few yards away, Matt's niece Taylor watched them, her eyes huge in her thin face.

Allison patted the dog's big head. "Good dog," she said uncertainly.

A corner of Josh's mouth crooked up, making him look like Matt. "I guess he likes you."

"Lucky me." She brushed at the smears, making them worse.

Josh grinned. "I don't get it. You're not his usual type."

Allison smiled back uncertainly. Were they still talking about the dog?

The back door banged open.

Allison looked up at Matt—clean, muscled, tanned hotness—and down at herself and sighed. So much for the hour she'd spent dithering over her clothes.

Josh took one look at his father's dark face and blurted, "Fezz got away from me."

"It wasn't his fault." Allison jumped to the boy's defense. "I surprised them."

Matt surveyed Allison, a smile lurking in his eyes. "I'd say it was the other way around. Let me get you a towel."

"She doesn't need a towel. She needs a change of clothes." A slim woman in jeans, her salt-and-pepper hair styled in an attractive short cut, followed Matt outside. When she smiled, the corners of her warm brown eyes crinkled. "Tess Fletcher."

Allison wiped her palm on the back of her skirt before shaking hands. "Allison Carter."

"And you know my dad," Matt said as the older man came out onto the porch.

Captain Ahab.

"Hi, Mr. Fletcher."

"Tom." His faded blue eyes twinkled. "I see you've been baptized into the family already."

Allison smiled back ruefully. "I've at least been accepted into the Church of Dog."

"Here are your flowers." The little girl, Taylor, held up the battered bouquet.

Her heart warmed helplessly. "Thanks. Um . . . These are for you," she said to Tess.

"How thoughtful." Tess accepted the bruised and decapitated flowers without batting an eye. "Matt, why don't you take Allison upstairs while I put these in water? I'll bring up something she can change into."

"It's not necessary," Allison said, determined to be a good sport. "If I could just . . ." *Take a shower.* "Use your washroom, I'll be fine."

"Don't argue with Mom," Matt said. "It's easier that way."

Josh nodded. "Resistance is futile."

Tess gave them a slitty-eyed look that promised retribution later. "The Mary Read room, I think," she said to Matt. "I'll be right up with the clothes."

Allison was carried into the house on a wave of kindness, sucked into a tide of Fletchers. Five of them. She was outnumbered and overwhelmed.

The kitchen smelled amazing, like an Italian restaurant. It had the same mix of old and new that charmed her on the rest of the island, wide plank floors and modern granite countertops, a scarred oak table and a yellow bowl full of ripening tomatoes and mail.

"Through here," Matt said.

The hallway was the same, not soulless, not perfect, a little frayed around the edges, with homey touches everywhere. A leaded glass transom cast bars of light on the faded floral rug in front of the door. Bright pillows softened a built-in bench tucked into a corner of the stairs. A sea grass basket cradled a haphazard collection of shells.

She knew it was an inn, a temporary resting stop on your way to someplace else. But it looked like a home, like the home she'd always dreamed of, enduring, lived in. Solid, with strong bones and just enough polish to promise something more.

Her gaze slid sideways. Kind of like Matt.

Yearning tightened her chest.

"Beautiful woodwork," she said, gliding her hand along the banister.

The stairs were dark with age, the handrail burnished to a soft gleam.

"Should be." Matt smiled his crooked smile, making her stomach squeeze. "I spent four months of my life stripping paint off those spindles."

"Your family did the restoration yourselves?"

"Most of it, yeah. In pieces, during the off-seasons, me and Dad and Sam. Sam Grady."

The handsome builder from the bar, with the cocky grin and TAG Heuer watch.

"He worked for you?" she asked, surprised.

Matt shook his head. "Sam was just around. His home life wasn't . . . great. His dad remarried right before we moved to the island. Sam and his stepmother weren't getting along so well, so . . ." Matt shrugged. "My parents kind of adopted him."

They reached the second floor landing, with a pretty cushioned window seat and an old cupboard fitted out as a coffee bar.

Matt stopped at the end of the hall. "This was my sister's room."

Allison looked at the neat brass plaque on the door and raised her brows. "'Mary Read'?"

"Eighteenth-century female pirate. All the rooms have pirate names." He pushed open the door. "That's Mary on the wall. Right next to the photo of Meg."

Allison crossed the bedroom to study the engraving of the woman with the cutlass. But it was the other picture that drew her, the photo of Matt's sister in a black cap and gown, her blue eyes leveled at the camera, a grin splitting her face. Behind her was a classic brick portico hung with crimson banners.

Allison blinked. "Your sister went to Harvard."

He came up behind her. "For undergrad. She got her MBA from Columbia."

Allison turned to face him. "When I made those comments about Josh going to college . . . Why didn't you say something?"

"Why?"

"Well, because . . . I just assumed . . ."

"That because Josh's father charters boats for a living his family is a bunch of ignorant rednecks?"

Yes. No. Heat swept her face. He was standing too close. She couldn't think. Matt had warned her about making assumptions. But she'd been so determined to help she hadn't listened.

"It doesn't make any difference that Josh's aunt got an advanced degree from a fancy school," Matt continued evenly. "Or that his daddy had to drop out of State. Or that his mother's on the faculty at Chapel Hill, though if you asked me that has something to do with Josh not wanting so much to do with college. What matters is what's right for Josh."

She moistened her lips. "You're right. You're absolutely right."

His gaze arrowed to her mouth, his quiet blue eyes dark and turbulent as the sea. Her blood rushed in her ears.

And then his mouth came down hard on hers as he backed her against the wall and kissed her. His mouth was hot and hungry, darkly flavored with need and frustration. Her heart pounded. Her knees went limp as string. He kissed like a starving man, imprinting her with his heat, pressing her up against the cool plaster wall. It was stunning to be kissed like this, a little crazy, a little rough. She'd never been wanted like this, desperately.

She quivered and held on, her hands reaching into his hair.

"I brought your . . . *Oh.*"

Matt's mother.

Oh, God.

Allison jerked. Matt raised his head, but he didn't let her go, wouldn't let her get away. It was a blatant display of possession, inappropriate and oddly thrilling. She squirmed.

"I'll just put these on the bed," Tess said, her tone dry. "Unless they'll be in the way."

Matt held Allison's gaze a moment, his eyes dark and hot, before he eased his body away. "Thanks, Mom."

"Five minutes before the lasagna comes out of the oven," she said.

Her footsteps faded down the hall.

"What do you think you're doing?" Allison hissed.

Matt glanced back down at her, his lids heavy. A corner of his mouth kicked up in a smile. "Kissing you. I've wanted to since you got here."

Another dark thrill chased through her. "Your whole family is downstairs."

"Well, that's why I waited," Matt said reasonably.

She bit back a smile. "What will they think? Your mother. Josh."

"My mother will think we're involved. Which is why you came, remember? And Josh already knows."

It was hard to remember anything with her blood still pumping, her head still spinning from his kiss.

She pressed her lips together. She could still taste him on her mouth. "If you invited me to save my reputation, you'd better get downstairs."

"I didn't . . ." Matt stopped.

Her heart drummed in her chest. She held her breath in anticipation. "You didn't . . . what?"

"Nothing." He smiled again crookedly. He glanced down at his wet shirt front and then at the bed. "Need help changing?"

She squelched an unreasonable feeling of disappointment. "No. Out."

MATT GRABBED A fresh shirt before he rejoined his family in the kitchen. No point in inviting comments from Josh or, God love him, his dad.

Allison came downstairs a few minutes later wearing a pair of Josh's jeans rolled twice at the bottom and a shirt of Tess's just tight enough to make Matt wonder what she was wearing under it.

Or not wearing.

His mind flashed back to Friday night, to the memory of her breast in his hand, soft, warm, velvet.

His mother kicked his ankle. "Matt, why don't you carry the salad into the dining room?"

Wincing, he accepted the bowl.

"Everything smells delicious," Allison said politely. "Can I do anything?"

"Just grab your wineglass," Tess said. "I think we're ready to eat."

Matt stood back to let Allison through to the dining room, watching her walk, appreciating the way Josh's old jeans hung on her waist, clung to her butt.

Tom followed the direction of his gaze. "Nice catch. I wouldn't throw her back."

Matt smiled and shook his head. "She's not a fish, Dad."

"No, she's not." Tom winked. "Got you hooked, anyway."

He opened his mouth to deny it. Found the words stuck in his throat.

Unease rippled through him.

Inviting Allison to Sunday dinner had been his idea. But he didn't want his family reading too much into her visit.

The dog, aware of his disgrace, waited until they all were seated before attempting to slink under the table.

"Fezzik, quit," Matt said quietly.

With a sigh, the dog retreated to the kitchen doorway, collapsing with his head on his paws.

"It's all right," Allison said. "I don't mind."

"No dogs in the dining room while we're eating," Tess said.

"Except at Christmas," Josh put in. "And Thanksgiving and Easter. Which are the only times we eat in here anyway."

Tess turned a little pink. "No *wet* dogs in the dining room at any time," she said.

"It must be nice having a dog," Allison said to Josh. "I always wanted a pet growing up."

"You didn't have pets? Like, not even a hamster or something?"

"My parents didn't believe in keeping animals in the

house. I brought a kitten home once. But . . . Well." She stabbed at her salad with her fork.

"I have a cat," Taylor volunteered.

This was the first Matt had heard about it.

Allison smiled at her. "What's your cat's name?"

"Snowball."

"And where is Snowball now?"

Taylor lowered her gaze to her plate. "I don't know."

Ouch.

Allison met Matt's eyes for one brief moment before she turned her attention smoothly back to Josh. "So, is your dog's name really Fezzik?"

"Yeah. It's from a movie."

"*The Princess Bride.* I know. Did you ever read the book?"

He shot her a grin. "Is it a kissing book?"

She must have recognized the quote, because she laughed.

"That was Josh's favorite movie when he was little," Tess said. "We used to watch it together when he stayed home sick from school."

"Isn't there a movie of *The Scarlet Letter*?" Josh asked. "Maybe I should watch that. You know, instead of reading the book."

Allison raised her eyebrows. "Demi Moore rescued by Indians? Please." She turned to Tess. "This is wonderful lasagna. I don't think I've had it with sausage before."

And as easily as that, she turned the conversation.

Maybe it was a teacher thing, Matt thought.

Maybe it was something else. Call it class, manners, breeding. But there was more to her than mere politeness, a genuine warmth, an actual interest, that made people respond.

"Lasagna al forno. It's a family recipe," Tess said. "My parents owned a restaurant in Chicago. My brother runs it now."

Allison glanced from Tess to Tom. "Then how did you two meet?"

"I was at Great Lakes," Tom said. "Naval Station. Walked into Saltoni's for dinner, walked out with the waitress."

"He was a big tipper," Matt said.

Tess looked fondly at her husband. "We were married two weeks later."

"Wow." Allison blinked. "That must have been an adjustment."

"Sure was. I thought I'd be a bachelor all my life," Tom said.

Tess rolled her eyes. "She means for me."

"And for your family," Allison said. "How did your parents react to you relocating to North Carolina?"

"We didn't right away," Tess said. "Tom had fifteen more years in the Corps, so we moved around a lot. We even stayed with my folks awhile when he was in Lebanon. I think they were grateful when we finally settled in one place."

"It seems like a wonderful place to raise a family," Allison said.

Matt reached for his wineglass. Kimberly sure hadn't thought so.

"That's why I brought Josh back. Eat your salad," he said to Taylor.

"I don't like this lettuce."

"Then eat the carrots."

"So, what brings you to the island, Allison?" Tess asked. "You must have had opportunities to teach elsewhere."

"This isn't my first teaching job. I interned one summer at the childhood development center of the Yankton Sioux in South Dakota. And I spent two years in rural Mississippi with Teach for America. What I discovered is that I love to teach, I enjoy natural surroundings, and I want to be part of a tight-knit community. Basically, I came here hoping to find all of that in a school system with more resources and slightly less isolation."

"Then you haven't been here after a hurricane," Tom said. "We're not just isolated then. We're completely cut off."

Tess shot him a look across the table. "Don't you listen to him. We didn't get hit nearly as hard last time as the folks on Hatteras."

"Road washed out," Tom said. "And the bridge. Couldn't get any cars or supplies across for two weeks except by ferry."

Allison nodded. "I read about that. I also read that even before help reached you, the island had already organized rescue and cleanup efforts."

"That's what we do," Tom said. "A man's got to help his neighbors."

Allison leaned forward, earnest and animated. "That's my point exactly. You're all fiercely independent, but there's this enormous sense of connection with each other as well as with the environment. That's really what attracted me, those deep bonds, that sense of belonging." She smiled at Matt. "You told me once the island was the first place that felt like home to you, that it was in your blood. Well, it's gotten under my skin."

For a moment, meeting her eyes, he felt he couldn't breathe.

That's it, he thought. That's it exactly.

"'It is the Force,'" Josh said in a deep voice. "'It surrounds us, it penetrates us, it binds the galaxy together.'"

Allison laughed. "Thank you, Obi-Wan. The Force is strong in you."

The boy grinned.

She fit in, Matt realized, unsure how he felt about that. Pleased? Relieved? Regretful? She got on with his family. She belonged on the island.

But for how long?

By her own admission, she was still testing things out, trying things on.

Most visitors to Dare fell in love with its beauty and its beaches. Seduced by the rhythms of the island, maybe they even flirted with the idea of staying. But by vacation's end, most of them were ready to scurry back to their real lives on the mainland, to big box stores and reliable cell phone service, to twelve-screen movie plexes and four-star restaurants.

Sure, they might indulge in a summer romance with the idea of island life. But few embraced the hardworking reality, the sweat, salt, and uncertainty, of wresting a living from the sea.

They didn't stay. The first long, dull winter, the first hurricane, sent them packing.

Across the table, Allison was teasing Josh, talking with his mother.

Odds were she wouldn't stay, either.

Matt stared down at his plate, which at that moment looked a hell of a sight more appetizing than his future.

Ten

"THANK YOU. I had a good time," Allison said as Matt walked her away from the inn down the garden path. She carried her wet clothes in a plastic Piggly Wiggly bag over one arm, leftovers in another, the recipe for lasagna al forno tucked into her purse next to her blinking cell phone. A quick glance at the display revealed her mother had called.

No doubt with a full report on Johnny-the-divorced-anesthesiologist. Allison pushed the thought away.

Matt slanted a look at her. "You sound surprised."

She collected herself to smile at him. "Sunday dinners have never been the highlight of my week," she said lightly.

"Sundays can be tough," he said, "without family and friends around."

She appreciated his attempt at comfort. She didn't need it, but it was . . . nice. He was a nice man with a really lovely family. Which made her own rather strained relationship with her parents seem even more pathetic.

"Usually I just grab a sandwich or something. I have

papers to grade. Lesson plans to write. Honestly, I prefer it that way."

"You don't miss your mother's cooking?"

Her mother's staff had Sunday afternoons off. To be with *their* families, Allison realized now.

"My mother doesn't cook. Sunday dinners are always at the club," she said.

A memory slapped her of hard white rolls and smooth white tablecloths, of sitting on her best behavior next to Miles, miserable in the jacket and tie required by the dining room.

She made herself joke. "At least now my parents can't send me to wait in the car when I screw up."

Matt took the grocery bags from her and set them on the grass.

She frowned, confused and resisting. "What are you . . . ?"

Putting his arms around her, he pulled her against his chest. His unexpected gentleness made her want to weep.

She closed her eyes instead.

"You were supposed to have dinner with them today," he said. "They wanted you to drive home for the weekend to meet some guy."

She nodded against his shirt, surprised all over again by his ability to listen. To remember.

"They want parental bragging rights," she explained. "They don't like my job, they're disappointed in my friends, they think I've wasted my opportunities. The least I can do, in their minds, is provide them with a big society wedding and a son-in-law they can talk about to their acquaintances."

"They want the best for you," Matt said.

"By their standards, maybe. Ever since I graduated from college, they've been trying to fix me up with the kind of man they think I should want." She raised her head from her chest, shaking herself out of her funk. "As long as he's a high status white male with an investment portfolio, a penis, and a pulse, he's good enough for their daughter. Every time I go home, dinner turns into this bizarre ritual, a cross between an arranged marriage and a job interview."

Matt laughed. "Most parents want to see their children married and settled."

She smiled, relieved to return to firmer emotional footing. "Yes, but yours are more subtle."

"I think they've just given up."

Right. Because he didn't do long-term relationships. The thought was vaguely depressing. She took a step back, finger-combing her hair.

Matt picked up the grocery bags. "Anyway, they approve of you."

"Mm." She shot him a sly look. "Your father thinks I'm a good catch."

A slight flush stained his cheekbones. "You heard that?"

"I'm a teacher. I hear everything."

Hooked, Tom Fletcher had said. The prospect left her oddly breathless.

Of course, their parents' generation thought that way.

Allison wasn't trolling for some trophy husband to stuff and mount over her fireplace.

"My mother always claimed to have selective hearing," Matt said. "That way she could pretend not to hear Luke and me when we bitched about doing chores."

"Your mother is a wise woman."

"She likes you. She doesn't give her family recipes to just anybody."

Allison's heart gave a happy little hop. "Too bad I get my cooking skills from my mother."

"It's not that hard."

She tilted her head. "You cook?"

He smiled his lazy smile. "I learned to, for Josh. I can manage more than peanut butter sandwiches and scrambled eggs, anyway."

There was no one in Allison's life to cook for. To care for. But she didn't have to be defined by her family. Isn't that what she'd come to Dare Island to prove?

"I guess if I can read, I can follow a recipe. I'm up for trying new things."

"Good." He stopped under the blooming crepe myrtle. Took her by the shoulders and drew her in. "Try this."

He kissed her.

She was prepared for the familiar rush of blood, the blast of heat. But his mouth was warm and soft on hers, testing, tasting, tempting her with little bites. Not a demand this time. A question. Her body loosened, moistened, as his tongue coaxed hers to play. She sucked in her breath and kissed him back, *yes*, answering with her body and her mouth, *yes*, promising him everything she had, *yes, please, yes.* His arms tightened. She felt him, the hard, lovely planes and angles of him hard against her breast, belly, thighs. *Matt.*

"Matt . . ." She opened her eyes to a pink haze of crepe myrtle and lust, a sweet, melting ache inside her. "Where are we going with this?"

"I don't know." He kissed the corner of her lips. "Does it matter?"

The ache was a hollow, begging to be filled.

"I'm not sure," she whispered.

"I know where I want it to go. I want to come home with you. I want to touch you, Allison. Make love with you."

He wanted her.

"I want that, too." Of course she did. "But your parents . . . Josh . . . What will you tell them?"

"I don't have to tell them anything. We're not kids, Allison. Let me take you home."

Her heart thumped. *Yes. All right. Why not?* She'd had sex with other guys for less reason and certainly with less attraction.

But Matt wasn't like any other guy. Sex with Matt would mean something. She shivered deep inside.

"Give me half an hour," she said. "I'm not, um, prepared for company."

He smiled and stroked her hair from her face, his touch gentle. "It's okay. I'll take care of it."

He thought she was talking about birth control.

Her eyes went a little misty. She'd told Gail she wanted an honest, adult relationship. Not only was Matt adult, not only was he responsible, he was sparing her the embarrassment of plopping a big box of condoms in front of the teenage checker at the Island Market. Who, with Allison's luck, would almost certainly be a student in one of her classes.

"That would be good. Thanks. But I have a few things to do. To get ready."

Change her sheets. Light some candles. Clear the tornado debris from her bedroom.

"You look perfect to me," he said.

Her heart expanded like a balloon in her chest.

"Half an hour," she said. "You can follow me."

"And how will you get home?" he asked. "You can't carry all these leftovers on your bicycle."

She half turned, gesturing to the silver Mercedes coupe under the trees. "I brought my car."

Matt's gaze flickered over her shoulder and back to her face, his expression unreadable. "That's yours?"

She nodded.

He released her. "Nice."

She felt an absurd impulse to apologize, to explain. "It was my high school graduation present. From my parents."

He didn't say anything.

"I hardly ever drive it. I'm afraid of running out of gas. It's a diesel. My father thought it would be more economical, but half the time I can't find a gas station with a diesel pump."

"Bring her down to the dock. I can fill her up for you. Most boats take diesel."

"That would be great. Thank you."

He stuck his hands in his pockets. "No problem."

She felt something slipping away, a mood, a moment, an opportunity. Maybe she shouldn't worry about the wardrobe bomb blast in her bedroom. Maybe she should drag him home with her and the hell with her cluttered bedroom and dirty sheets. But then he'd be stuck at her place without a car.

"I really appreciate it," she insisted.

Matt smiled at her. "What are friends for?"

The word trickled through her like melting ice. *Friends?*

But sure, yeah, friends was okay.

If she were going to make a life here, she needed friends. They could be friends. Adult friends. Friends with benefits. She knew him well enough now to trust that whatever came next—or after—Matt was a man whose friendship was worth having.

She smiled back.

"See you in half an hour," he said.

MATT PARKED HIS truck in front of the Armstrongs' empty vacation rental, two doors down from Number 214.

Not that he was sneaking around or anything. No harm in being discreet.

Allison's cottage loomed in the dusk. Yellow light spilled from her windows, threw barred shadows from her porch. His heart beat like a schoolboy's.

In the shadows beneath her deck, the silver Mercedes gleamed like a shark.

It was a good thing they'd had a chance to cool off, he thought. To slow down.

Allison was a smart, beautiful woman. She was also a lot younger than he was. Probably less experienced. He'd had relationships . . . Well, he'd had encounters that hadn't lasted as long as the two-and-a-half dates he'd shared with Allison. But from her perspective, things must be moving pretty fast. He didn't want her to get the wrong idea.

He wasn't looking to fall in love, wasn't interested in marriage.

He would never let himself feel that desperate need, that stunned, bewildered, punch-in-the-gut loss, again.

He'd learned his lesson. Don't get too close to someone who could leave you. Don't depend on someone who could let you down. Don't peg your future, don't risk your kid, on anybody who wasn't family. Keep things simple, keep things light.

But Allison deserved to know that as long as their relationship lasted, as long as she stuck around, she would be the only woman he slept with.

He would treat her with all the care and gentleness he was capable of.

And with respect, now and after.

He rang the doorbell.

He should have brought wine, he thought now that it was too late. Or flowers . . . No, she'd done that. Or candy.

The door opened and there she was, long blond hair, smiling brown eyes, and . . . *Hello, breasts.* She'd changed the jeans and T-shirt for a pink dress, elastic on top and loose on the bottom, that molded to her curves and exposed a lot of bare, perfect skin.

Deliberately, he returned his gaze to her face, shoving his empty hands in his pockets so he wouldn't do something stupid like grab her. "Hey."

Very smooth.

"Hi." She stepped back to let him in.

Her house was furnished like every other beach rental, plenty of faded blue cushions and wicker, but somehow she'd

VIRGINIA KANTRA

turned the standard décor into something uniquely hers. A
bright cardigan tossed over a chair, her messenger bag
tucked under a desk. A framed museum print, a woman in
an old-fashioned dress looking out over the ocean, hung
over the sofa. Thick white candles burned on the table. The
room even smelled like her, like vanilla and spice. He
wanted to sniff her, lick her, all over, the curve of her neck,
the swell of her breasts, the inside of her thigh.

Down, boy. He couldn't jump her the minute he walked
through the door.

The display shelves around the TV were crammed with
books, fat, bright paperbacks jammed in with college text-
books, childhood classics mixed with mystery and romance.
He wandered closer to look at the titles, hands in his pockets,
searching for the thing to say that would make his visit seem
less like a booty call.

"Lot of books," he observed.

"Occupational hazard." He felt her move up behind him,
a whisper of heat along his skin. "I don't feel at home without my books."

"You have to travel light in the military. We moved
around too much to hold on to things. But we had this one
kids' book—some duck family living in a park—I must have
read that story to Meg and Luke about a million times."

"*Make Way for Ducklings* by Robert McCloskey."

"That was it."

He'd bought a copy for Josh's first birthday, trying to give
his son . . . What? A sense of continuity, a feeling of home.

"But that's so perfect."

He glanced at her over his shoulder, a little taken aback
by her delighted tone.

She smiled at him warmly. "It's about a pair of mallards
who decide to raise their family on an island. No wonder
you liked it."

"I guess. Yeah." He'd sure as shit never thought of it that

way. He moved his shoulders, uncomfortable with the direction the conversation had taken. He hadn't come over tonight to talk about children's books.

"Do you like poetry?" she asked.

He looked down into her cleavage. Up into her eyes. Respect, he reminded himself. He could manage a few minutes of conversation before falling on her like a dog on a bone. "I haven't read much."

"Edna St. Vincent Millay?"

Never heard of her. "No."

She smiled. "Would you like to?"

Was she kidding?

"Now?"

"I think now is an excellent time." Standing back from him, she grasped the hem of her pretty pink dress and pulled it over her head. And there she was.

Naked.

His heart stopped. Sweet Jesus, she was beautiful.

And naked. Hard to miss that. Her nipples peaked, pink against the creamy white of her breasts.

And blond, honest-to-goodness natural blond between her long, smooth, honey-colored thighs.

Her naked thighs.

"What do you think?" she asked, a hint of mischief in her tone.

He couldn't think. All his blood had deserted his brain and gone south.

"I think . . ." He cleared his throat. *Come on, dickhead. Speak.* "As long as you're naked, we can do whatever you want."

Her smile lit her beautiful face. "I mean about the quote."

Quote?

"It's Millay." She turned slightly, her arms still lifted over her head. The position raised her breasts, her bare, amazing, twenty-five-year-old breasts, taut and smooth and . . .

She had a tattoo. Running along her ribs just under the pale bottom curve of her right breast, unexpected, erotic. Two lines of dark text inked into her silky skin, and some kind of flower lying on its side, its petals half open.

"'I will touch a hundred flowers and not pick one,'" he read.

"It's from a poem about taking a perfect moment and accepting it for what it is. Not trying to hold onto it, not grasping at happiness." Her gaze met his. "Just . . . being glad. Happy."

He looked into her eyes, intelligent, warm, hopeful, and didn't know what she wanted him to say.

He didn't know if he could make her happy or not.

He sure as hell hadn't made Kimberly happy.

"This moment feels pretty damn perfect to me," he said.

It wasn't poetry, but maybe it was the right thing to say anyway, maybe it was enough, because she grinned. "I bet I can make it feel even better."

Oh, baby.

She moved closer, all the way close, her soft breasts pressing against his chest. His arms came around her automatically, his rough hands on the smooth skin of her back. The world spiraled down and coalesced with her as its center, Allison, her flushed, pretty face, her soft pink lips, the heat and humor in her eyes.

He couldn't hide what she did to him, the evidence hard against her stomach. Her hands were on the back of his neck, urging his head down. She leaned up to kiss him, taking his mouth in soft, hungry bites.

His blood pounded as he kissed her back. His hands slipped down to cup her sweet ass as she tugged his T-shirt from the back of his jeans, working the fabric to his shoulders. He wanted to be inside her, to bury himself inside her, to make her part of him, his.

He broke off kissing her long enough to yank his shirt

over his head. While he was temporarily blinded, bound by his shirt, he felt her fingers busy on his buckle, cool and smooth against the hot skin of his stomach. His muscles jumped. His zipper rasped. She covered him with her hand.

Jesus.

He'd promised himself to take it slow.

But this . . . But she . . .

She shoved at his jeans, pulled at his boxers. His erection sprang free, dark and eager. She dropped to her knees, making this sexy hum, *Mmm*, in the back of her throat that nearly destroyed him.

He threw his shirt into a corner, threaded his hands in her hair. "Allison . . ."

He barely recognized his own voice. Begging. *Stop?* Or *Don't stop?*

She licked her lips and took him into her mouth.

HE WAS HOT and thick, salty and delicious, hard against her tongue.

His legs were planted like tree trunks, but Allison could feel the tremor in his muscles as she sucked him, worked him. It was such a rush, such a turn-on, knowing she could make big, strong Matt Fletcher tremble at her touch.

Kneeling between his feet, she rubbed her face against him, drunk on his scent, dizzy with power. Loving the feel of him, hot stone and satin against her cheek.

"Oh, God, Allison." His fingers tightened in her hair.

He tugged her head up.

She smiled into his eyes, feeling almost incandescent with heat and satisfaction. "I'm not finished."

A choked laugh escaped him. "I will be if you keep that up."

Taking her shoulders, he dragged her up against his long, hard body. They kissed, his mouth hot and seeking. His thigh thrust between her legs. *Heaven*. His tongue tangled with hers.

"Let me . . ." he said.

He hopped on one foot. They staggered, clumsy with laughter and lust, as he struggled out of his shoes, stripped off his jeans.

She reached for his hand. "Bedroom."

He grabbed for his pants. "Condom."

Most of the boys she'd had sex with needed to be reminded to use birth control.

But then, Matt was no boy.

Something she appreciated even more when she saw him like this, naked, his broad chest—no manscaping for this guy—his hard muscled stomach, his thick shaft jutting between his thighs.

Straightening, he hauled her off her feet and into his arms. A thrill ran down her arms and spine.

"So romantic," she teased breathlessly as he carried her into the bedroom and sank with her onto the mattress.

But it was. It really was.

At five-ten and almost one hundred and forty pounds, she didn't get swept off her feet very often.

"I'll show you romantic," he promised.

His lips moved down, hot against her neck, ticklish on her stomach, but she didn't need that. She needed him, Matt, inside her, now. Wanted him as hot, as desperate, as crazy for her as she was for him.

She rolled with him, nearly clipping his jaw with her knee. His head dropped back against the pillow. She scrambled over him, straddling his thighs, stretching over his head for one of the condoms he'd tossed on the bedside table, practically shoving her breasts in his face. He liked that, turning his head to suckle her, making her catch her breath. So hard. So good.

She wriggled back, propping herself with one hand on

his hot, muscled chest. Sinking on her heels, she ripped open the packet and covered him.

His eyes darkened. "Sweetheart . . . Let me . . ."

She panted. "No."

Leaning forward, she took him in hand, rubbing his hot length against her, making him feel how wet she was, how ready. He grasped her buttocks firmly as she shifted and . . .

Sat.

They both groaned at the same time. Reality narrowed down to this moment, to him, in her. She felt too full to breathe.

Matt held still deep inside her. His eyes sought hers. "Okay?"

Warmth unfurled inside her. She felt burnished inside and out with flower petals. She loved the look of concern on his face, loved . . . "Very okay."

To prove it, she began to move slowly up and down, setting a rhythm. His big hands were hard on her hips as he pushed inside her, as he pulsed inside her, filling her, flooding her senses. She arched back, feeling him, wanting him in every nerve and tissue. He rocked her, faster and harder, moving inside her, part of her, hers. She was drenched, drowning in him.

Swept away.

She cried out as he slammed up into her, holding her tight. His release shattered them both. She came, clenching around him as he clutched at her, absorbing his shudders in her own flesh, colors running in her head like the sun sliding into the sea.

MATT LAY EMPTIED. Stunned. Satisfied.

In his experience, there was no such thing as bad sex. Some of it was less good, that was all.

And some . . .

He blew out his breath. Allison's warm, pliant body sprawled over him, her skin damp, hair silky against his jaw, across his chest.

It wasn't just the sex, he thought. Or the end of his four-month moratorium. It was her. Allison.

She was as full of contrasts as the sea, the bright surface and cool depths. Every time he thought he had her figured, she surprised him. Like that tattoo she wore, waiting to be discovered under her pastel cardigans.

She stirred him up, he admitted. Stirred feelings he hadn't let himself feel in a long time. He was drawn to her warmth, challenged by her determination to embrace life, to try things out, to take things on, to put herself out there.

To be naked, in every way.

She murmured and burrowed deeper into his neck.

She felt so good he didn't want to move. He could stay like this for the rest of the night, for the rest of his life, forever.

The thought stuck in his mind, a quick, warning tug, like a big fish testing his line.

She yawned and stretched on top of him, making his skin prickle with awareness.

"You cold?" she asked sleepily. "We could get under the covers."

He didn't need to get under the covers. It's not like he could spend the night. He never spent the night. "I'm fine."

"Just 'fine'?"

Wrong answer, he thought. After rocking his world, she deserved better than a lukewarm, lame ass "*fine*." "I'm great. You're wonderful. That was . . ." He searched for a word.

Her lips curved against his neck. "Fast?"

He laughed. She had definitely challenged his staying power, but he knew damn well he hadn't left her behind. Besides, he could feel her smiling. "I was going to say, 'amazing.'"

She raised her head. "You sound surprised," she said, the way he'd said to her after dinner.

"Maybe I am."

Maybe he had harbored some outdated ideas about schoolteachers. The way she'd gone down on him . . . his body stirred, reacting to the memory and the feel of her plastered against him.

She watched him, a hint of uncertainty in her gaze.

He stroked his hand down her hair, brushed the back of his fingers along that dark, erotic tattoo. "Mostly I'm just happy."

Her smile bloomed.

He added, "Not to mention grateful."

The light in her eyes set off a warning knell in his head like a channel buoy.

Deep waters here.

He ignored it.

Nothing had really changed. His life hadn't changed. He knew that, and she understood it. *Accept it for what it is,* isn't that what she'd said? *One perfect moment.*

Or as many moments as he could get before she went away.

He grabbed another condom from the nightstand and rolled her under him.

Eleven

NIGHT BLANKETED THE island. The sky pulsed with fistfuls of fat diamonds undimmed by city lights.

Matt made his way to the cottage, navigating the familiar path easily in the dark. His body felt loose and relaxed, his head light and clear.

She hadn't asked him to stay.

He stuck his hands in his pockets. That was fine. That was good. He was a man who liked his space, in bed and out. Besides, they both had things to do in the morning, Allison had said with a smile.

No pressure.

But it had been surprisingly hard to leave her for his cold truck, his empty bed. He couldn't remember ever regretting leaving a woman before.

He climbed his steps, glancing automatically over his shoulder at the wide, black windows of the inn. His parents' room, dark. The kitchen, dark. The family room . . .

Matt frowned at the silver light flickering against the

glass. The television? It was after midnight. His parents were in bed. Josh, too, or his son had some explaining to do.

But somebody had left on the TV.

Matt crossed the yard and climbed the steps to the deck. No harm in checking it out.

In recent years, the town had incorporated and hired a police chief. But his time was mostly spent directing traffic, assisting the Coast Guard, and busting up underage drinking parties on the beach. Theft was rare on Dare Island. Everybody knew what belonged to everybody else, so stolen goods were rapidly identified and returned to their owners. Tess, however, had grown up in Chicago. Even after all these years, she still locked up at night. Quietly, Matt let himself in the back door with his key.

A tiny bulb shone over the stove. Red numerals on the coffeemaker glowed in the dark. Matt moved lightly through the kitchen, following the spilling silver light and the rising, falling voices from the television.

The family room was lit with the glow of the TV. On-screen, a couple of women with artificial tans and smiles sat around a studio coffee table, discussing the amazing effects of some skin-care product.

Matt looked for the remote and spotted Taylor curled on the couch, wrapped in one of his mother's afghans, his brother's hat on her head.

Asleep.

The sight of her punched a hole in his chest. Her wary blue eyes were closed, her bony shoulders relaxed, her pointed chin soft and delicate. For once, she looked younger than her ten years and more vulnerable. She looked like a girl.

He didn't know much about little girls, but did know she couldn't spend the night on the couch.

He sighed. Tomorrow he would ask what the hell she was doing sneaking downstairs on a school night while his parents were in bed.

Tonight, he would tuck her in and hope she wasn't completely wiped out in the morning.

The remote had slipped to the floor. He picked it up and turned off the TV, setting the control by the set. The room plunged into darkness.

"Taylor?" He kept his voice low, so he wouldn't startle her. "Come on, honey, time for bed."

No answer. He hadn't really expected one.

Scooping her up, afghan and all, he moved with her toward the kitchen. He'd carried Josh like this, years ago. Through colic and fevers, tears and bad dreams, coming home from fireworks and after late night fishing trips. The memories crowded in, evoked by her soft dead weight and her little kid smell, grass and sweat and shampoo.

She exploded in his arms, thrashing and screaming. "Let me go! Let me *go*! Leave me *alone*!"

Matt nearly dropped her in surprise.

Her small fists flew, bashing him in the mouth.

His head snapped back. Instinctively, he tightened his hold.

"Easy. Taylor. Ouch." With his gut tied in slippery knots, he tried to soothe her, tried to contain her, tried to put down this tornado of blanket and limbs without letting her hurt herself.

He knelt, keeping one arm loosely around her. Reaching into the flailing, wailing storm, he found her shoulder and gave it a shake.

"Hey, Taylor. It's okay, kid, you're all right."

Her wide, terror-filled eyes met his, her mouth still open to scream.

"Uncle Matt?" she whispered.

"Yeah."

Those eyes—Luke's eyes—flooded with tears, gleaming in the dark. With a sob, she flung herself at him, her skinny arms fastening in a death grip around his neck.

Jesus. He rocked her, giving comfort.

The overhead light snapped on.

"What on earth is going on?"

Tess stood in the kitchen archway, belting the sash of her robe, her salt-and-pepper hair sticking up in every direction.

Matt shrugged as best he could with Taylor clinging to his neck. "No clue."

"Taylor, sweetie." Tess rustled forward to stroke her granddaughter's hair, to feel her forehead with an expert hand. "What's wrong? Do you feel sick? Are you all right?"

Taylor shook her head against Matt's shoulder.

"Is that, no, you're not sick, or no, you're not all right?"

"Mom." Matt spoke patiently. "Give us a minute, okay? We both just had the crap scared out of us."

"That makes three of us," Tess said. "I thought somebody was being murdered."

Taylor's muscles were rigid.

"So naturally you decided to investigate in your bathrobe." Matt smiled at his mother, keeping his tone deliberately light. "Come on, Mom, you've seen all those scary movies. You know that when the heroine hears a bump in the night she's not supposed to go down into the basement."

As he talked, he could feel Taylor's grip easing, her trembles fading away.

Tess met his gaze. "We don't have a basement," she said, matching his relaxed tone. "Anyway, I'd like to meet the monster who's a match for me and my frying pan."

"You or Taylor." Matt explored his throbbing lower lip with his tongue, tasting blood. "That's some right hook you've got there, kid."

TAYLOR STOLE A cautious look at Uncle Matt. He didn't sound mad. But you never could tell with grown-ups.

"Sorry," she mumbled.

"No problem." He smiled at her crookedly, touching the back of his hand to his mouth.

She winced. He was bleeding where she'd punched him. "I didn't mean to hit you."

"It's okay," he said, and she almost believed him. "Your dad and I used to pound on each other all the time. Of course, I won, being older and bigger and all. But he was a scrapper. Like you."

She smiled back, relieved and guilty, still not sure if she was in trouble or not.

"So." He was still smiling, but his eyes were serious. "You want to tell me what that was all about?"

Panic clogged her throat. She couldn't. Her heart pounded. She couldn't tell anybody.

"I . . ." She darted a look at Grandma Tess, standing there in her bathrobe. "I had a bad dream."

He nodded. "I figured that much. What were you doing downstairs?"

Taylor swallowed around the hot lump in her throat without answering.

"This is the third time I've found her sleeping on the couch," Grandma Tess said.

Uncle Matt's eyes narrowed. "Why didn't you tell me?"

Grandma Tess shrugged. "What could I say? I thought she'd get over it. You always did." She patted Taylor's shoulder. "Come on, sweetie, let's get you back to bed."

Back to the dark and the quiet, where bad things could happen.

Taylor's stomach clenched. She shook her head.

Grandma Tess looked at her kindly, the way grown-ups did when they didn't have a clue. "Honey, we talked about this. You can't stay down here."

"You do."

"She's got you there," Uncle Matt murmured.

"Because my room is down here," Grandma Tess said. "My bed. You can't sleep on the couch every night."

"My mom would let me. She let me sleep on the couch at home all the time."

Which was a lie, but they didn't know that. Taylor's throat burned. They didn't know anything.

The two adults exchanged glances over her head.

"Maybe she doesn't want to be up there alone," Uncle Matt said, and Taylor felt hopeful and scared at the same time, because if he got that part right, who knew what else he might guess?

Thinking about it made her head hurt. She was too tired to think, tired of lying, tired of crying, tired of being scared.

"I don't know why I can't sleep in front of the TV," she said in a whiny voice. Maybe if she whined they'd leave her alone. It worked with Grandma Jolene. "You'd let me sleep in front of the TV if I was having a sleepover."

"Not on a school night," Grandma Tess said.

Uncle Matt rubbed his face with his hand. "Look, it's late. We could all use some rest. Why don't we just move one of the guest TVs into her room for now and figure out the rest in the morning?"

"No cable," Grandma Tess said.

"Fine. Then give her a night-light and a radio."

Grandma Tess sighed. "I'll get something."

She held out her hand to Taylor. She had nice hands. Her nails weren't painted pink like Mom's, but they were short and clean and didn't scratch. Taylor liked her, but she wasn't Mom, nobody was Taylor's mom anymore, her mom was dead.

Grandma Tess smiled. "We'll find a light, and then I'll tuck you in."

A light would help—maybe—but Taylor wasn't taking any chances. "I want Uncle Matt."

She didn't want to sound mean, but she was really tired.

If Uncle Matt stayed with her, it would almost be like having her father there.

She wasn't afraid with Uncle Matt. Even on the motorcycle. Uncle Matt was calm and strong. Grandma Tess was nice, but she couldn't keep Taylor safe any more than Grandma Jo could.

"Sure." Uncle Matt tugged the brim of her cap down over her nose, the casual gesture better than a hug. "Let's go."

She pushed the cap back on her forehead. "You'll stay with me?"

The two grown-ups looked at each other again, but she kept her gaze fixed on Uncle Matt. *Please, oh, please, oh, please . . .*

"I could do that," he said slowly. "Just until you fall asleep."

"You promise?" she insisted.

His eyes narrowed. She squirmed a little under that steady look, but her fear was too huge to let her back down.

"Yeah," he said, "I promise," and she relaxed.

Grown-ups lied all the time, but she figured she could trust Uncle Matt.

"Good," she said, and trudged with him up the stairs.

JOSH WAS EATING cereal at the kitchen counter when Matt stumbled toward the coffeepot the next morning.

The boy smirked. "Rough night?"

Matt glowered blearily at his son before hooking a mug out of the cupboard. His system screamed for caffeine. He'd be out all day with a group of serious fishermen trolling for stripers, holding the old *Sea Lady* steady just outside the choppy waters of the inlet where the migrating fish would feed. To navigate the shallow chop, Matt needed to be alert.

He needed coffee.

He sipped. Winced.

"Your lip is busted," Josh observed.

Matt grunted.

Josh's eyes gleamed with mischief. "You always told me no meant no."

He'd raised a damn wiseass, Matt thought.

Under other circumstances, the realization would have made him proud. But not when Allison had to face the boy in class this morning.

He gulped more coffee. "I was up all night with the kid. Taylor."

Josh swallowed. "Puking?"

"Nightmares."

Every time Matt thought she'd drifted off, every time he'd tried to leave, Taylor had forced herself awake. Finally, he'd accepted his fate and napped on a chair in her room.

"Sucks," Josh said sympathetically.

Matt nodded, rubbing the crick in his neck.

"I thought you were with Carter last night," Josh said.

"Miss Carter," Matt corrected automatically.

"Whatever." Josh buried his face in his cereal bowl.

Matt took a deep breath. He didn't want to get into a discussion of his love life with Josh. He'd always kept those two parts of his life separate, sex over here, family over there, no contact between the women he slept with and the son he loved.

But the issue had to be addressed now that Josh had brought it up. Now that Matt and Allison were . . . His mind fumbled with labels, searching for a word that wouldn't be either insulting or inaccurate. *Dating? Sleeping together? Involved.*

He never wanted to lead Josh on, to raise expectations he didn't have a prayer of satisfying.

Eight years ago, when Kimberly remarried to a fellow professor, her new husband had encouraged her to invite Josh for a visit. Matt had been terrified. When he'd granted Kimberly visitation rights in the divorce agreement, he'd never imagined she would voluntarily seek contact with their son. At eight years old, Josh had been a cheerful, open-hearted boy ready to bestow affection on anybody who asked. Everybody loved him. He'd been excited at the prospect of meeting the mother he didn't remember and his two new stepsiblings. In the weeks before the visit, Matt had wrestled with nightmare scenarios of Josh being drawn into one big, happy blended family in Chapel Hill.

But all his worry had been wasted. The visit was not a success. Kimberly had no interest in Transformers or video games or, it turned out, their son.

At the end of five days, when Matt drove halfway across the state to pick up Josh, the boy clung to him as if he'd never let go.

Josh never cried. Never complained. But for weeks afterward, he'd been very, very quiet.

It broke Matt's heart. He had resolved then he would never introduce another woman into his son's life who could let Josh down.

But Allison was different.

She was Josh's teacher. They had to deal with each other on a daily basis. And deal with the talk that was bound to make the rounds, especially after Friday's little episode under the pier got out.

Matt drank his coffee, studying his son over the mug's rim. "Is that a problem for you?" he asked quietly. "Me seeing her?"

Josh lowered the bowl. Wiped milk from his mouth. "Does it make any difference?" he asked, not bitter, not snarky, just . . .

Curious, Matt decided.

It was a serious question. It deserved an honest reply.

"It could. You come first, Josh. Always have."

The tips of Josh's ears turned pink. "Jeez, Dad. You are so lame."

Fletcher family shorthand for "I love you, man."

"Yeah," Matt said. "I love you, too."

"Anyway, Carter's cool. *Miss* Carter," Josh said before Matt could correct him. "It's okay if people know that you're banging . . . Sorry, that you're *seeing* her." He grinned, sliding off the stool to carry his dirty bowl to the sink. "It would be bad if she were ugly or something. Because then you'd be, like, an even bigger loser. But since she's hot, it's okay."

Matt cuffed him lightly on the back of the head. "Watch your mouth. Especially at school."

"I know. I will. I *will*," he repeated when Matt narrowed his eyes. "I told you, she's cool."

Matt let it drop. For now. "You finish your homework?"

"Yeah." Josh cocked his head. "Are you guys going to compare notes on me now?"

"All the time," Matt told him solemnly. "In fact, you're all we ever talk about. I can't wait to see her tonight to hear about your day."

Josh laughed.

Satisfied, Matt poured himself another mug of coffee.

He did want to see Allison tonight.

And not for a parent-teacher conference.

"GO AHEAD," ALLISON said as she sat down with Gail Peele in the faculty break room. "Ask. As a friend, you are entitled to the inside scoop."

Gail Peele unwrapped her sandwich from home. "As your friend, I could pretend not to know what you are talking about. But that wouldn't be any fun. How was your hot date under the pier with Matt Fletcher? And please don't be afraid to give details. Jimmy and I have been married ten years. I could use a little inspiration."

Allison felt heat rise in her cheeks even as she laughed.

"We were not under the pier. He took me for a picnic at the beach."

Gail nodded. "Beach picnic is good. Usually he takes his dates off island. To Beaufort, maybe, or Morehead City. And he never, ever takes them home to meet his family."

Allison felt a flash of gratitude toward Matt. He was right. His invitation to Sunday dinner hadn't stopped the talk. But it had definitely changed the conversation.

Still, she felt compelled to say, "Sunday dinner wasn't really a date."

Gail set down her sandwich. "Honey, from Matt, that's practically a declaration. So, how was it?"

"Dinner?" Allison grinned, aware of Suzy Warner at a nearby table leaning closer to listen. "It was wonderful. His parents are really nice. His mother made lasagna."

"These are not the details I was hoping to hear."

"She gave me her recipe."

Gail pursed her lips. "Okay, better. And then?"

Allison raised her eyebrows. "How do you know there's a 'then'?"

"Because with Matt there usually is. Also," Gail added before Allison could take offense, "today you look all sleepy, smug, and satisfied. Kind of like my cat after she's found a fish head in the garbage."

Allison laughed. "What a lovely analogy. So." She took a deep breath. "After dinner, Matt came over."

"Now you're talking. And?"

"And . . ." She couldn't stop the smile from spreading on her face. Okay, she was smug. "I jumped him."

Gail sat back in her chair. "I don't need to ask how that went."

"It was . . ." Allison searched for words. It was wonderful to have a girlfriend to confide in, to share these new and lovely feelings with. "Intense, you know? Like he sees me, like he wants to be with me and nobody else. When he looks at me . . ." She pressed her hand to her heart, half embarrassed by the cliché, still stunned by the weight of her feelings. "I feel it. Here."

"Oh, my." Gail fanned herself. "I may need to go home and jump Jimmy after all. When are you seeing him again?"

"I don't know," Allison confessed.

Gail frowned faintly. "You don't think . . ." She paused delicately. "You don't want some kind of commitment?"

"Not after two dates."

One night, she thought.

"Right now, I'm just enjoying the moment. Taking things as they come." *He wants me. He makes me happy. Isn't that enough?* She met Gail's gaze. "But the next move has to be his."

Twelve

ALLISON WAS SITTING on her couch that evening, working her way through eighteen five-hundred-word essays on *The Scarlet Letter*, when her cell phone rang.

Matt, she thought, with a bump of heart.

Or not.

He hadn't called all day. Not that she was waiting by the phone. Okay, she was waiting by the phone, but . . .

His number blinked on her display screen.

"Hi, Matt," she answered happily, breathlessly. "I was hoping I'd hear from you."

"Yeah." A pause. "I meant to call earlier. The day got away from me."

He sounded tired, she thought, pleasure morphing to concern. "Anything I can do to help?"

"Thanks, I'm handling it." His setting of a boundary was no less clear for being polite. Automatic. "The thing is, I'm not sure I can see you tonight."

She controlled her disappointment. She was not going to overreact simply because he'd taken her at her word.

One perfect moment. Accept it and move on.

"I understand."

"I don't think you do." His voice was patient. Weary. "I want to see you. I don't know if I can get away."

"Oh." She shifted the papers on her lap, readjusting her position and expectations. "Listen, neither of us got much sleep last night. If you need to crash, I understand. I don't expect you to rearrange your schedule just because I answered the door naked."

He laughed. "Don't underestimate the power of you naked, babe." His voice was warm now, and amused. "As long as we're seeing each other, you have the right to expect that I'll call. That I'll see you as often as I can, whenever you want. Tonight, if possible. Okay?"

"Very okay," she said, the words an echo of last night, and hung up feeling better.

HE'D BEEN SUCKERED, Matt thought, watching Taylor's rigid little body under the quilt.

He could have resisted tears. Maybe. He was prepared for defiance. But that brave quiver of her chin, ruthlessly controlled? The stoic silence as he'd tucked her into bed?

He was toast.

I'll stay until you fall asleep, he'd promised.

Yeah, because that had worked so well last time.

He touched his swollen lip. Next time he sent a MotoMail to Luke, he'd hit him up for hardship pay.

The lights were dim, the radio playing softly. The kid would not—or could not—sleep. And her refusal to shut her eyes for more than a minute was putting a serious crimp in Matt's plans for the night.

Baffled, frustrated, he shifted his weight in his mother's chair.

Fezzik twitched his tail out of the path of the rockers, lurching closer to the bed. After a moment, the dog raised his head and poked it over the edge of the mattress.

"Quit," Matt ordered quietly.

With a sigh, Fezzik collapsed, laying his head flat between his paws. Matt knew just how the dog felt.

Taylor's pale little face popped up from her pillow. "What was that?"

"Fezzik just wanted to say good night. Go to sleep."

Her head dropped down, but she whispered, "G'night, Fezzik."

The dog's tail thumped.

"Fezzik," she said again.

The dog lurched up, shoving his head back on the bed.

Taylor giggled.

The sound—happy, girly, *normal*—caught Matt right under the ribs. He rubbed his jaw so she wouldn't see him smile. She needed to get to sleep. "Both of you settle down."

For a while, they did.

Fezzik inched closer, haunches wriggling. Matt watched as Taylor oh-so-casually slid her hand down the side of the mattress. The dog angled his head, his big tongue swiping her wrist. Another giggle.

Matt managed a frown. "No more noise now, I mean it."

"'Anybody want a peanut?'"

He shook his head, the smile escaping. "You've been watching movies with Grandma."

"With Mommy," Taylor said, blindsiding him. "She liked that one."

Her dead mother. He looked at her helplessly, seeing all over again how small she was, how vulnerable. How could Luke have left her?

Fezzik propped both front legs on the bed, tail wagging.

Taylor looked at Matt. "I think he wants to come up."

Matt swallowed the lump in his throat. "Probably. He used to sleep with Josh before they both got too big for one bed."

"Oh." She stroked the dog's rough head.

Fezzik panted in approval.

Matt watched them, floundering in a flood of affection and worry. "He could stay with you, if you want."

"You mean, like a guard dog?"

Something tickled the back of Matt's neck like a spider. "Why do you want a guard dog?"

Taylor's eyes slid from his. "I have bad dreams," she mumbled.

She'll get over it, Tess had said. *You did.*

His mother knew best. God knew she had more experience with kids and deployments than Matt.

But Taylor wasn't only dealing with a father away in a war zone. Her mother was dead. Her whole world had been turned upside down. No wonder she didn't feel safe.

Matt frowned. Luke ought to be here. His rare calls, his infrequent emails, might satisfy Mom, but they weren't enough to reassure Taylor. *Maybe I can get him to Skype when he gets back to the main camp.*

In the meantime, if it made the kid feel better to think of the dog as protection from Things That Went Bump in the Night, then Matt could play along.

"Sure. He can be your guard dog."

Taylor's hand dropped from Fezzik's neck. "He's your dog."

"No," Matt said firmly. "He's the family dog. You're family."

Her eyes, Luke's eyes, met his before she gave him a small, sweet, heartbreaking smile that was hers alone. "Okay. Then I guess he can stay."

* * *

MATT LOOKED TIRED, Allison thought. Fatigue or stress had deepened the fine lines around his dark blue eyes and dug in between his brows.

"I didn't know if you'd still be up," he said. The yellow porch light picked out streaks of gold in his dark blond hair, glinted off the stubble on his jaw. "I took a chance, drove by and saw your light on."

"I was just grading papers." She opened the door wider. "Come in."

He stood in her entry as if he wasn't sure of his moves. The slight awkwardness in a man so confident was unexpectedly endearing.

"What's in the bag?" she asked.

He held up the small brown paper lunch bag he carried. "Snickerdoodles."

She smiled. "You don't have to court me with cookies, Matt."

His answering smile started in his eyes. "Maybe I want to. Besides, these reminded me of you."

"Um . . . Pale? Round? Bland?"

"The smell," he explained. "Cinnamon, vanilla. Sugar."

He leaned forward to kiss her, a gentle, unhurried, hello-how-are-you-kiss that stole her breath and disturbed her heart.

She sighed when he was done. "That's sweet."

His gaze was on her mouth. "Yeah."

"Do you want to . . ." She glanced toward the bedroom door.

"Not yet. Have a cookie."

She searched his face, not sure what he wanted. Needed. If he hadn't come for sex . . . "I'll get us some milk. Unless you want coffee."

"With cookies? You're kidding, right?"

He followed her into her narrow kitchen, his hands in his pockets, not touching her, just *there*, big and warm and solid, watching her.

"What happened to your lip?" she asked as she got glasses down from the cupboard.

"I got beat up by a girl. Taylor," he explained with a smile. "I woke her up from a bad dream and she let me have it."

Allison frowned in concern. "She has nightmares?"

"Be a wonder if she didn't," Matt said. "With everything she's been through the past couple of months."

"This must be a difficult time for her, especially with her father gone."

"We're handling it."

His tone didn't encourage questions. But if she were going to share herself with him, she needed more from him than physical intimacy. She studied his face. Maybe he needed more, too.

She tried again. "Of course, your family has experience coping with deployments. Your father is an ex-Marine."

"No such thing. Once a Marine, always a Marine. So yeah, we're used to it. But this is the kid's first time."

"Didn't her mother tell her when her father went overseas?"

"Nope."

"Wow." Carefully, she poured milk into the glasses. "So this is a big adjustment for all of you."

"That's one word for it." Matt rubbed the back of his neck. "Until Dawn died, Luke didn't even know he had a daughter."

Allison's jaw jarred as her image of the Fletcher's picture-perfect family splintered and shifted like the pieces of a kaleidoscope. "How did he get custody then?"

"Dawn—Taylor's mom—named Luke as guardian in her will. Her parents are contesting it."

Allison put away the milk in the fridge. "Oh, no. How can they? I mean, if Luke is Taylor's father . . ."

"Doesn't matter. Not if some judge decides Taylor is better off with Dawn's folks. The Simpsons are saying the kid shouldn't have to live with strangers."

She wanted to take his side. But fairness made her say, "You can't blame them. Taylor is all they have left of their daughter."

Allison winced. She sounded like her mother.

Matt leaned against the counter, arms crossed over his chest. "Their daughter didn't want them to have her."

She turned to face him. "Why not?"

"I don't know. It's not like she talked to me. I haven't seen Dawn since she was in high school."

Allison wiped her hands on the thighs of her jeans. She could understand why a young single mother would want her daughter raised among the rock-solid, loving Fletchers. But with Luke serving in Afghanistan . . .

"Doesn't that strike you as a little, well, odd? All those years, Dawn never even told Luke they had a daughter together. So why give him custody now?"

Matt's big shoulders moved in a shrug. "Maybe she felt guilty."

"Maybe." Allison frowned, her mind still rattling and spinning like a hamster wheel in a third-grade classroom. "Is it possible something, you know, happened? Something that would convince Dawn that Taylor was better off with your family than her own?"

His eyes were grave. Unwavering. "Like what?"

Allison floundered as all the ugly home-life issues teachers dealt with every day crowded in on her. Estrangement. Alcoholism. Abuse. Behavioral problems. "I just wondered . . . If Taylor's having problems sleeping . . ."

"The kid has nightmares," Matt said. "So did you, you said. So did I, when my dad went overseas. You don't have to search for reasons when they're staring you in the face. Her mother died. Her dad's deployed. Before Luke left, he told me to take care of her. Which is what I've been doing for the past two hours."

"That's why you're late. You were putting her to bed."

"Yeah."

Allison's misgivings dissolved in a little glow. Taylor was safe and cared for. She wished every child she'd taught could claim the same.

Cupping Matt's face in her hands, she laid her lips on his.

His hands settled warmly at her waist. "What was that for?" he asked when she leaned back.

"Because you're such a nice guy."

He smiled at her with his broken lip. "Uh-oh. Usually when a woman says that, she's moving you to the Friend Zone."

"We are friends," Allison said. He'd come to her as a friend. Confided in her like a friend. The realization warmed her.

The wrinkles at the corners of his eyes deepened. "More than friends."

The glow grew brighter.

You have the right to expect that I'll call, he'd said. *That I'll see you as often as I can.*

It was easy to imagine that he had feelings for her. Tempting to believe that they had a real relationship. A future.

But that wasn't part of their deal. One perfect moment was all she'd asked for, all she'd promised.

Was it reneging to wish for . . . Well, *more*?

Allison shook her head. That was her parents' way, to constantly raise the bar until they were never satisfied, until whatever she did was never enough. She'd sworn never to do that to anybody.

She was not going to do that to Matt.

CAROLINA HOME

Carrying the milk into the living room, she cleared a section of the couch so he could sit.

He frowned at the stack of papers on the floor. "I interrupted your grading."

"No, I was done." *Almost.* She patted the cushion next to her, pleased that he'd spared a thought for her work. "It's a small class. American Literature. Speaking of which, Josh really surprised me."

Matt lowered himself onto the couch and opened the bag of snickerdoodles. "Because he turned in his homework?"

"Because his essay was so good." She accepted a cookie.

"You must have inspired him."

The compliment felt good. "I thought maybe you threatened him."

Matt smiled. "Nope."

She nibbled her cookie, which was delicious. Maybe she could learn how to cook. "Well, he totally exceeded my expectations. He wrote his paper in . . ." She broke off as Matt lifted her bare feet from the floor and swung them into his lap. "What are you doing?"

Matt's big, warm hands engulfed her feet. "Rubbing your feet."

She tried to pull them back. She'd never had a man massage her feet before. She was used to doing for others, not having others do things for her. To her. She felt oddly exposed and vulnerable. "You don't have to do that."

His grip tightened on her ankles. "Tell me about Josh."

"Well." She cleared her throat. "I assigned the class a five-hundred-word character sketch on *The Scarlet Letter.* Josh wrote his in the first person, as if he actually were Dimmesdale. Which wasn't the assignment, but it was creative and . . ." She shut her eyes. "Oh, God, that feels good."

"Glad to hear it. He's okay with us, by the way."

She opened her eyes. "What?"

173

"Josh."

"You discussed us with Josh?" Her voice squeaked embarrassingly.

Matt's hand moved up her calf, under her jeans, and gave a little squeeze. "I didn't give details. But he's bright enough to figure out the broad outlines on his own."

Good for Josh. Maybe when he figured it out, he could fill her in.

But it was hard to think, to worry, with Matt's broad hands reducing her to putty. His thumbs found a sensitive spot on the ball of her foot, and she groaned with pleasure. He tugged on her legs until she was half lying along the couch, her head against the armrest.

She shifted against the cushions, guilt seeping through her satisfaction. "I should . . . do something."

He stroked her legs. The muscles in her thighs went lax. "Why?"

"Because . . ." Her brain blurred as he scraped a fingernail over her zipper. "Well, because I . . . Because you . . . I don't expect to just lie back while you take care of everything."

"You don't expect much." He massaged her slowly, tiny circles through her jeans. Her legs eased open. "Makes me feel like I have something to prove."

She stirred, damp and restless. "If you don't expect things . . ." She inhaled as he pressed. "You can't be disappointed."

"Yeah." His eyes gleamed. He tugged at her jeans, pulled down her panties. "I'd hate to disappoint you."

She swallowed, lifting her hips to help him. Not that he seemed to require much assistance. Obviously he knew what he was doing, she thought as he kissed a trail down her stomach. Which was a relief, except that with all that practice he must be used to partners who actually . . .

He nuzzled her, his beard growth delicately abrading her skin, his mouth hot and seeking.

She gulped. *Partners who participated.*

She ought to reciprocate, she thought hazily as he learned her. She ought to reach for him. But Matt didn't seem to find anything lacking in her response, and after a while she stopped thinking, stopped caring. There was something deliciously decadent, sinful, self-indulgent about giving herself up to him, no straining, no striving, no wondering *does he like this* or *should I do that*, only Matt's mouth and Matt's hands and the way they made her feel.

Her body coiled tighter and tighter. He lifted her, his big hands bracing her buttocks, her legs on his shoulders, his head between her thighs as he sucked, flicked, licked inside her. The lamp burned her eyes, everything hot and wet and golden, searing behind her closed lids. She touched him, her fingers in his hair, until even that effort was too much, until her hands slid away and her arms rose and fell, beating at nothing like a gull trying to fly. He thrust a finger inside her, then two, his mouth hot, insistent, *there*, and a tether snapped inside her, and she soared.

He raised his head, his breathing heavy. She felt him shifting, reaching, heard the sounds of him putting on a condom while she lay there, doing nothing, too satisfied to move, and then he was back, warm and heavy on top of her, hard and sure between her thighs, moving on her and into her with blunt strength, and she let him, let him do everything, no work, no worry, no responsibility.

Only Matt.

She cried out and came, again and again.

When it was over, she settled slowly back to earth, her mind drifting, her body floating with pleasure.

He levered himself on one elbow. "It's getting late."

Cold reality trickled back.

Here it comes, she thought. *Gee, honey, look at the time. I better get back to my place. Life. Houseplants.*

Matt kissed her forehead. "Mind if I crash here for a couple of hours?"

She opened her eyes to find him smiling down at her, his blue eyes lazy and warm. Her heart turned over in her chest.

"I don't mind at all," she said and twined her arms around his neck.

"CAN I TALK to you a minute?" Allison asked Josh the next morning as her fourth period class broke up.

Which of course set off another round of the curious looks and snickers that made their conversation necessary.

She sighed.

Josh ambled to her desk, books on his hip, sun-streaked hair in his eyes.

Allison waited until most of the other students had departed before she said, simply, "I'm sorry."

Pink still tinged his cheekbones, but he said, "'S okay."

"I didn't realize that asking you to read your assignment out loud would get that kind of reaction from your classmates."

"They'll get over it." He offered her his father's sweet, crooked smile. "I am."

Nice kid.

"The thing is . . ." Gail had warned her against showing favoritism in class. But Josh's work was too good to be ignored. Wasn't it partiality to withhold recognition where it was deserved? "You did an excellent job with the assignment. Very creative. I want you to understand that my calling on you had nothing to do with . . ."

Me sleeping with your father. She cleared her throat.

Josh shrugged. "Hey, at least it got some laughs."

Thalia looked up from the back table, where she was sorting through the student newspaper's files. "Because it was funny."

"Thanks," he said dryly.

She rolled her eyes. "Not Miss Carter calling on you. Your essay, the way you made Dimmesdale sound like this horny poseur. That was funny."

"You're a good writer," Allison added.

"Thanks," Josh repeated, more warmly this time.

Thalia cocked her head. "You ever think about writing for the school paper?"

"Hell, no."

She flushed to the roots of her red hair. "Right."

"It's not a bad idea," Allison said, backing her up. "We need more writers. Particularly since we've added the blog."

"I have work after school. And basketball's starting up soon."

"In November," Allison said.

His eyes gleamed through his thick lashes. "We have conditioning before that."

"See, that would be interesting to know about," Thalia said gamely. "You could do a guest blog. Or a series. Kind of an insider's view of the team."

"I don't know if Coach would go for that."

"You could ask," Allison said. "I could talk to him, if you like."

"I guess I could think about it," Josh said and escaped.

Thalia grinned. "Thanks, Miss Carter."

"He hasn't said yes," Allison cautioned.

"He didn't say no, either. At least now I've got a shot at spending time with him outside of class."

"There's a big difference between spending time with someone and a commitment," Allison said.

Listen to yourself, she thought.

"Aren't you always telling us to be open to new experiences? Maybe the paper is Josh's new experience." Thalia flashed another grin. "And maybe Josh is mine."

Allison bit her lip, not sure if she should be encouraging this kind of experience among her students. "I just don't want to see you get hurt."

Thalia shrugged. "Even that would be an experience. I'm tired of being smart and alone. Better to have loved and lost and all that, right?"

Allison looked at her bright, expectant face and didn't have the heart to tell her otherwise. Maybe Thalia was right and everything would work out the way she hoped.

And maybe the girl was setting herself up for heartbreak. Maybe this whole love-and-loss business was one experience she'd be better off without.

It was too soon to tell.

For either of them.

Thirteen

HE NEEDED MORE sleep.

Matt set his purchases on the counter of Evans Tackle Store: hooks for trolling baitfish and two large coffees to go for him and Tom.

Two weeks of getting up in the middle of the night to change beds was getting old.

Especially when he had to be up at five in the morning.

The tourist section of the store was still dark, the bright T-shirts hanging like shrouds, the key chains and shot glasses glinting in the shadows. In mismatched chairs on the other side, men in waders and sweatshirts talked about their neighbors, their trucks, the latest restrictions on commercial catches, and the current NOAA weather report. The air was thick with the tang of oil and tobacco, the hum of the lights and refrigerator, the drip and gurgle of the coffeepots.

"You listen to every damn weather advisory, you'll starve," Randy Johnson, a commercial fisherman, complained.

"And if you ignore them, you'll drown," quipped George Evans from behind the register. He rang Matt up. "Hey, Matt. Haven't seen you in here lately."

"Matt's got other fish to fry in the mornings," put in one of the men around the table.

"Hear he's hooked on the new teacher," Randy Johnson said.

"Couple of weeks now, isn't it? Must be a record."

"He's so pretty with that gaff in his mouth, we ought to string him up and take his picture."

Matt shrugged off the ribbing and paid for the coffees. Let them have their fun. He and Allison were fine. He and Allison were great. He didn't have to make promises, she didn't make demands.

"I'd buy you a drink," Sam Grady said behind him. "But you already have coffee."

Matt turned. "Sam." Surprise lightened his voice. He didn't usually see Sam here. "Just fueling up. Got a party of two going out for king mackerel today. You can come along if you want to crew."

"Wish I could. But I only dropped in to say good-bye. Driving to a work site in Cary today."

"Trouble on the job?"

Sam grinned, quick and sharp. "You could say that. Ever since the old man checked himself out of the hospital, all he can do is bitch about every decision I made while he was laid up. I've got my own business to run. I can't stick around and drive up his blood pressure. Maybe he'll relax when I'm gone."

Sam's dad was a dick. Time and illness hadn't changed that. Absence wouldn't either. But pointing that out wouldn't help Sam.

"Give me a call when you get back," Matt said instead. "We'll get us some blues, some brews."

"That'd be good. If you can spare the time from Hot Teacher."

Matt eyed his oldest friend. "You know my rule. Never let a woman interfere with fishing."

"Bullshit. Jenny Vaughan, sophomore year," Sam said promptly. "You blew off pier fishing for a pair of breasts."

Matt grinned. "Hey, they were my first breasts." His first everything, he remembered. Pretty, fun-loving Jenny. "Anyway, she's married now. Two kids and another on the way."

"And so it goes." Sam shook his head. "Watch yourself, pal. Heard you were thinking of taking the plunge again yourself."

Hot coffee burned Matt's mouth as he gulped. "What?"

"You and Hot Teacher."

Matt felt a spurt of something like panic. "No."

Sam raised his brows. "Okay."

Matt swallowed again to relieve the sudden dryness in his mouth. "We've only been seeing each other a couple of weeks."

"Nobody else, though, right?"

"So? That's only because there's no one else I want to be with."

"Sure," Sam said lightly. "Let me know when you've moved on. Maybe I'll come back and cheer her up."

"Try, and I'll kick your ass," Matt said.

Sam grinned. "Relax. Your girlfriend's safe from me. She's not my type anyway."

Matt rubbed his jaw. He would have said Allison was exactly Sam's type. They had the same advantages, the same background; classy, moneyed, privileged.

"Too much like dating my sister," Sam said.

Sam's half sister Chelsea was the princess of the family, with sweet ways and an even sweeter smile. Matt winced. She was also barely twenty-one.

"I would never hit on your sister," Matt said. "Any more than you would hit on mine."

Sam started to say something. Shook his head.

"What?" Matt said.

"Nothing."

Matt narrowed his eyes. "You never did."

"What do you think?"

"I think Meg wouldn't have anything to do with you. She's too smart."

"Too smart for both of us."

"Besides, if you touched her back then, I'd have to kill you."

"You think I don't know that?" Sam's eyes danced. "You better hope Hot Teacher doesn't have a brother."

"She does. They don't see each other."

"Uh-huh. Since when did you start exchanging family histories with your dates?"

Matt shrugged. "It came up."

"Listen to you. She's got you wriggling on the line and you don't even know it."

Matt frowned as he carried his coffees a hundred yards down the waterfront to Fletcher's Quay.

Sam was just yanking his chain about Meg. About Allison.

Maybe he did enjoy Allison's company. Maybe he had gotten into the habit of looking for her at the end of the day, of dropping by to see her at night. That didn't mean he was hooked.

So he'd filled up her gas tank. Big deal. She'd gotten up twice in the dark hours before dawn to fix scrambled eggs and coffee before he stumbled home.

So what if she was spending time with his son? Hard to avoid that, given her job. She'd actually gotten Josh interested in some after-school project, writing for the paper.

But these were only minor course adjustments, Matt told himself. He was hardly sailing off with her into the sunset.

He could want her, he could enjoy being with her. But he'd learned the hard way that he was better off if he didn't need her.

If he didn't let himself depend on anyone but family.

"JOSH, DO YOU have your lunch?" Tess asked before she could stop herself.

Josh grinned tolerantly, bending to kiss her cheek. "Yep. Packed it last night. Thanks for breakfast, Grandma."

She smiled up at him, her tall, beautiful grandson. "My pleasure."

She stood at the back door to watch him walk the garden path to Lindsey Gordon's waiting car. He looked so much like Matt at the same age that her heart gave a little squeeze. He waved before he climbed into the car, but she could see he'd already left her in his head, all his attention focused forward, on the girl, on the road, on whatever it was that occupied the thoughts of teenage boys. Sex, probably. She hoped he and that girl weren't getting too serious.

Tess made a small sign of the cross, a blessing in the air, as they drove away, the way her own mama used to fifty years ago.

One child down, one to go.

She turned back to Taylor sitting at the kitchen table, wearing an oversize shirt and jeans, Luke's cap planted defiantly on her blond head. Where it would remain, Tess knew, until Taylor crossed the school threshold.

"Almost time to go, honey," Tess said.

Taylor looked at the clock on the stove. "I have eight more minutes."

Tess smiled. She considered it a healthy sign that Taylor

felt acclimated enough, secure enough, to object to a change in her routine.

"I need to make an early start this morning," Tess said. "I'm leaving right after I drop you off."

Taylor's blue eyes narrowed. "Where are you going?"

"Just over to the mainland."

"For how long?"

Tess looked up from her to-do list, alerted by the child's suspicious tone. Of course. Too many adults in Taylor's short life had left and not come back. It was enough to give anybody trust issues.

Or nightmares.

She brushed a hand over Taylor's head, pretending not to notice how the girl stiffened under her touch. "Not long. I'll be back before you're home from school."

"Why do you have to go?"

"Well . . ." Now Tess was the one to check the clock.

Why did children always start conversations at the most inconvenient times? Right before bed or when guests were coming or while you were on your way out the door? Matt and Meg and Luke had been the same.

But you had to talk when they were ready, Tess thought. And Taylor hadn't ever been ready before.

"I have an appointment in Beaufort," Tess said, trying to sound breezy and failing. "With Kate Dolan." *The lawyer.* "Your mom's boss."

Taylor's small, pale face pinched. "Are you going to give me back?"

Tess's jaw dropped. "Give you back?"

"To Grandma Jo."

"No." Tess was genuinely shocked. "Never. Your daddy wants you to stay with us, baby. You live here with us now."

Taylor's bony shoulders became a fraction less rigid. "Okay."

Tess drew a deep breath, conscious of having blundered,

unsure how to make things right. She had never had to live through the knock at the door, the car at the curb, the two Marines waiting on the porch with grave faces and the news: *Killed In Action.* But she understood Taylor's fears. Living on base, Tess had seen that car pull up to other curbs, the grief detail stand on other porches. She'd delivered cakes and casseroles, offered hugs and tears, prayers and practical help to other families whose fathers would never come home. Sometimes the best you could do was to listen.

"Is there anything you want to talk about, honey?"

Wary blue eyes surveyed her from under Luke's Marine cap.

Tess tried again. "About your dad or, well . . . anything? Your mom?"

Taylor shook her head.

Something was wrong. Tess felt it in her bones. She couldn't explain it, couldn't define it, couldn't dismiss it.

I need to know, Tess thought, but she couldn't force Taylor to open up to her. Matt was just as much in the dark as she was. Luke didn't know anything. Anyway, Tess didn't want to worry him while he was in a war zone with a bunch of vague suspicions that might not amount to anything at all.

She knew the Simpsons. Ernie liked to drink too much on a Friday night and Jolene was a little scattered, but she had a good heart. They'd made their mistakes as parents, letting that boy of theirs run roughshod over the little kids, letting Dawn run wild. But then, Luke had run a little wild, too, and Tess herself hadn't been able to do a damn thing to stop him.

Taylor fed bacon to Fezzik under the table while Tess pretended not to see. But she couldn't look the other way on this conversation.

This afternoon she was taking her questions to the lawyer. Perhaps Dawn had confided in her.

Tess studied her grandchild's down-bent head. "Everything's going to be all right." It was a promise. "I just want to talk to Miss Dolan."

No answer.

Tess supressed a sigh. "I figured while I was over there I'd do some shopping in Morehead City," she said lightly. "We have a big group this weekend, the Kellers. It's their fiftieth wedding anniversary. They're coming to stay with their kids and grandkids and I want to get some special touches to put in their room. I thought while I was at the mall I could pick up that comforter we looked at for your bedroom."

Taylor shrugged.

Tess refused to be discouraged. She had hoped that decorating Taylor's new bedroom would help the child feel at home. "Did you see something in the catalog you like better?"

"No, it's okay. At least it's not pink."

"Right," Tess said. "Because pink would show dog hair."

Taylor snorted and stuffed the last of her toast in her mouth.

A wave of pure love swept over Tess. Taylor was tough. She would be all right. They all would be all right.

Girls could bounce back from almost anything. Look at Meg. It was boys you had to watch and worry about, who carried their damage silently inside.

While Taylor scrambled to get ready, Tess indulged herself by adding a few girly items to her list: T-shirts, a hoodie, maybe a pair of leggings. Nothing pink. Meg hadn't been a fan of pink, either.

"Can I have a piece of cake?" Taylor asked as they drove to school.

Tess slanted a look at her granddaughter riding shotgun. "What cake?"

"The wedding cake."

The Kellers. "It's an anniversary party, honey. Cakes are just for newlyweds."

"Why?"

"Well . . . It's tradition. So the husband and wife start their new life together with a little sweetness."

Taylor slumped in her seat. "That's dumb. If I was having a party, I'd want a cake."

"You're right," Tess said. "After fifty years, you deserve a cake."

Fifty years. She and Tom had been married forty.

Maybe while she was at the mall, she'd hit Belk's lingerie department, do some shopping of her own. Tess smiled to herself. Tom deserved something, too, for putting up with her for all these years.

And he'd never been a fan of cake.

"You have a good day!" she called as Taylor slipped out of the car. "I'll pick you up after school."

She stayed at the curb to watch Taylor drag off her hat and march into the building, shoulders straight under the straps of her backpack.

Tess pulled out of the car pool line, already revising lists in her head, reviewing what she would ask Kate Dolan. The Spinners' "Then Came You" played over the radio, the way it had that summer when Tom walked into her parents' restaurant.

Tess cranked up the volume and drove down island toward the bridge, singing loudly and out of key along with the radio.

THE LONG LINE on the port side twitched as the baitfish darted frantically beneath the surface. The *Sea Lady II* was fourteen miles out in the warm waters of the Gulf Stream, finally catching some action.

Up on the bridge, Matt watched as the tip bent and the line took off. He yelled to Scott, the nearer of their two passengers. Scott grabbed at the rod, fumbling as he tried to jam the butt end of the rod into his fighting belt.

Matt shook his head. The lighter rods made for a better

fight, but the thirty pound test line reduced the margin for error. "I'm going down," he said to Tom. "He's going to lose it."

The radio crackled behind him as he came off the bridge. Scott had braced his knees against the side of the boat as the line screamed out, the big fish fighting for freedom.

"Tighten the drag just a little," Matt coached. "That's the way."

Pump and reel, pump and reel, recovering the lost line. One minute. Two. Their other passenger, Bill, hung over the side, watching the battle.

As Scott cranked, Tom descended from the bridge. "We're heading back to shore."

"Screw that," Scott puffed.

Bill glanced over his shoulder. "No way. He just hooked this baby."

Matt turned and saw his father's face, gray and set as concrete. "What?"

The old fear—of a knock on the door, of a Casualty Assistance Officer in dress blues coming up the walk—hollowed Matt's chest. "What is it? Is it Luke?"

Or—a fresh wave of panic—one of the kids.

Josh.

Tom met his gaze. "Your mother." His throat worked as he swallowed. "There's been an accident."

"SO BOTH MEN try to conceal their crimes." Allison perched on her desk, gently swinging her feet, addressing her fourth period class. "Dimmesdale becomes an articulate, inspiring minister. Bigger becomes a brutal murderer. Is that a function of individual choice? Or are they simply fulfilling the roles society created for them?"

She was encouraged by the way her students flung themselves into the discussion.

"Dimmesdale tries to confess. He even tells Hester to, you know, name the kid's daddy."

"Because he doesn't have the balls to do it himself."

"At least he doesn't chop her up and put her in the furnace."

A tap on the door interrupted them. She glanced toward the hall. Principal James Oates's ruddy face peered through the glass into her classroom.

Sliding from her desk, Allison hurried to the door. "Mr. Oates."

"Miss Carter." Oates was a large, gentle, rather remote man with a ginger mustache, his round face folded in serious lines. "I'd like a word with Joshua Fletcher. Tell him to bring all his things."

Her students nudged each other with their elbows and shifted in their chairs.

Allison flashed a glance at Josh. He shrugged, all innocence.

"Of course." Allison lowered her voice. "Is anything wrong?"

He blinked. "I think it would be best if I talk to Josh first. I'll speak with the staff later today."

A rush of protective feelings washed over her, fierce and surprising. She took a step forward, crowding Oates back, into the hall. She closed the classroom door behind them, fueling the noise inside. "Josh isn't in trouble, is he?"

"No, no." Oates hesitated. "Well, I guess I can tell you."

She caught the faint emphasis on the last word. Tell her because she was Josh's teacher? Because she was sleeping with Josh's dad? She didn't know. She didn't care as long as she could help Josh.

"Matt Fletcher called," Oates said. "Tess Fletcher was involved in a car accident on the mainland this morning. Matt needs Josh to watch his cousin Taylor after school."

Allison sucked in a distressed breath. "Oh, no. Is she . . . Is Tess . . ."

"Alive," Oates said. "But it's pretty serious. Carteret General life-flighted her to the trauma center in Greenville. Matt and Tom are driving up there to be with her."

MATT WATCHED THE waiting room clock outside the surgery doors, his eyeballs gritty and his hands cold. Sometimes he paced and Tom sat. Sometimes he sat while Tom paced.

He needed to move. His heart pumped with adrenaline. His skin crawled with frustration. He wanted to do . . . something, anything, to fix this. But he was useless, his hands tied by ignorance and lack of training.

The dread of not knowing pressed on him even harder than the weight of helplessness.

The three-hour trip from Fletcher's Quay to Pitt County Memorial Hospital had stretched like a nightmare. But at least while Matt was driving he'd been able to focus on traffic. At least he'd had something to do.

He jammed his hands into his pockets. He couldn't even call out on his phone. Cell phone reception in the building was crap. He'd called his sister from the cafeteria when he'd gone downstairs to fetch the coffee that sat, cold and unnoticed, at his father's side. He'd finally gotten through—briefly—to Josh, telling him Grandma was okay, the doctors were doing everything they could, Josh should watch Taylor, Matt would call again soon. He and Tom had agreed there was no point in contacting Luke in Afghanistan until Tess was out of surgery.

Nothing he can do, Tom grunted, closed inside his own pain. *Don't worry him*.

Matt retreated to the window and stood staring out at the parking lot. Nothing any of them could do until they knew for sure that Mom . . . That she . . .

He rubbed his bristly face as if he could scrub away his fear. Head-on collision with an SUV. The other guy's fault. Damn drunk driver, dead on the scene, since his stupidity had extended to not wearing his safety belt. Tess had suffered blunt abdominal trauma with internal bleeding, the nurse had explained when Matt rejoined Tom after parking the truck.

The words rolled over them like boulders, crushing in their import. *Chest tube. Pelvis. Fracture. Hemorrhage.*

Tom had signed everything the nurses put in front of him, his face lined and aged, his words and movements rigidly controlled. Matt had no idea how much his father actually comprehended. He took the clipboard to read the forms himself, chilled by the standard warnings. Whatever they did to his mother beyond those closed doors might not work. All procedures carried the risk of bleeding. Complications. Infection. Death.

Assuming her injuries didn't kill her first.

Matt glanced again at the clock. Where the hell was the nurse? She'd promised to come back as soon as she knew what was going on inside, promised the doctor would be out to talk to them soon. But the minutes bled by, and no one came.

Tom's hands shook. He gripped them together between his legs, his elbows resting on his knees, staring sightlessly at the carpet. Matt couldn't remember ever seeing him like this. Not when Meggie broke her arm trying to fly from the garage roof, not even when he'd come home from the Gulf. For the first time in his life, his father looked frail. *Old.*

He was a tested combat leader, trained for battle in uncertain and chaotic conditions. Military families prepared for the worst and hoped for the best.

But none of them were prepared for this.

Men who made their living from the water developed a certain fatalism, broader than acceptance, deeper than faith. *The sea giveth and the sea taketh away.*

But Matt had never imagined in a million years that his

mother might be taken from them so soon. Tess was their rock, their anchor, calm in crisis, constant through moves and deployments. Without her, they were lost. Adrift.

Matt swallowed the ache in his throat.

"Dad." He touched Tom's arm, searching helplessly for the magic words, his mother's words, that would make everything all right. "What do you need? What can I do?"

Tom met his gaze, his eyes like stone. "Pray."

ALLISON SQUARED HER shoulders and knocked on the cottage door. The sound of crashes and explosions from the television inside penetrated to the stoop.

The last time she was here, she'd been invited for Sunday dinner. Now the woman who had welcomed and fed her was fighting for her life.

Allison couldn't do anything for Tess. But she could try to help Josh.

She knocked again, louder.

A dog woofed once.

Josh answered the door, game controller in hand, big-screen battle raging behind him. Doing his teenage best, Allison thought, to keep his mind off what had happened, to keep his cousin distracted. *Good boy.*

He nodded. "Miss Carter."

"Hi." There was a fiery crash on the TV behind him. She did her best not to wince. "I came to see how you were doing."

"I'm fine."

Sure you are, she thought. You and your dad. Always fine.

She offered the box she held. "I brought pizza."

"Thanks." As if recalling his manners, Josh stepped back to let her in.

Taylor hunched on the couch behind him, clutching the

other controller, Fezzik at her feet. On the coffee table in front of her, on the counter behind her, crowding the table and set on the floor, were dishes, plastic-wrapped deli trays and bags of sandwich buns, foil-covered casseroles and baskets of fruit, cakes, cookies, fried chicken, a . . . ham?

Allison blinked. "Wow."

Josh surveyed the outpouring of support with her. "Yeah. People like to bring food around here. Mostly when somebody dies." He smiled, but his voice was bleak.

Allison's heart squeezed.

"We should get some of this labeled and into the freezer," she said, deliberately brisk. "Your grandmother might be glad not to cook right after she gets out of the hospital."

Josh looked more cheerful. "I guess."

"Got masking tape and a marker?" Allison asked.

"Duct tape."

She smiled. "That'll work."

Taylor watched Allison from the couch while Josh rummaged in the kitchen for supplies.

"Hi, Taylor. How are you doing?"

Taylor gave her a dark look from under the bill of her cap. *Okay, stupid question.*

She had nightmares, Matt had said. In a few short months, the little girl had lost her mother, said good-bye to her father, been uprooted from her home. And now her grandmother was in the ER.

Allison tried again. "You want to help me start a list?"

Taylor regarded her suspiciously. "What kind of list?"

"What people brought over, what dishes they came in," Allison said patiently. "So you can give the dishes back and say thanks to the right people."

"Josh already said thank you."

"We should still write a list."

Keep them busy, she thought. Keep them from brooding. With all three of them working, organizing the donations took less than half an hour. Most of the casseroles came labeled already, so they could quickly be added to the list and carried across the yard to the inn's freezer. The rest Allison divided depending on whether the items needed refrigeration or not.

"You want to keep out this fried chicken for dinner?" she asked Josh.

"Nah." His smile was so much like his father's it took her breath away. "I'd rather have pizza."

She turned on the oven. "We'll keep the chicken in the fridge, then. Your dad might be hungry when he gets home."

"Maybe. I don't know when he'll be back."

She slid the pizza onto a cookie sheet to reheat. "When was the last time you talked with him?"

"Before you came. He's not allowed to use his cell phone where he is, and reception sucks anyway. He had to call from outside."

"How's your grandmother?" she asked quietly.

A quick shoulder jerk. "It was a bad wreck. She's out of surgery, Dad said. He hasn't seen her yet."

Four . . . No, five hours later? Dear God. Matt must be out of his mind with worry and grief.

How is he? she wanted to ask, but she would not lay the burden of her concern on Josh's young shoulders.

"He sounds okay," Josh volunteered, surprising her. "But it's hard to tell with Dad. He's tough."

She smiled and risked a pat on his arm, trying not to overstep her boundaries as his teacher. Trying not to undermine his boy's dignity. "Must run in the family."

Josh looked at her, his face unguarded, open, only sixteen. Sudden tears glittered in his eyes.

She remembered her brother, Miles, who felt everything and had no way to show it, and she thought of Matt, weariness in his eyes, saying flatly, *We're handling it.*

Maybe so, she thought. But Josh shouldn't have to handle this alone.

She put her arms around him, and he ducked his head against her much shorter shoulder to hide his tears.

MATT STOOD TO stretch. Outside, the sky was fading, but the harsh lights of the waiting room held time still and the dusk at bay.

His sister Meg blew into the cold stale air like a summer squall, dark and fast and crackling with energy.

"Dad!" She went into his arms and hugged him tight. "How's Mom?"

Tom raised a shaking hand to stroke her hair, his granite composure cracking. He closed his eyes.

Matt's heart wrenched with helpless pity. He was reluctant to take the lead, to take control with his father standing there. But Tom had never been one for talking. Without Tess, he was speechless.

All Matt's life, his parents had been there, an unquestioning support, an ever-present backup, a port in the storm. Now that their roles were reversed, he had to be there for them.

Matt cleared his throat. "You missed the doctor. Mom's out of surgery."

"Matt." Meg flew to his arms.

He held her hard, absorbing her strength and the smell of the world outside the hospital. She was still wearing what he thought of as her City Girl clothes, black skirt, big bag, knotted scarf.

She raised her head from his chest, her blue eyes damp. "Are you okay?"

She sounded so much like Mom Matt almost lost it.

He ignored her question. "We didn't expect to see you till tomorrow."

"My secretary found a flight from Newark to Raleigh. I rented a car and drove the rest of the way."

"Expensive," Tom said, finding his voice.

She shrugged. "I can afford it. I wanted to be here."

And his sister didn't let anything stand between her and what she wanted, Matt thought, amusement warming the coldness inside him.

"So." Her gaze lasered in on Matt. "What's up with Mom?"

Tom turned away again to stare down the hall.

"Steering wheel broke her rib and her hip. Pelvis," he corrected, dragging the heavy words from the depths of his fear, trying to arrange them in order for Meg. "The surgeon said they repaired the most life-threatening injury and the rest will just take patience and time. She had a lot of bleeding. The, um, rib punctured her lung."

"Any damage to her spleen? Her liver?" At his narrowed look, she held up her BlackBerry. "I had time to research abdominal trauma on the plane."

Of course she did.

"Liver," he said. "They removed part of it."

Meg's eyes widened. "Oh, God, Matt."

"It's okay," he said, even though it wasn't, not really. "She can actually grow it back. Kind of like a starfish. The doctor said she'll have to have another operation in a couple of days on her hip. But they stopped the bleeding. That's the most important thing. Her prognosis is good, they said."

"Have you seen her? Talked to her?"

He shook his head. "The nurse says we can't go back yet."

Meg lifted her chin and narrowed her eyes, transforming in the space of a breath from devastated daughter to stone-cold city girl. "We'll just see about that."

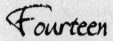

Fourteen

MATT PULLED IN behind the cottage and sat in the truck, raw and unsettled and too tired to move. Caffeine jangled through his system. Fatigue gnawed down to his bones.

If he closed his eyes, he could still see his mother, small and frail, as white as the sheets that covered her, a tube down her throat and another in her chest, hooked to machines that blinked and beeped and breathed for her.

So he kept his eyes open, staring into the darkness beyond his windshield.

Meg had argued against him driving home tonight. He'd been up for twenty hours straight. Her secretary had already booked them two rooms in a hotel near the hospital. *We don't need two crashes in one day*, Meg had said fiercely.

But Meg was the one who had to stay at the hospital, the one who would argue and ask questions when the orthopedic team came in the morning, the one who could advocate for Mom and hold Dad's hand.

Somebody had to be there for Josh and Taylor.

Matt climbed stiffly from the truck. Which was why he was here in the dark hours before dawn and not at Allison's.

God, he wanted her, wanted to lose himself in the blind, hot rush of sex, wanted to bury his grief and fear in the warm welcome of her body. Wanted her energy, her optimism, her comfort.

But wanting wasn't needing, he told himself.

He had people who needed him. Family who depended on him. Josh had sounded okay on the phone when they talked around ten, but he could be faking it.

They all could be.

He walked up the path, feeling as creaky as an old man, and let himself into the inn. He'd told Josh to let Taylor sleep in her own room tonight and to bunk in an empty bedroom. Thank God they weren't expecting guests before Friday.

His tired mind grappled briefly with the problem of the coming weekend. How was he going to handle the charters, the guests, the kids alone?

He shut the thought down. He couldn't, wouldn't, go there now.

He climbed the stairs to check on Taylor. As he pushed open the door, Fezzik raised his head from the foot of her bed, ears alert, eyes gleaming in the glow of the night-light. On the job. Matt reached out and rubbed the dog's head, communicating thanks, taking comfort. Taylor curled in a tight, defensive ball under the covers, her blond hair sticking up like the spines of a puffer fish. Asleep, he thought, and some of the tension inside him eased.

He closed her door and went in search of Josh. A faint light shone from the Stede Bonnet Room. Josh must have left a light on and the door cracked in case Taylor woke and came looking for him. Matt smiled. He hadn't expected that kind of thinking from his son.

He flattened his palm against the panel, easing the door

open. The smell hit him first, cinnamon and vanilla. His pulse thudded. He rubbed his eyes.

A dim light from the bathroom fell across the curves and valleys of the bed. Rounded hip, slim arm, hair spilling across the pillow.

Not Josh, he realized, and suddenly felt a lot better.

Allison.

ALLISON WOKE TO a prickle of awareness like a whisper against her skin, like a change in temperature.

Adrenaline pumped through her. *The kids.*

She pushed herself up on one elbow, her gaze seeking the door. A tall, broad-shouldered figure was outlined against the moonlight from the hall.

Not Josh, she realized, and suddenly felt a lot better. *Matt.*

She stretched out her arm and clicked on the bedside lamp.

He looked tired, she thought, her heart twisting. Haggard. The yellow light cast shadows in the creases of his cheeks, the lines scored from nose to mouth. She wanted to press her lips at the corners of his eyes, in the hollow of his throat.

"Hi." Her voice was husky with sleep and concern.

"Hey." She saw the effort it cost him to smile. "What are you doing here?"

He didn't sound upset.

She returned his smile. "Well, I was trying to get some sleep," she teased, adding softly, "I'm glad you're home."

He still leaned against the doorway. As if he would fall down unless he was propped up. Swinging her bare legs out of bed, she went to him, sliding her arms around his hard waist, lending him her strength and support.

He wrapped his arms around her and held on, sharing her heat, stealing her breath, their hearts in rhythm. Gradually his rigid muscles relaxed.

"How's your mom?" she asked.

His chest expanded with his breath. "Better. Alive. She's busted up pretty bad. Goddamn drunk driver. Ribs, pelvis, lung, liver. The police said she was lucky she didn't crack her skull wide open."

"So, she's conscious?"

"Not really." He sighed, stirring her hair and her heart. "They've got her doped up, because of the pain and to keep her from fighting the tubes. She looks like hell."

"Then you got to see her?"

She felt him nod. "Before I left. She's only allowed two visitors every thirty minutes, and with my dad there . . . and Meg . . ."

"Josh told me your sister came," she said.

He nodded again. "Flew into Raleigh." His voice was raw with heartache, rough with fatigue and frustration.

She squeezed his waist. "And you came home to take care of the kids."

"Yeah. How're they doing?"

She took one of his big, callused hands between both of hers and tugged him toward the bed. *They're fine*, she almost said—the Fletcher family anthem—but he deserved more of an answer than that.

"Josh is great," she said. "Taylor was a little quiet all evening."

Matt obeyed her nudging, dropping onto the edge of the mattress. "She's always quiet."

Quiet, fine. But Allison suspected that there was more to Taylor's silence than simple reticence.

"How did Taylor's mother die?" she asked abruptly.

He stiffened but answered readily enough. "Brain aneurysm."

"Oh, God, that's awful."

He scrubbed his face with one hand. "Yeah."

"Did Taylor ever see her mother in the hospital?"

"I don't know. Why?"

"I wondered if maybe your mother's accident brought back any memories for her."

Matt's eyes sharpened, concern cutting through his fatigue. "She give you any trouble? Problems at bedtime?"

She hastened to reassure him. "We were fine. Taylor was fine. Did you know she sleeps with the dog?"

Matt nodded. "Protection. From monsters under the bed."

Allison felt a prickle of unease, stirred by instinct or her teacher's training. "Imaginary monsters? Or real ones?"

Matt frowned, uncomprehending.

He looked so tired. Her heart clenched. She didn't want to hit him with this now, when he was already reeling on his feet. But more than his feelings—or hers—was at stake. She had to think about Taylor.

"She wore sweatpants to bed," Allison said.

His brows knit. "So?"

"It's seventy degrees outside."

He shrugged. "You want me to buy her pajamas, I'll buy her pajamas."

Allison sighed. "I don't think Taylor needs pajamas. The sweatpants are a sign, like the oversize jerseys or the baggy jeans. Or the nightmares."

He shook his head. "Lots of kids—"

"Have nightmares. I know." The silence crowded between them. Should she say more? At this point her suspicions were only, well, suspicions. "There's also the fact that she doesn't like to be hugged."

Matt's eyes had darkened to navy. His face set like stone. "She hardly knows us. Not everybody's a hugger."

Allison's stomach dropped. But having come this far, she forced herself to go on. "I don't know anything about Taylor's situation before she came to live with you. But have you considered that she might benefit from professional help?"

"You mean a shrink."

"A child psychologist, yes," she said calmly. "Taylor's a strong little girl with a loving family. I'm sure she'll heal in time. But her experience is bound to leave scars. It doesn't help to ignore her wounds."

Or yours, either.

"Better than having some expert pick at the scabs. Taylor needs her parents. No therapist in the world can change that. And I can't give them to her."

The frustration in his voice tore at her chest. He was such a good man, with so much love to give. But his feelings were buried as deeply as Taylor's.

"You're there for her," Allison said softly. *The way you're there for everyone else.*

"I don't know what to do for her."

"You could start by talking to her," she suggested. "More than anything, Taylor needs to know that she can confide in you. That she doesn't have to deal with whatever's upsetting her alone."

She could see from his face that the idea made him uncomfortable, but he nodded slowly. "Yeah. I can do that."

She looked down at him, at the harsh stubble of his jaw, the tender line of his mouth, and felt her heart unraveling and spooling at his feet. "I'm sorry," she said. "I didn't mean to hit you with this tonight."

He shrugged. "I had to hear it sometime."

The silence collected again like shadows in the corners of the room. Matt sat, his gaze turned inward, his thoughts far away while she waited, aching for him. Yearning for him.

He roused, raising his head. "Did I thank you for coming over?"

The tension inside her eased. "You couldn't keep me away," she said honestly.

"I appreciate it." His gaze captured hers. "You being here for the kids."

For them.
For you.
I love you.

The realization loomed inside her, solid as a rock sticking out of the ocean, staggering in its simplicity.

She loved him. Loved his quiet steadiness, his uncomplicated directness, his commitment to family, his determination to do the right thing. Loved Matt, the whole man.

She wanted to sing with her discovery, to shout, to babble promises.

But tonight wasn't about her. Or even about them. She couldn't burden him with her feelings now while he was raw and reeling.

She would not tell him.

She rested her hands lightly on his shoulders, feeling his muscles heavy and warm under her palms.

She would show him instead.

"I didn't think they should be alone." She stroked a line from his neck to his shoulders, digging her fingers in a little to loosen the knots of tension there. "Nobody should be alone at a time like this."

ALLISON'S SCENT SWAM in Matt's head.

She stood between his knees, her hands moving over him with slow, sure purpose, kneading his taut muscles, her touch soothing and arousing at the same time. He felt the brush of her breath on his temple, her fingers tracing his spine, and wanted to groan with pleasure, wanted to rest his head between her soft, warm breasts and sink into her comfort like a child sinks into sleep. He ran his hands over her instead, hips to waist and down again. Her legs were long, bare, smooth. The hem of his T-shirt flirted with the tops of her thighs. *Nice.* He slid his hands over and under it, finding the taut, warm curve of her ass, the stretchy strip of her thong. He dipped his fingers under the elastic, following the sweet, deep indentation, down, down.

She shivered. "I borrowed your shirt to sleep in," she whispered. "I hope you don't mind."

A smile worked its way up from deep inside him. "Nope."

He rubbed his face against her, bringing his hands up to skim her rib cage, to cradle the soft weight of her breasts. He scraped his thumbs over her. Her nipples peaked to tight attention under the worn cotton. "It looks good on you."

She threaded her fingers through his hair. Tugged his head up. "You can have it back if you want."

Her teasing roiled him deep inside. He wanted . . . too much. He wanted everything.

"I don't want to take anything away from you."

Not his shirt. Not her future.

Her smile gleamed, bewitching him in the dark. "Maybe I want you to have it."

She stepped back. He watched, heavy and motionless, as she closed the door. The snick of the lock cracked against the stillness. Turning, she gathered the hem of his shirt and pulled it over her head.

Her beauty swamped him. Desire crashed over him in a wave, drowning fatigue, sapping any thought of resistance. He had never brought a woman home. Never made love under his parents' roof or in the house he shared with his son. But he wanted her here, now, like this, with an urgency he hadn't felt since he was a teenager, with a desperation born of a man's loneliness and need.

She swayed toward him, naked except for that wicked strip of lace and the inked words dancing along her ribs.

She crouched at his feet. "Let's get these shoes off."

His blood pounded in his veins as her fingers fumbled with his laces. Her shoulder brushed his thigh.

She drove him crazy.

He didn't need her to undress him and put him to bed like

a child. He didn't want her to take care of him or seduce him. He wanted her *with* him, under him, slippery with sweat and desire. His control snapped. He reached for her, jerking her up and into his arms, falling back with her onto the mattress as they both grappled with his buckle, as they fought to free him of his clothes. She yanked on his shirt. He shoved at his jeans. He rolled with her, naked, dipping his fingers under the barrier of lace to find her warm and wet and ready.

He couldn't wait.

He spread her thighs wide, opening her to his gaze, to his body. She squirmed, her hips arching to meet him. He took himself in hand, pulling aside the stretchy bit of lace to rub against her, giving her a taste of what she wanted, he wanted, teasing, tormenting, pleasuring them both. She writhed, wrapping her strong legs around him, and he slipped briefly, too briefly, inside her.

His mind blanked. Her heat scorched him. He was dying here, she was killing him, the denial and discipline of sixteen years going up in smoke. She melted around him, both of them burning up. Playing with fire.

Her eyes opened wide. "Condom?"

He froze, desire a hard ache. He had to . . . He needed . . . *Damn it.*

He withdrew from her—*agony*—and almost fell off the bed grabbing for his jeans, digging for his wallet. She reached for him, stroking his back, touching his thigh, shaking with muffled noises of laughter and impatience as he wrestled with the damn latex, making him feel better even before he got the job done. He lunged for her, sliding thick inside her laughter and her heat, roughly, no holding back, taking her, reclaiming everything he'd lost sixteen years ago. He thrust inside her as her body closed around him, shuddering under him, taking him, too, making him forget the day and all responsibility. Until at last he spilled deep inside her, spent.

Home.

* * *

ALLISON'S PHONE ALARM chimed on the bedside table. 6:00 AM. She reached quickly to turn it off, careful not to disturb Matt sleeping beside her.

Matt.

She turned her head, her heart doing a little dance, her inside parts a squeeze.

He sprawled beside her, sated and relaxed, the faint light from the bathroom illuminating his tanned features. With his bare, hair-roughened chest and the stubble on his jaw, he looked less like a charter boat captain and more like the "gentleman pirate" the room was named for.

She grinned. *Yo ho ho.*

For a moment she entertained a fantasy of the two of them sailing the high seas on a voyage of discovery, locked alone in a cabin for days on end while Matt plundered her body and she explored his. New worlds . . .

She smiled and shook her head. The reality was different but just as novel. Exciting, even. In the real world, Matt's world, there was a family, children in the house who had to be fed and readied for school. She sobered abruptly, thinking of Taylor. Children who needed her.

She needed to be needed. She wanted to help.

She gathered her clothes and dressed in the bathroom.

Fifteen minutes later, she was spreading peanut butter onto sandwich bread when she heard something over the gurgle of the coffeepot.

She turned her head. "Hey, Josh. What are you doing up?"

The boy stood in the kitchen door, barefoot and disheveled. "I heard a noise. I thought maybe Dad was home."

"He got in really late last night. He's upstairs sleeping now. Your grandfather's at the hospital with your grandmother and Aunt Meg."

Josh's throat moved as he swallowed. "Is Grandma . . . ?"

"She's going to be okay," Allison said firmly. "Still in ICU, but your dad wouldn't have left if she weren't going to be okay. He can fill you in when he wakes up."

Josh ambled forward. "What are you doing?"

"Making lunch for you and Taylor." She dropped apples into their bags. "I'm going home to shower and change and then I'll be back in about forty-five minutes to take you both to school, all right?"

Josh regarded her thoughtfully. "You know, you don't have to do all this."

He sounded like his father.

She smiled. "I want to do it."

"Grandma taught me to pack my own lunch when I was seven."

Heat flushed her face. "I wasn't . . . I'm not trying to take anybody's place." *His grandmother's. His mother's.* "I just want to help."

He leaned against the counter, looking at her with Matt's blue eyes. "That's cool. But I've got this. It won't kill me to walk Taylor to school today."

"Oh." She wiped her hands on a dish towel, jarred from her fantasies for the second time that morning. "I guess I'll see you at school, then."

"See you." He waited until she was almost to the door before he added slyly, "Allison."

Oh, boy. She turned. Maybe she couldn't take the place of his mother or grandmother. Maybe nobody could. But she was still his teacher. She needed his respect. "At school, it's Miss Carter."

He nodded, accepting that. "What about here?"

What *about* here? she wondered. She couldn't take advantage of the Fletchers' situation to push in where she wasn't wanted. This was about what they needed, not about her playing a role. She winced. Playing house.

"What do you think is appropriate?" she hedged.

His eyes gleamed between thick blond lashes. "Not Mom."

Ouch.

"Of course not."

"Because she never packed my lunch for me."

"Never?" Allison asked before she could stop herself. She knew—because Gail had told her—that Josh's mother had walked out on them when Josh was a baby. She had the opportunity to get details here, but she was pretty sure that pumping your lover's teenage son for dirt on his mother carried a penalty, like going to hell. "She must have sometime. Maybe when you visited her."

"I don't. Visit," he explained. "Not since I was eight."

Allison's jaw dropped in distress.

"She still sends checks." Josh smiled wryly. "Every year, on my birthday."

Allison didn't know what to say.

Matt was all about family. What must it have done to him, to be married to a woman who could reject family so completely, who could ignore her own child?

"Checks are always nice," she said faintly. Her own parents used money as the currency of affection.

"Yeah. The thing is . . . we're used to not having her around."

"Right," Allison said, not feeling any better.

"Last night . . . when you came over . . ." Josh said and stopped.

He'd cried in her arms. He was probably mortified, remembering.

"You were great," she said. "You took good care of Taylor."

"Thanks. But it was nice." He met her gaze. "You being there."

"Oh." A wave of emotion seized her by the throat. His admission was acceptance on a level she hadn't expected, validation of a kind she hadn't known she needed. It made her smile. It made her hope. All her life, she'd been searching for her true calling, her true course. And now suddenly her future rose in front of her like land on the horizon, growing brighter, closer, clearer with every moment.

It took her breath away.

She cleared her throat. "Anytime."

Fifteen

THE SNOW FELL faster and faster, big fat flakes swirling in the darkness beyond the windshield, trapping Tess in the cold shell of her parents' car on Lake Shore Drive. She couldn't get out. She couldn't get home. All she could hear was the rasp of her breath, foggy in the stale air, and the howl of the storm, the hiss of black and white as scrambled as the signal of an old TV. Even her fear was muffled, smothered in blankets of white.

She thought vaguely that there must have been an accident. That's why she was stuck here on the bridge in a blizzard. She had a memory of flashing lights and urgent voices, gone now, all gone. Now there were only drifts and the abandoned cars of panicked commuters trying to get home.

She shivered, alternating between hot and cold, searing blasts from the heater, icy shafts from the windows, her toes freezing, her chest burning up. She couldn't breathe. She tried to swallow and gagged. Pain swirled, white and thick as the snowflakes.

Something moved up ahead, a flicker in the storm, a young woman, a girl, translucent, shifting in and out of the storm, under the bridge lights, her long hair lifting in the wind. She should really wear a hat, Tess thought, just as the girl turned, smiling, and she recognized her, pretty seventeen-year-old Dawn Simpson.

Tess shuddered, floating between weightlessness and dread, the cold sinking into her bones. That wasn't right. Dawn must be in her twenties now.

Dawn was dead.

Tess opened her mouth to call out, to ask Dawn what she was doing dancing in a snowstorm in Chicago, but her voice made no sound. Her mouth was cracked and painful, her chest on fire. She tried to move away from the pain, and the fire flared and reformed, consuming her from the inside.

Someone rapped on her window.

Tess almost shrieked.

But it was Tom, appearing in his dress blues out of the snow, handsome as the day they married. *My hero.* Somehow he'd found her through the storm. He stood beside her rattletrap car, peering through the foggy glass.

"You're doing great, Tess. I'm proud of you."

A compliment. Despite her pain, Tess almost smiled. That was different. Nice. She tried to roll down her window to tell him so and frowned. She couldn't move her arm.

Lights hummed. Machinery beeped.

She felt a touch on her hair, light as snow. *"The surgery went great, babe. They got you all fixed up now, plates, pins, screws, the works."* He cleared his throat. *"You got yourself a regular hardware store in there."*

Beneath the joke, the encouraging tone, she heard the strain tightening Tom's vocal cords.

Poor, dear, taciturn man. He never had been any damn good when one of the kids was sick or in the hospital.

Hospital.

She opened her eyes, remembering.

Her husband hovered over her bed, feathering her hair from her forehead with trembling fingers, his face lined and worried. Old. She blinked sudden moisture from her eyes, sadness pooling in her chest. When had they gotten so old?

"They took the tube out of your throat now, too," he said, holding her hand in his strong, rough, callused hand, his touch warm and familiar. "You can breathe on your own now. And talk. Can you talk to me, babe?"

The tube down her throat had been replaced by soft prongs under her nostrils. Clear lines ran into the back of her hand and the crook of her elbow, soft restraints bound her wrists. So she wouldn't tear at the tubes in her sleep, she remembered the nurse saying.

She moved her lips without sound.

Tom scowled. "How do you feel?"

Like hell, she wanted to say. Like she'd been hit by a truck. Or an SUV. Pain radiated from her chest, throbbed in her hips. She felt battered, bruised, taken apart and manipulated.

She licked her cracked lips, swallowed the lump in her aching throat. "Fine," she croaked and coughed.

Tom looked stricken.

She squeezed his hand, doing her best to smile. "Feel . . . fine."

Her husband's fierce gaze flooded with sudden tears. "Glad you're back, babe."

He laid his gray head beside their joined hands on the mattress and cried.

"Hi, little girl."

"Dad. Hi." Allison juggled her phone as she stood in line

at the bakery. Her father never called. "Is everything all right? Mom?"

Taylor pulled on her arm. "Can I have something to eat now?"

Allison covered her phone. "You can pick out one snack." Catching Josh's eye, she held up one finger and then pointed toward the bakery case.

He nodded in understanding. "Come on, brat."

". . . misses you, of course," her father said. "She was very disappointed when you canceled your visit."

Guilt needled her. "I miss you guys, too."

"Then you'll be happy to hear my news."

Allison kept an eye on Taylor as the woman behind the counter wrapped up two enormous bear claws. Was she ruining the kids' appetites for dinner? "News?"

"I'm here in North Carolina visiting a project, a mixed-use development outside Wilmington. The Riverside Club. Herb Stuart, the architect, is an old friend. Your mother is flying down for the weekend. I've reserved an extra room so you can join us."

"I . . . What? When?"

"We have dinner reservations for eight. And then tomorrow you can entertain your mother while Herb and I check out the golf course."

Taylor was back, squinting up from under the brim of her Marine cap. "I want to pick out the cupcakes."

"Fine. You have to choose a variety, though. Three dozen minis, please," Allison said to the counter lady.

"What?" her father asked.

"Daddy, I can't."

"Of course you can. It's all arranged. Riverside will be a new experience for you." Richard Carter chuckled. "I know how you like new experiences."

"Dad, you should have asked me before planning something like this."

"Your mother wanted to surprise you. I thought you'd be pleased."

"It's a lovely thought. I appreciate it, I do. But I have another commitment."

"Well, of course I wouldn't want to interfere with your plans," her father said stiffly. "You can come down tomorrow."

"No, I can't. Not anytime this weekend, I'm afraid." She covered the phone again. "Not *all* chocolate, Taylor."

"I like chocolate."

"These aren't for you. These are for the guests. Maybe some of them don't like chocolate."

"Is it that man you're seeing?" her father asked.

"Excuse me?"

"That'll be forty-two dollars and sixteen cents," said the woman behind the counter.

"Your mother mentioned you were dating someone," Richard said. "Bring him along. I'd like to meet the man who's taking up all of my little girl's time."

"Hey, Al—Miss Carter, you got any money?" Josh said.

"Is that him?" Richard asked.

"No, that's Josh. Matt's son." She thrust her wallet at Josh. "Take this."

"He has children?"

Oh, hell. "Listen, Dad, I really have to go."

"Allison . . ."

"I'll call you," she promised. "I love you. Bye."

"Who was that?" Josh asked as she shoved her phone and wallet into her bag.

"That," Allison said grimly, "was my father."

"Are you in trouble?" Taylor asked. Above her cinnamon-streaked cheeks, her eyes were blue and worried.

Allison pulled herself together and smiled down into Taylor's wary little face. "I'm good," she said. "Everything's fine. How's that bear claw?"

* * *

MATT RESISTED THE urge to knock before opening the door to his parents' bedroom off the kitchen. "I put you in Mom and Dad's room."

His sister Meg stopped in the sunshine streaming through the kitchen windows. "I'm not in Mary Read?"

Her old room upstairs.

"Booked for the weekend," Matt said. "We're full up except for the family rooms. Big anniversary party."

Meg nodded her understanding. "So you couldn't cancel. Well, at least business is good."

She adjusted her purse strap and marched past him into their parents' room.

Only to stop dead, staring at their mother's robe tossed over a chair. Matt winced. Everything was the way Tess must have left it on Tuesday morning, her robe on the chair, her book by the bed, her towel on a bar by the open bathroom door.

Matt set his sister's suitcase carefully on the bed. "Sorry. I didn't have time to clean in here."

"It's okay." Meg's lips quirked. "That's what I'm here for."

He returned her smile. He knew damn well that when Meg left Dare Island she'd been determined never to clean another toilet, to fold another towel, again. But here she was. *Back to back to back.* Gratitude made him say, "I can give you a hand for the rest of the day. Josh, too, when he gets home."

"Good. If we're full up, we're going to need all the help we can get." Meg crossed to her bag and unzipped it. "What about tomorrow?"

Matt rubbed his jaw. "Both boats are booked. Jimmy Peele's captaining the old *Sea Lady* for me, but with Dad at the hospital I'll need Josh to come along as mate."

Meg pulled a pair of sneakers from her bag and turned to look at him. "So I'm on my own?"

"The Kellers are staying two nights. You won't have to change their sheets," Matt said, feeling guilty. "Just make the beds and, you know, straighten up a little."

"I know what to do," she said, tying her shoes. "God knows I did it often enough growing up."

She moved into the kitchen at New York speed, muttering and opening cupboards. Matt followed in her wake.

"Okay, somebody has to go shopping," she said, surveying the inside of the fridge. "I don't have time to bake cookies before check-in, and we've got nothing in the house for breakfast."

"Give me a list," Matt said.

"Great. Thanks." She grabbed the pad and pencil by the phone and started writing. "You know, Matt, we need to start thinking about the long term. Mom's car was totaled. I rented something for Dad so he could get to and from the hospital, but . . ."

How could she write a list and talk to him at the same time?

"Randy Scott is looking to sell his Nissan Altima. I told him I was interested."

Meg raised her head. "Will Mom's insurance pay for that?"

"Doesn't matter. Dad can drive it for now, and if he decides he wants something else for Mom, it will be a good car for Josh."

It wasn't a Mercedes. Or the Jeep that Josh had been talking about. But the sedan was safe and reliable, without too many miles on it. Josh could deal.

"Okay." Meg nodded slowly. "That takes care of transportation. That still leaves us shorthanded at the inn. I need to go back to work as soon as Mom's out of intensive care. We'll have to hire somebody."

Matt set his jaw. "We can't take on somebody full-time at the end of the season. Mom and Dad can't afford it."

"News flash, big brother. Mom and Dad aren't here. It'll be weeks before Mom can come home. And Dad won't leave her."

He felt the conversation getting deeper, the levels of complication piling up, until he was in over his head.

Keep it simple, he thought.

"We'll make it work," he said.

"How?"

"We'll figure it out. I can move some charters, maybe get part-time help. Lots of captains just sitting at the docks this time of year. Right now we just have to get through the weekend."

"What about Taylor?"

His shoulders tightened. It had been three days since his conversation with Allison, three days in which Taylor had slept with the dog and played video games with Josh, eaten her vegetables under protest and done her homework without complaint. Three days in which Matt had barely found time to take a piss, let alone schedule a heart-to-heart with his ten-year-old niece. "What about her?"

"I've never met her. How is she going to react to having another stranger take care of her?"

The tension in Matt's neck and shoulders ratcheted up a notch. "She'll be fine. She's a good kid. She won't give you any trouble."

"Matt." Meg put her hands on her hips, looking so much like their mother it was creepy. "Her mother just died. Her father, who she barely knows, is getting shot at in fricking Afghanistan. She's living with people she just met, and her grandmother is in intensive care. If she doesn't give me any trouble, then something is seriously wrong with her."

He didn't want to hear it. But Meg was right.

It doesn't help to ignore her wounds, Allison had said the other night. *Taylor needs to know she doesn't have to deal with whatever's bothering her alone.*

"I'll talk to her," he said.

Meg's brows rose. "You?"

"Who else? Unless you're volunteering."

Meg laughed. "God, no."

Allison would have said yes, he thought. She said yes to everything. He didn't know how they would have made it through the past three days without her. But she wasn't family. She had her own life, her own work, her own obligations to attend to. He couldn't keep laying his shit on her, too.

No, this one was on him.

"Oh, crap," Meg said, looking out the window. "They're here already."

Matt frowned. "The Kellers?" David and Sharon Keller had a six-hour drive from Lynchburg, Virginia. He was sure they'd asked for a late check-in.

"One of the daughters, I think. Or a granddaughter. Looks like Baylor Barbie traded in her pink convertible for a Mercedes."

The back of Matt's neck prickled. *Mercedes?* That was . . .

The kitchen door opened and Allison stood in a flood of sunshine, looking young and fresh and impossibly beautiful, her arms full of flowers and a wide grin on her face.

Matt's heart lifted at the sight of her, the weight dropping from his shoulders, the tension easing in his neck. Whether he admitted it or not, whether he wanted it or not, she made things better simply by being there.

Her gaze sought his across the kitchen. "Sorry we're late," she said cheerfully. "I stopped by the grocery store on the way home. I figured you'd need a few things."

Meg reacted like a cat hit by a bucket of water, with swift, stiff, disdainful suspicion. "Who are you?"

ALLISON BLINKED AT the short, chic, semihostile woman glaring at her from beside the kitchen counter.

Matt's sister. She recognized the blue eyes, cropped hair, strong jaw of the smiling Harvard grad in the picture upstairs.

She wasn't smiling now.

Well, this was a stressful time for her, Allison thought fairly. For her whole family. No wonder Meg was feeling protective. *Circle the wagons.*

Allison pasted on her most disarming parent-teacher smile and introduced herself. "Allison Carter. I'm . . ." She hesitated, searching for a nice, neutral label that wouldn't threaten Matt's sister.

Matt's friend? Girlfriend?

"Josh's teacher," Matt said. "She's been helping us out since the accident."

Well, that was certainly neutral, Allison thought, swallowing hurt.

"And she brought you flowers," Meg drawled. "How sweet."

Allison stuck out her chin. "These are for the Kellers. Matt mentioned this weekend is their fiftieth wedding anniversary. I thought the bouquet would be a nice touch for their room."

"Pretty," Matt approved.

"She didn't throw them at the dog this time, either," Josh joked as he carried in the bag of groceries from the car. "Hey, Aunt Meg."

"Josh!" Meg's hostility melted into smiles as she hugged her nephew. "God, you're so tall. Good-looking, too."

Taylor followed Josh into the kitchen, carefully balancing a pink bakery box from Jane's Sweet Tea House. "We bought cupcakes. Allison let me pick them out."

Allison glanced from Matt to Meg. She'd only offered to drive the kids from school so Matt could be home when his sister arrived. Maybe she should have asked, she should have waited, instead of blundering blindly in with what she thought was needed. "I thought . . . since there wasn't time to bake cookies . . ."

"What a good idea," Meg said coolly. Her smile warmed when she looked at Taylor. "I'm your Aunt Meg. Let's see what you've got."

"Good job," Matt said quietly as his sister huddled with Taylor over the box.

Allison expelled her breath. "Thanks."

"Sorry about Meg. She's used to being the Queen Bee in the family."

Family.

Every pinch Allison had felt, the hurt, the irritation, the injured pride, dissolved into gooey warmth.

"You're her brother. This is your family business. I totally understand her feeling territorial."

"That's no excuse for taking it out on you. I'll talk to her."

"Don't worry about it, Matt. I can take care of myself."

He drew back slightly. "Sure."

What had put that faint distance in his eyes, that reserve in his voice?

"I mean, you have enough people to take care of," she said.

"Right."

She watched Taylor with Meg, arranging cupcakes on a plate. Saw Josh, swigging milk in front of the open refrigerator as he put the groceries away. She didn't want to go. She wanted to be here, with them, part of this.

She searched Matt's face. "Do you want me to get out of your way?"

"No." His slow, rare smile took her breath away. "I want you to stay for dinner. If you can stand to eat ham again."

She laughed. The donated ham had provided them with two meals and three packed lunches already. "Maybe we can heat up a casserole this time."

"Forget dinner. We need to get ready for check-in," Meg said. "We have guests coming."

"We still have to eat," Matt said calmly. "Eventually."

"I could put dinner together," Allison offered. "While you do . . . whatever you have to do."

"Do you cook?" Meg asked.

"No," Allison admitted. "But I can warm a casserole and make a salad."

Taylor made gagging noises.

Meg looked at her, alarmed. "What?"

"She doesn't like salad," Allison explained. "You can have carrot sticks," she said to Taylor.

Meg nodded. "Fine. You can stay."

HE WAS GOING to strangle his sister, Matt decided over dinner.

As long as Meg had guests to impress, she'd played the part of the perfect innkeeper, friendly, energetic, and efficient. She'd made beds and dinner reservations, answered questions and arranged for special meals. She'd provided videos, a crib, and a babysitter for the Kellers' grandchildren.

Eventually, though, the Kellers trooped off happily to the restaurant of their choice. Meg sat down to eat with Matt, Allison, and the kids.

And promptly started the questioning.

"So why Dare Island?" she asked Allison over hamburger casserole. "Did you come here on vacation?"

"No, I just saw the job posting and liked the idea of an island school."

"Where did you teach before?"

Allison set down her fork, responding pleasantly to his sister's interrogation. "I didn't start out as a teacher. I had to find my way into it. I did a lot of volunteer work, food pantry, Habitat for Humanity, that kind of thing. Then I got this summer internship with a women's shelter in South Dakota, working with the childhood development program. That convinced me to try teaching. So after graduation, I spent two years in Mississippi with Teach for America."

"Not much in that, is there?"

"Actually, it was very rewarding."

"I meant financially," Meg said.

Allison raised her eyebrows. "I don't consider money as the only, or even the most important, factor in making career decisions."

Meg's gaze flickered to the diamond-faced watch around Allison's wrist. "Easy to say when you have it."

Allison gave a small, polite smile. "I've been very fortunate."

"Obviously," Meg drawled.

Matt glanced around the table, wondering when his sister had reverted to being a First Class Brat, wondering how much of the tension the kids were picking up. Josh shoveled in food, oblivious, but Taylor's small face was pinched and watchful.

"Allison's a great teacher. Josh is lucky to be in her class," he said.

"Good for him. Good for her. No offense," she said to Allison. "It's just that I could never afford to flit around the country following my bliss. I had to work to pay the rent."

"Says Miss Central Park West," Matt said.

"Hey, it took me a long time to get there. Everything I have, I earned. Unlike some people."

Enough was enough.

"What is your problem?" Matt asked. "Allison's been busting her ass all day, first at school, then here. You should be grateful. You should thank her."

Meg's face reddened. "I am. I do. Thank you."

All right, then. Matt dug into his dinner.

But Meg, being Meg, couldn't leave well enough alone. "I'm just saying that people who come from a certain kind of background don't understand how things are for the rest of us."

"I understand more than you realize," Allison said. The good manners Matt had noticed before, that made her so easy to talk to, kept her spine straight and her tone mild. "I didn't go to Harvard, but one of the things I learned flitting around the country is that you might want to take some time, get to know a person or a situation, before you start making judgments."

Recognition sparked in Matt. Those were his words, almost the exact words he'd used to her over their first beer at the Fish House.

She looked across the table at him and grinned.

She had more than class, he thought. She had guts and heart.

Most people buckled to Meg. But no matter what his sister threw at her, what life threw at her, Allison found a way to keep smiling.

Matt smiled back, wishing he had more to offer her than warmed-up casserole with his sister and kids.

"WHEN I'VE BEEN a bitch, I say I've been a bitch," Meg announced the next morning.

Allison straightened from cleaning the toilet and turned. Meg stood behind her in the door to the William Kidd room, wearing two-hundred-dollar jeans and an apron.

Allison lowered the dripping toilet brush. "*Dirty Dancing.* Movie quote," she explained. "So?"

Meg scowled. "So, what?"

"I'm waiting for you to say it."

Meg laughed, humor chasing the storm from her face.

"I like you. Even if you are younger, prettier, and way nicer than me."

"And . . . ?" Allison prompted.

"I'm not getting away without a real apology, am I?" Meg asked wryly.

Allison considered. "I can excuse your being rude to me. You had a long drive and a long day yesterday, and you're under a lot of stress. But your attitude made things more difficult for Matt last night. So . . . No."

Meg nodded. "Fair enough. I was a bitch," she said sincerely. "And I'm sorry. Can we be friends now?"

Allison smiled, relaxing. "I'd like that."

"It's okay if we don't hug, though," Meg said. "At least until you put down the toilet wand."

Allison laughed.

Meg tilted her head. "The Kellers are all off fishing, bike riding, and touring the lighthouse. I have leftover coffee cake and a fresh pot of coffee in the kitchen. Feel like a break?"

"I drink tea, and I'd love to take a break with you," Allison said.

THE KITCHEN GLEAMED. The dishwasher hummed. All traces of the breakfast Meg had prepared and served to the eleven adult Kellers and their seven children had been cleared, wrapped, washed, and organized away.

"I'm impressed," Allison said, sitting at the kitchen table. "Also intimidated."

Meg cradled her mug and stretched out her legs. "Now you're sucking up. I like it."

"I'm just being honest. Did you ever think about going into hotel management?"

"Oh, God, no. I had enough of that growing up. Do you

VIRGINIA KANTRA

know what those entry-level jobs pay? There's more money in insurance."

"And that's important to you."

"Yes," Meg said, one word, fast and definite, in a way that shut down further discussion.

"This coffee cake is delicious," Allison said.

"Thanks." Meg's eyes suddenly, unexpectedly, filled with tears. She blotted them with the corner of her napkin. "Shit. It's Mom's recipe."

"How is she?" Allison asked sympathetically.

Meg sniffed and crumpled the napkin. "I talked to Dad this morning. Mom finally convinced him to catch a few hours of sleep at the hotel last night. The orthopedic guy says she's making a very fast recovery. They think they'll be able to remove her chest tube and move her into a step-down unit in a couple of days."

"That's wonderful."

"Yeah." Meg rubbed the crease between her brows. "Of course, she'll be in the hospital or rehab for weeks. Maybe months. And Derek is already putting pressure on me to come back to New York."

"Derek is your boss?"

"That would be awkward. We live together," Meg explained. "*And* we work together, but I don't actually report to him."

"I'm sure he misses you," Allison said politely.

"Yeah. The company just acquired Parnassus Insurance—maybe you read about that? I write the press releases—and things are crazy at the office right now."

"I meant personally."

"Well, sure," Meg said. "He actually talked about coming down with me, but he's on the transition team. There's no way we both could be gone. He really needs me in New York."

Allison nodded, not sure what to say. They needed Meg here, too.

But Meg had a career, an apartment, a lover demanding her attention. Allison completely understood. She'd refused to let her own life be dictated by her parents. How could she suggest that Meg put everything on hold indefinitely?

"Where's Taylor this morning?" she asked.

"The Kellers' daughter Lisa has a couple of kids around Taylor's age. She invited Taylor to tour the lighthouse with them." Meg shot Allison a droll look. "Apparently she felt having an outsider along would stop her kids from fighting."

"Oh, yes," Allison murmured. "Because that always works."

Meg grinned. "Hey, I've already admitted I was awful. In my defense, I was trying to protect my brother. I don't want to see him hurt."

Family was a big part of who Matt was. The man Allison wanted, the man she loved. If she took him on, she realized, she'd also be taking on his entire family: Josh, Matt's parents, his brother and sister, his niece.

That future she had envisioned, waiting like a bright island on the horizon, suddenly got more crowded. And more complicated.

"Okay, I respect that," Allison said. "Actually, I envy you. I wish I had that kind of relationship with my own brother. But Matt can take care of himself."

"Himself and everybody else. Which is part of the problem."

Allison thought of Matt rescuing her by the side of the road, rubbing her feet, filling her gas tank. Matt, with his slow, rare smile, making her come. Making her happy.

"How is that a problem?"

Meg set down her mug. "Look, you seem like a nice person. You obviously care about Matt. But he's thirty-six years old. He knows who he is and where he belongs. His family is here. His roots are here. You, on the other hand, are what, twenty-three?"

"Twenty-five."

"Okay. Not to sound condescending or anything, but you're young. You're still finding yourself. You've got things to do, places to go. You're not going to want to spend the rest of your life on Dare Island. I sure didn't."

"That doesn't mean I won't."

"What's keeping you?"

Allison's heart beat faster. "You mean, besides Matt?"

Meg's gaze was shrewd and not unkind. "I know my brother. Has he ever once asked you to stay?"

The coffee cake in Allison's mouth was dry as dust. "We've only been seeing each other for a few weeks. It's a little soon to be talking commitment, don't you think?"

"With Matt, it's always too soon. Commitment is not his strong suit."

Allison swallowed. "He's committed to his family."

"Exactly. He's never made room for anyone else."

"He must have once," Allison objected.

Meg looked at her blankly.

"He was married," she explained.

"At nineteen. To a girl like you. Nice girl, nice clothes, nice family." Meg grimaced. "Okay, maybe Kimberly wasn't so nice. But you're the same basic model—blond, smart, sure of yourself. One thing you can say about my brother, he's consistent."

That sounded terrible, Allison thought. It sounded . . .

Her stomach hollowed.

True.

Sixteen

MATT SQUATTED BESIDE the Harley to change the front brake pads, absorbing the quiet along with the tang of grease and metal.

Taylor perched on a bench, looking up every now and then from her homework.

I'm old enough to look after myself, she'd said this morning when he had announced his intention of picking her up after school. *I've done it before. Mom gave me my own key.*

Maybe.

But he didn't like the idea of her being home alone. She was safe here. The kids on Dare still ran free, roaming wild like the island ponies, the older ones looking out for the younger. But Taylor was so . . . little compared to Josh, small and female, vulnerable in ways he was only beginning to understand and didn't know how to deal with.

Matt popped off the brake clips.

God, he wished Allison was here. She would know what to do. What to say.

They'd barely seen each other the past couple of days. He was busy, she was busy, and when they did get together there were always other things, other people around, demanding his attention. Not much fun for her.

The problem was, he'd gotten used to her being there at the end of his day. Not that he needed to dump on her, exactly. He had other people around to talk to. If he wanted to swap stories, he could go down to the tackle shop. But he missed their conversations, missed sharing something besides the weather, the latest fishing quotas, or sports scores. Missed seeing Allison's face, hearing her enthusiasm as she talked about her students or the island.

He missed sex.

Allison, bless her, didn't complain. Maybe she was okay with the idea of taking things easy for a while. Maybe she didn't ache for him the way he ached for her.

The thought didn't make him feel any better.

Couldn't be helped, Matt told himself as he reached for the brake cleaner. He'd gone a damn sight longer than this without sex before. Occasional abstinence was part of being a dad, especially a single dad, like colic or fourth grade science projects or taking your kid to the dentist, something you got through with as much humor and patience as you could muster.

He shook the can as Taylor watched silently from the bench.

She's too quiet, Meg had said before she left for Greenville yesterday morning.

More than anything, Taylor needs to know that she can confide in you. That she doesn't have to deal with whatever's bothering her alone, Allison had told him the other night.

He didn't know what the hell to say to her. But maybe he didn't need to talk. Maybe he could just listen.

He sprayed brake cleaner until it ran dripping onto the newspaper under the bike. "How you doing, kid?"

"Fine."

Good. Except he had a feeling Allison would expect him to ask more. He scrubbed at the brakes with a toothbrush. "Everything okay at school?"

"Uh huh."

"Is there, uh, anything you want to tell me?"

Taylor narrowed her eyes. "Am I in trouble?"

That surprised a half smile from him. "Nope. Not at all. I just thought . . . Anything bothering you? Anybody bothering you?"

She shook her head.

Right. He scrubbed harder. "Because you know you can talk to me anytime."

"Okay."

"About anything."

She gave him a dubious look.

He didn't blame her. He tried again. "Or if you maybe wanted to talk to somebody at school . . ."

"I don't talk to the kids at school."

Matt filed that one away under Things to Deal With Another Time. "Not a kid. Another grown-up."

"You mean Allison?"

Allison would be good. She was smart and caring and female. She would know instinctively the right things to say to a little girl. She sure as hell wouldn't be fumbling with the brakes, searching for words.

Matt shook his head. Taylor was his responsibility. His brother's child. And right now, with Luke in Afghanistan and Tess in the hospital, Matt was all Taylor had.

"I was thinking more like a guidance counselor." Or a psychologist, like his ex-wife. He winced. Not that trying to talk to Kimberly had ever done Josh a damn bit of good.

"I knew I was in trouble," Taylor said darkly.

Matt grinned as he slid the clip from the brake reservoir.

"No, you're not. I just thought maybe you'd like to talk to somebody about your feelings and sh—stuff."

"No."

He sighed. "Just think about it, okay?"

She didn't answer.

He wrapped a rag around the reservoir, wishing little girls came with an owner's manual, a set of simple diagrammed instructions.

"Why do you do that?" she asked.

"In case it expands and leaks." Machines, he could talk about. "Brake fluid's corrosive. You don't want to touch it with your hands."

"Oh."

He pushed in the pistons with two fingers and reached for a new brake pad. Too bad Taylor's problems weren't the kind you could fix with a set of tools.

"Can I help?"

He looked up. She perched on the bench, her head to one side, watching him with bright, cautious expectation. Like she was a pelican and he was cleaning fish.

Scraps. The kid was hungry for scraps of attention. Affection. His throat closed. She deserved more than that from him. From all of them.

He swallowed hard. "Sure. Bring over that can of anti-seize."

He showed her how to put anti-seize on the pins, line up the holes, and snug down the bolts. And then they did the whole thing over again on the other side.

"You've got to pump the lever, see?" He reached around her to demonstrate. Her hair had that little kid smell, a compound of sweat, sunshine, and shampoo that reminded him of Josh's baby years. "To engage the pistons."

She nodded and squeezed the brakes, her little face squinched with concentration, her tongue between her teeth.

"Do you ever actually ride that motorcycle?" Allison

asked from the shed door, her voice rich with amusement.
"Or do you just use it to impress women with your mechanical competence?"

Matt turned his head. Allison stood in the doorway, her big brown eyes warm and alight, so beautiful that for a moment he forgot to breathe. He exhaled slowly. "I thought you had a thing, meeting, after school today."

She nodded. "Student newspaper."

Taylor hopped to her feet. "Hey, Allison."

"Hi, sweetie. The graphics art club needed the computer lab," she said to Matt. "So I dismissed the kids early to work on their individual projects. I told Josh if he and Thalia wanted to work here I'd buy them pizza."

"Thalia Hamilton? The organic farmers' kid?"

"Josh and Thalia are writing an article on optimizing athletic performance through diet."

"Over pizza." He was amused.

Her answering smile revealed her teeth, white and even. "I am not above bribery. Anyway, that's three food groups, dairy, grains, vegetables. Want some pizza?" she asked Taylor.

"Do I have to eat the vegetables?"

"Only in tomato sauce."

"Okay."

"Go see Josh. He'll hook you up." Allison's gaze met Matt's. "If you're done here."

"We put on new brake pads," Taylor said proudly.

"I can see that," Allison said. "They look very . . ."

"Safe," Matt supplied, smiling.

"Thank you. Very safe."

Taylor looked at him from under her cap. "Are we done, Uncle Matt?"

If she were Josh at that age, he'd have ruffled her hair, maybe given her a hug. He tapped the brim of her cap instead. "For now. We'll do the rear brakes next time."

His heart squeezed at the doubtful look in her eyes. What did she think? That he would bail on her? Too many adults in her life had done that.

"Unless you don't want to," he added.

She shook her head so vigorously her cap almost came off.

He smiled at her. "So what's the problem?"

"No problem." Her answering smile, shy and crooked, snagged in his chest like a fishhook. "Can I have pizza now?"

"You bet. You earned it. Good job, kid."

"Thanks." She hopped toward the door.

"Okay if your uncle Matt and I go out for a little while?" Allison asked.

Taylor paused on one foot, looking back. "On the motorcycle?"

"Maybe," Allison said.

"Sure." Another lightning grin. "More pizza for me."

She ran off.

Matt rose slowly to his feet, feeling the pull in his thighs and his shoulders. "I thought you were seeing your parents tonight."

Allison watched Taylor skip up the steps and bang through the back door of the cottage. "We didn't make any firm plans. I can't drop everything on a school night to drive three hours into Wilmington and three hours home. I'm totally free and off the clock. Now you are, too." She turned back to him and smiled, making his blood run hot. "Thalia offered to help Josh babysit."

Matt hooked his thumbs into his jeans pockets. "Why would she do that?"

"Well, if the pizza wasn't sufficient inducement, I'm guessing she wanted to spend time with your son."

His brows rose. "And you figured Josh's love life could use a push."

Her cheeks turned as pink as her shirt. "Actually, I thought ours could."

His brain shifted gear as his blood went from simmer to boil. "You did."

"I've never been on a motorcycle before." She stepped up to him, her breasts almost touching his chest. Her scent, vanilla and spice, punched him in the lungs. "Want to take me for a ride?"

He rested his hands on her hips. "Baby," he promised hoarsely, "I will take you anywhere you want to go."

Her smile bloomed. She looped her arms around his neck, pressing all that soft warmth against him, making his heart pound. "How about my place?"

Heat hazed his brain. But he couldn't just disappear with her for an hour and get naked. He had responsibilities.

He inhaled. "I should probably . . . You sure the kids are okay?"

"*Mm.*" She kissed his neck. "Thalia has four younger brothers and sisters. I think she can keep Taylor in line."

Taylor.

"I talked to her," he said.

"I saw." Her hair tickled his jaw.

"It didn't do any good," he confessed. "She won't tell me what's bothering her, and she doesn't want to see a counselor."

Allison raised her head. "There's more than one way to communicate, Matt. Taylor is obviously coming to trust you. I'd say you're doing fine."

Her approval, her optimism, made him feel good. So did the way she rested her weight against him, her breasts, belly, thighs.

He cleared his throat. "What about Josh?"

Teenagers and an empty house were not a good combination. He'd been a teenager. He knew.

Allison looked him in the eye. "Josh and Thalia are not a couple. Anyway, he's your son. Do you really think he would try something with Taylor right there?"

"No," Matt admitted.

"All right, then. I figure we have almost two hours before dinner. I say we make the most of it."

He could do that. No promises, no commitments, just making the most of whatever time they had.

Even if it was no more than an hour stolen from the rest of his life.

He handed her a helmet and then showed her how to put it on. He jumped the start and flexed his wrist, and the bike roared and rattled to life. Allison slid on behind him, wrapping her arms around his waist.

The afternoon was soft and bright. The air rushed at them, rich with salt and sharp with juniper. The bike thrummed and throbbed, the black road unspooling, the landscape sliding away, as if he were eighteen and free and had everything ahead of him.

He knew the freedom was only an illusion, of course. But it felt good to travel the road with Allison pressed against him, leaning into him on the curves.

ALLISON STRETCHED BETWEEN her sheets, basking in sunshine and contentment, as warm and melty as butter on pancakes, watching Matt step over their discarded clothes on his way to the bathroom.

"Nice butt," she called.

He turned his head, all the lines smoothed from his brow, his smile cracking across his lean, stubbled face, and her breath actually caught, he was so beautiful. What they had shared was beautiful.

Meg was wrong.

Matt did care about her, this was special, she was different from all his other women. He couldn't touch her like that, be with her like this, and not care.

And to hell with all the women in literature and throughout history who had probably told themselves the same thing.

She lay there listening to the sound of running water, shivering a little with longing and regret, because the past hour had been wonderful, nothing in the world was as wonderful as making love with Matt and now, for now, it was over.

He came out of her bathroom, naked, broad and solid and unself-conscious, and she melted some more.

He picked up his jeans.

Oh, well. She sat up.

"You don't have to get up," he said.

She glanced at her bedside clock. Five thirty. "Yeah, I do. I doubt the kids left enough pizza for dinner."

"Meg made a stew. Yesterday, before she left for Greenville. I'll heat some up."

Oh.

Allison plucked at the sheet, mentally regrouping. "Have you talked to her? How's your mom?"

Matt's head disappeared briefly inside his shirt as he tugged it over his head. "Mom's doing good. They removed the chest tube today. As long as her chest cavity stays clear, they should be able to move her to a step-down unit tomorrow."

He sounded distracted. He hadn't yet put on his shoes, but with every word she felt him drawing away, going away from her in his mind.

She struggled to follow. "Does that mean Meg will go back to New York?"

"She has to. She's got stuff to do. Work stuff."

So do you, Allison thought. "I hope she'll take a little time for herself."

"Not much chance of that."

"She mentioned things were busy at the office. But it's not going to help her to pile on more stress. Ultimately, she needs a balanced life. We all do. You, me, everyone."

"You sound like a guidance counselor."

Allison refused to be offended. "Does that bother you?"

"No." He looked away. "Maybe. My family's not some project, Allison."

"Of course not." But she needed to make Matt see that his sister wasn't the only one who needed some time to process her feelings, to regain some balance in her life. She tried again. "I'm just saying it may benefit Meg to get back to her normal routine, but she also needs some space. You know, to deal with everything that's been going on."

Matt sat—not next to Allison on the bed, but in a chair across the room—to pull on his socks.

Okay, so he didn't want to talk about his sister or his feelings or his family's trauma.

Not a problem.

Allison threw back the sheet. "Give me five minutes to shower, and I'll come with you."

His gaze dipped. She flushed as he took her with his eyes, making her feel beautiful. Desired.

He shook his head. "You don't have to. I should hit the road."

Alone? she thought.

"I'll see you later, then," she said brightly. She was not going to indulge in hurt feelings. Matt had a lot on his mind. A lot on his plate. This wasn't about her. "I probably should drive my own car, anyway."

"I mean, you don't have to come over tonight."

A chill chased over her. "What are you talking about?"

He pocketed his keys and wallet. "Like you said, you need to get back to your routines."

Her mouth gaped. "I wasn't talking about me!"

"Yeah?" He shot her a dark, unreadable look. "What was all that talk about needing your own space?"

"That wasn't . . . I didn't . . . What just happened here?"

He scooped his jacket off the floor. Shrugged into it. "I had a good time. I thought you did, too. We both needed the break. But break time's over, and I've got a pile of shit to deal with at home."

He might as well have slapped money on the dresser.

She grabbed the sheet and wrapped it around her, feeling suddenly exposed and angry. Hurt, too. "I am not just a *good time*. I am not somebody you sleep with when you need a fucking break."

He scowled. "I didn't mean it like that. I just meant you don't have to spend every spare minute taking care of me and the kids."

"What else should I do with my time? I'm not one of your summer flings. I'm not here because I need you to show me a good time. I'm here. I'm staying. Don't make this out to be less than what it is. Don't make me out to be less than what I am."

His face darkened with frustration. "Damn it, Allison, I'm not taking advantage of you. Not more than I already have."

"I'm offering to help."

"How much help? For how long? You don't know." He ran his fingers through his thick, sun-streaked hair. "Hell, I don't know. It could be weeks before Mom gets out of rehab. It could be months before things get back to normal. You could be in for way more than you bargained for."

"And you think my help comes with an expiration date? You think I'm suddenly going to turn on you and say, 'Oh, sorry, Matt, I can't do this anymore, it's too much' ?"

His eyes flickered. His face set.

He did, she thought, her heart twisting. That's exactly what he thought. What he was afraid of.

But he said, "No, I don't. You've been great. You've done everything anybody could ask. Hell, you've done things I didn't even know needed doing." His eyes were dark and level. "But I won't let you shortchange yourself or your work because of me."

Her breath deserted her. Her anger died. He was such a good guy, she thought.

Such a dear, good, *pigheaded* guy.

"So, what, you're going to do it all yourself? Take care of your parents and the kids, run the inn and the boat business by yourself?"

His jaw set, mule stubborn. "If I have to."

"That's what I'm trying to tell you. You don't have to. You need help."

"Then I'll hire somebody to cover at the inn. Part time, on the weekends."

She crossed her arms over the sheet. "That's not enough, and you know it. I'm not going to shortchange my students. But I'm not going to stand by and do nothing while you work and worry yourself to death."

He glared, clearly frustrated. "What do you want me to say?"

"I want you to accept my help!"

"That's it?"

"Yes!" she snapped. Their gazes locked, both of them breathing harder. After a long moment, she looked away, muttering, "Well, and it wouldn't kill you to say thank you."

He crossed the room to her. She felt his heat. Stared at his shoes.

His arms came around her gently as he gathered her close, fitting her against him, breast and belly and thighs, two halves of one whole. He pressed a kiss to her hair.

"Thank you," he said softly.

With one finger under her chin, he urged her head up. His eyes were deep and turbulent as the sea. He inhaled once, sharply, and then laid his lips on hers, his kiss gentle, seeking, hungry, taking and giving in equal measure, and she opened her mouth and kissed him back, promising everything, giving him everything.

When he raised his head, she was trembling.

The smallest smile indented one corner of his mouth. "Thank you very much."

"You're welcome." Her voice shook. She cleared her throat. "What are friends for?"

Not the words she longed to say. She was in love with him, the idiot. It would have been nice to tell him so.

But if a simple offer of help made him jumpy, a confession of love would send him running screaming for the hills.

At least he wasn't shutting her out of his life.

At least he hadn't said no.

For a guy as stubbornly independent as Matt Fletcher, she thought hopefully, it was a step in the right direction. A very small step, but a step forward, all the same.

NOW THAT ALLISON had wrung an admission from Matt that he needed her help, she was determined to deliver.

She finished making up the bed in the Anne Bonney room, bundling the dirty sheets into the hall. Most of the inn's guests wouldn't arrive until the next day, Friday. But because of their school schedules, she and Josh had to turn the rooms tonight.

The drone of the vacuum cleaner penetrated the hall. She poked her head into the next room where Josh was working to the beat of his iPod. "I'm done in Bonney."

He pulled out his earbuds. "What?"

"You can do Anne Bonney next."

He flashed her a grin. "She's not really my type."

She rolled her eyes. "Whatever, funny man."

She moved along to the second floor landing, where the

paneled and upholstered window seat provided a view of the water. An old wardrobe housed the coffee and tea service for the upstairs bedrooms.

Allison cushioned two used mugs on top of the dirty laundry, tucked in the depleted thermoses of milk and half-and-half along the sides. As she hefted the basket, the door-bell chimed.

"Josh?"

No answer. He probably couldn't hear over his music and the vacuum. Allison clomped downstairs with her load.

"I've got it!" Taylor dashed through the hall.

Allison rounded the banister as Taylor tugged open the front door. "I'll be right with you," she called over the laundry piled in her arms. "Welcome to Pirates' Rest."

"Allison?" The word vibrated with appalled disbelief.

Her stomach sank. She lowered her basket.

Two people stood on the worn William Morris carpet in the hall, the woman champagne blond and petite, the man tall and handsome with heavy brows and a beak like the Muppets' Sam the Eagle.

Her parents.

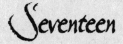

Seventeen

"So I SAID to your father, if Mahatma won't come to the mountain, the mountain simply has to come to Mahatma," Marilyn Carter said to Allison as they entered the restaurant for dinner.

"Mohammed," Allison said. "Not Gandhi."

"What?"

"The mountain comes to Mohammed."

"Don't correct your mother," Richard said.

"Sorry. It was really . . . sweet of you to come."

Marilyn pursed her lips. Coral, to match her dress. "We wanted to surprise you."

Allison smiled feebly. "Well, you certainly did that."

"Your table is ready, Mr. Carter," the black-clad host announced.

Allison had made eight o'clock reservations at Brunswick, the one fine dining establishment on the island. The chef was a local celebrity with two cookbooks and a guest appearance on *Iron Chef* to his credit. The dining room was white linen and exposed brick and lots of glass that opened on lovely vistas of the harbor and garden. It was hard to tell which at night. Discreet candles glinted off massed wine-glasses and precisely ordered flatware.

Allison hoped her parents would be . . . not impressed by her choice. They were never impressed by her choices. But placated, maybe, by the familiar trappings.

She hoped Matt wouldn't hate it.

"How did you know where to find me?" she asked after the waiter had left with their drink orders.

"We didn't," Marilyn said. "That is, we had your address, but Daddy and I were going to check into our hotel before we called you."

"Full up," Richard said with displeasure. "The desk clerk suggested we try the inn. It's not the kind of place we would normally consider staying. Certainly not the kind of place we would expect to find our daughter employed as a maid."

"I'm not employed there, Dad. I'm helping out while Matt's mother is in the hospital."

"Speaking of Matt, when is your young man joining us?" Marilyn asked. "Although I suppose I can't really call him that, can I?"

"Mine?" Allison asked before she thought.

Marilyn's smile sharpened. "Young."

Oh, boy.

Allison wiped her damp palms on her napkin. This evening was not going to be fun. She should have told her parents that Matt couldn't come, he was busy, he was sick, he was out of the country . . .

"He had to put Taylor to bed," she explained. "I'm sure we'll see him soon."

She saw him crossing the dining room, broad and solid in khaki slacks and a perfectly appropriate navy blazer, and felt like a lost crash survivor spotting a rescue plane.

He nodded to her mother, shook hands with her father, smiled into Allison's eyes. "Nice dress."

She looked down at her scoop-necked blue silk dress, chosen, like her earrings and the restaurant, to appease her parents. "Thank you."

He leaned in as he sat down, murmuring, "Remind me to take it off you later."

She grinned at him, suddenly feeling better about everything.

THE DINING ROOM was cool, the atmosphere around the table icy. Matt was glad he'd worn his jacket.

The waiter appeared with the Carters' drink orders. Allison, Matt noticed, stuck to water.

If his parents were like the Carters, he'd want to keep a clear head around them, too. That, or he'd get blind, staggering drunk.

"Hey, Matt. Carolina Pale Ale?"

Matt nodded. "Thanks, Greg."

"I thought I'd order wine for the table," Richard Carter said. "Unless you'd prefer your beer."

Matt let his gaze dip briefly to Richard's Scotch. He was used to rich assholes. As long as they were paying for his boat and his time, he could deal. Since Allison's dad was picking up the tab for this dinner, Matt could deal with him, too.

"Wine is fine," he said.

"We'll start with a bottle of the Cab," Richard said.

He ordered filet, Marilyn fish. Matt scanned the prices and got the pasta.

"You probably eat fish all the time," Marilyn said to Matt. "You must tell me how you get that smell off your hands."

"*Mother*," Allison said.

"It's okay." Matt smiled at Marilyn. "Actually, I have a trick I learned from my grandfather. You cut a lemon and rub your hands with the lemon and some sugar. Takes the smell right out."

"Interesting," Marilyn said.

A silent busboy deposited hard white rolls on each plate with the seriousness of a priest distributing communion. Until he got to Allison.

He grinned. "Looking good, Miss Carter."

Her death grip on her napkin eased. "Thanks, Miguel."

Richard frowned. "You know this young man, Allison?"

"Miguel is in one of my classes. How's the paper coming?" she asked.

The kid shrugged. "Well, you know . . ."

"Due Monday," she reminded him.

"Yeah, yeah."

"We need more water here, I think," Richard said.

Marilyn leaned forward as Miguel returned with the pitcher. "His English is very good," she whispered loudly.

Allison flushed. "Of course it's good, Mom. His family lives here."

Matt squeezed her leg under the table. She clutched his hand like a lifeline.

Their appetizers appeared from the kitchen, shrimp cocktail for Richard and three salads. Matt sat back as Allison's father ran the conversation like a pool hall hustler, small talk cracking and ricocheting around the table. *Aim, shoot, sink.*

When their entrees arrived, the game got serious.

"So, Matt, tell us what it is that you do, exactly," Richard said.

Matt knew the drill. He'd been through it before, with Kimberly's parents. "I'm a fourth-generation fisherman on the island. I inherited one boat from my grandfather, added another a couple of years back. We concentrate on charter sport fishing, with a little commercial fishing in the off-season."

"And that's enough to provide you with a living," Richard said.

"Me and my family," Matt said steadily. "Yes."

"Ah, yes, your family." Richard sipped his wine. "Allison tells us you have a son."

Allison sat up straighter. "Joshua. You met him at check-in, Dad."

"Big boy. He's what, eighteen?"

"Sixteen." Matt drank his water, any appetite he'd had gone. If this was typical Carter mealtime conversation, no wonder Allison hated Sunday dinners.

On the other hand, her parents were only grilling him because they cared about her. Meg had been just as obnoxious.

"So you must be around forty," Richard said.

"Thirty-six," Matt said politely.

"Eleven years older than Allison," Marilyn said.

Allison glared. "Are we going around the table revealing everybody's age, Mom? Because you haven't mentioned yours."

"That's enough," Richard said.

"It certainly is," said Allison.

Marilyn pouted. Well, it could have been the collagen in her lips, but Matt thought she was pouting. "I simply remarked on your age difference, dear. It is rather a lot."

"Really? How old is Johnny Pearson?" Allison asked.

"Doctors are different," Marilyn said. "All that schooling . . . They're really not ready for marriage until they're forty."

"Which explains why he left his wife," Allison said.

"Where did you get your degree, Matt?" Richard asked.

"Matt attended NC State," Allison said.

"But I didn't get my degree," Matt said. "I left my sophomore year to support my family."

"Don't you think that was rather shortsighted?"

"It was the right choice for me and Josh at the time."

"Too bad your parents didn't help you stay in school." Richard waved his knife. "Marilyn and I have always felt it's the parents' responsibility to protect their children from the consequences of poor choices."

Matt set his jaw. "Actually, Mr. Carter . . ."

"Call me Richard."

How about Dick? "Actually, Richard, my parents helped us out quite a lot until I got on my feet."

"So then that's kind of a pattern for you," Richard said. "People helping you out. Your parents. Allison."

"Dad . . ."

"Allison has been more than generous," Matt said.

"For crying out loud," Allison said. "It's not like I'm giving you money out of my trust fund."

"But he's not paying you either, is he?" Richard asked.

"I don't want him to pay me!"

"Our little girl has always liked to volunteer her time," Richard said to Matt. "Of course, she never sticks with any one project for very long."

Matt's head throbbed. He could swallow the implication that he was a loser. A charity project. But Richard's dismissal of Allison stuck in Matt's craw.

"Allison is a great teacher. But she'll be successful at anything she does. She has a big heart and strong principles. She sees what needs doing and she rolls up her sleeves and gets it done."

Marilyn laughed lightly. "Well, we certainly saw her rolling up her sleeves this afternoon."

Allison closed her eyes. In embarrassment, Matt guessed, or pain, and he didn't know which one was worse.

Because he'd been here before. With Kimberly.

The thought was like a dull knife in his chest. He didn't want to be that guy, the guy who wasn't good enough for her family, the guy who screwed up her life.

He'd spent the past sixteen years making sure he wouldn't be that guy again.

Richard reached for his wineglass. "I agree with you. Our little girl has a bright future ahead of her."

"Yes," Matt said.

"But not here," Richard said decisively. "She won't stay here."

Allison sat stiff beside him, her mouth tight. Because she agreed with her father? The knife twisted. Or because she didn't want to get into a fight?

He could make her stay, Matt thought.

He wouldn't even have to knock her up.

All he had to do was appeal to that big heart of hers, take advantage of her need to be needed, and she would stay. For him.

He met Richard's dark, knowing eyes.

"I won't hold her back," Matt said.

"GEE, THAT WAS fun," Allison said as Matt walked her to her car. "Let's not do it again."

Matt didn't laugh, the way she hoped he would.

"Not a chance. I'm pretty sure your parents will be happy never to see me again," he said.

"I'm sorry." She touched his forearm, rigid with muscle. "They were awful."

"No, they weren't. They were being parents."

She sighed, relieved that he was so understanding. "I guess they mean well. They just . . ."

"Want what's best for you," he finished for her. He

stopped and faced her under the lights of the parking lot, his hands stuffed into his pockets. "And they know I'm not it."

Uh-oh. He looked serious. Her heart slammed into her rib cage.

"Is that what you think?" Her voice shook.

He met her gaze. "Yes."

Just that one word, flat, inescapable. Her pulse spurted in panic.

Get a grip, she told herself. He doesn't mean it, you can fix this.

Matt had always seemed so confident, so comfortable, so at ease in his own skin. But a dose of her father could shake anybody's confidence. "Look, I know my parents can be pretty . . . judgmental. But you can't believe everything they said—implied—about you."

"I don't."

She was confused. "You can't think *I* believe it."

He didn't say anything.

"Don't let them define you. They've never been right about me. They're not right about you, either."

"But they're right about this. Us."

"How can you say that?" she demanded. "Why would you think it?"

"Because I've been here before."

She stared at him dumbly.

His shoulders moved under his jacket. "When I was even younger than you. Kimberly . . . She was slumming with me. I was like some college experiment, a relationship that wasn't supposed to go anywhere with a guy who would never amount to much. Somebody as different from her parents as she could find. Somebody they'd never in a thousand years invite to dinner at the club. Maybe if things had had time to play out, she would have seen that, or I would have. But I screwed up."

"You can't blame yourself because she got pregnant. It takes two people to make a baby."

"Yeah. But I made things worse by wanting to marry her. I thought, my kid, my responsibility." He stared out over the dark parking lot. "Her parents warned her if she went through with it, her life as she knew it was pretty much over. But she didn't believe them until it was too late."

Allison crossed her arms to protect herself from the evening chill. "I am not your ex-wife."

"I know that." He looked back at her, his eyes shadowed. His voice deepened. Softened. "You've got so much heart. So much spine. I don't see you ever leaving somebody who loved you. I don't see you ever giving up or walking out, on a promise or a child. You'd stay whatever it cost you, whether staying was the right thing for you or not. Your parents are smart enough to see that. And I'm old enough not to ask you to."

She managed not to flinch. "I'm not asking you for a commitment," she said carefully. *Just don't shut me out. Don't send me away.* "I'm okay with the way things are."

His face was hard as stone. "Maybe you shouldn't be."

"You don't get to decide what's right for me. Any more than my parents do. I want to stay." *I love you.* She swallowed the lump in her throat. "All I need is to know that you . . . want me, too."

"This isn't about what I want."

"Why not?"

"Because I don't get what I want." His voice was flat and factual as a brick wall.

"That's just sad," she said. *Wrong.* "That is the saddest thing I've ever heard."

A muscle bunched in his jaw. "I'm not looking for your pity. I worked damn hard to get where I am. To get what I need. To provide for my kid. That's enough for me."

Was it? Everyone relied on Matt. Everyone expected he

would be there, would stand up for them, would shoulder their burdens without complaint. Without help. She wanted to be the one to share his load, to lighten his life.

Except he didn't want her help.

"What you're saying is, you don't need me."

He was silent.

Oh.

He was silent, and he was breaking her heart.

"*Say something,*" she demanded.

He looked away. "You were the one who said we shouldn't hold onto things. We shouldn't make this out to be anything more than what it is."

Her heart beat fast and hard in her throat. Her mouth was dry. "And what is it? According to you."

Because her definition clearly wasn't working.

Matt looked at her then, his eyes deep and regretful. "I guess it's over."

ALLISON WANTED TO stay home from school on Friday. Call in sick. Take a day off. Her head pounded, her eyes and throat were raw and swollen, and her stomach was upset. Classic crying jag hangover.

But her students needed her, even if Matt didn't. She owed it to them—she owed it to herself—to show up.

She took a deep breath, wrapping up the fourth period class discussion. "So through each of these characters, Hester, Bigger, Conroy, the authors are examining the question, How do we define ourselves? And how are we defined by others?"

The bell rang, releasing them to lunch. Allison looked down at her blotter so she wouldn't have to face the student tide looking as if she'd spent the night bawling her eyes out over Matt Fletcher. Maybe she would spend the period planning at her desk. She really wasn't up to the teachers' lounge today.

"Miss Carter, do you have a minute?" Thalia hovered by her desk, her face flushed, her eyes dangerously bright.

Allison summoned a smile. "Of course, Thalia."

"Hey, Miss Carter." Josh shouldered through the rows of desks like a ship escaping harbor, with confidence and easy grace. He looked like Matt, a younger Matt, a carefree Matt, a Matt who still believed he could have whatever he wanted.

I've been here before . . . When I was even younger than you.

Her heart clutched. "Josh."

"Dad told me to tell you we're good for this weekend."

"Excuse me?"

"He hired Mrs. Lodge to do the cooking-cleaning thing for a couple of days."

Lodge? Her mind fumbled. Cynthie Lodge. The waitress from the Fish House.

She felt actually, physically sick.

"So you don't have to help out," Josh continued with a wide, genuine smile. "He knew you'd want to spend some time with your folks while they were here."

"I . . ." *Message received.* "Thank you," Allison managed.

"No problem." He flashed his lightning grin. "Well . . . I just wanted to let you know. I'll see you around."

No awkward consciousness in his voice, no awareness of adult undercurrents, no wondering why Matt had chosen to communicate through his son instead of calling Allison's cell phone.

"You bet," Allison said.

Josh glanced at Thalia, some of his assurance leaking away. "See ya," he mumbled.

"Whatever," she said coldly.

The tips of his ears reddened as he walked away.

Allison raised her brows. "What was that all about?"

"I went to his house last night," Thalia announced. "To work on the article?"

"Okay," Allison said cautiously.

"And we were sort of joking around, you know? About food enhancing performance."

Oh, boy. "I take it we're not talking about athletic performance," Allison said.

Thalia smirked. "That, too. Anyway, we were eating this pizza, and Josh sprinkled pepper flakes on his slice and made some crack about how they made him hot. So . . ." She took a deep breath, her face pink and defiant behind her large black glasses. "I kissed him."

"Well. Wow." Allison regarded her student, admiring her courage. Worried about the social and emotional risk she was taking. "Did he kiss you back?"

"He did. I mean, he really *kissed* me, Miss Carter. Tongues and everything. It was great."

"Um . . . Congratulations."

"Yeah." Thalia's smile faded. "But afterward he got all weird. And he said he couldn't do this with me."

"This," Allison said, hoping they were still talking about a kiss.

"The boy-girl thing."

Allison sighed in relief and sympathy. "That's tough. Is there . . . someone else?"

"You mean, like Lindsey? No, he . . . he said he just doesn't see me that way."

Ouch. Maybe blindness ran in the family. "I'm sorry."

"Miss Carter, I don't know what to do. I really like him. I thought when we started hanging out . . . He said he liked me. I thought we were *friends.*"

Allison's heart ached for her, so young, so earnest, so hopeful. Memories assaulted her. *We are friends . . . More than friends . . . What are friends for?*

"I'm sorry," she said again. "Did Josh ever say anything to make you think he wanted something more?"

"Like, did he lead me on or anything?" Thalia shook her head. "But I thought . . . I guess maybe I led myself on. You know, convinced myself something else was there."

Allison winced. *Right there with you, girlfriend.*

Not that she would ever share her romantic failures with a student.

"Sometimes wanting something isn't enough," she said. "Sometimes you have to look ahead to getting what you need."

"You sound like my parents," Thalia said in disgust.

I sound like Matt. Allison pushed the thought away. "Are your parents focused on college, too?"

"I meant, quoting the Stones," Thalia said. She sang, "'You can't always get what you wa-ant . . .'"

A grin broke on Allison's face. She'd have to ask Matt if he knew his philosophy of life was based on the writings of Mick Jagger.

Assuming she ever talked to him again.

Thalia regarded her suspiciously. "You aren't going to say something now about how I'm young and I'll get over it?"

"No. I'm going to say that this was a new experience for you. New experiences can hurt. But they're what make you unique. They can change you. Make you stronger."

"Like Hester Prynne."

"Exactly."

They smiled at one another.

Joined in the Sisterhood of Women Rejected by Fletchers, Allison thought.

Thalia sighed. "I will probably get over him. Eventually. I mean, only two years until I go to college."

"There you go," Allison said.

Only seven months left to run in her teaching contract.

As silver linings went, it pretty much sucked.

Eighteen

"WHAT THE FUCK?" His brother's voice crackled through the laptop's speakers as Matt sat at the inn's kitchen table. Even through the jumpy, disintegrating Skype image, Luke's fury came through loud and clear. "You should have told me Mom was in an accident."

Privately, Matt agreed with him. But he'd let their parents overrule his judgment, and now he had to deal with his brother's questions and his wrath. "What were you going to do, Luke? You're thirty hours away. Assuming you could get another leave so soon. Mom didn't want you to know. Dad said you needed to focus on your mission."

"Because when Dad was overseas Mom never told him anything."

"Exactly," Matt said. He watched his brother absorb that before adding, "Just because we've got the technology now to keep in touch doesn't mean we should always use it. How'd you find out, anyway? Meg?"

"I got a MotoMail from Dawn's lawyer." Luke's tone was

clipped and angry, his face carved into sharp angles by the light hanging from the tent pole above.

Apparently lawyers didn't worry about the concentration of combatants in a war zone. "What does she want?"

Luke raked his hand through his short, bleached hair, brushing a swath through the desert dust. "Dawn's parents are claiming that with Mom in the hospital I can no longer provide a stable living environment for their grandchild. They're suing for temporary custody."

Anger stirred, and a deep, defensive protectiveness. "That's bullshit."

"Yeah. But it might be enough to sway a judge. Family court's in two weeks." Luke's eyes met his through the laptop screen. "You've got to be there for me."

"I'll be there," Matt vowed. *Back to back to back.*

"Thanks." Luke's fingers drummed on the table. "How is she?"

"Mom? She's good. They're moving her to a step-down unit."

"Yeah, you said. That's good." Luke nodded a couple of times, apparently unable to sit still. Or maybe it was the twitching internet image that made it seem that way. "I meant Taylor."

"You talked to her," Matt said. He'd made sure of that, giving Taylor the first precious minutes of the video visit before chasing her outside so that he and Luke could talk. "She's fine." Allison's words replayed in his mind. *It doesn't help her to ignore her wounds.* "She's adjusting," he amended.

"You'll take care of her." It was a statement, not a question.

"You know I will."

Something moved against the back wall of the tent, just outside of Matt's line of vision. Luke turned his head. "I've got to go."

"Right." Matt cleared his throat. "You keep yourself safe over there. Taylor's counting on you to come home."

Matt sat in the quiet of the kitchen, listening to the tick of the clock and the hum of the refrigerator, feeling drained. Empty. It had been three days since he'd told Allison they were through. Three days of listening for the sound of her voice and her footsteps, of missing her smiles and her comfort, of storing up things to tell her only to realize that she wasn't going to be there at the end of the day, he wasn't going to see her again unless he scheduled a damn parent-teacher conference or stalked her in the aisles of the grocery store. Three nights of rolling over and not feeling her warmth, of staring at the ceiling and not hearing her breath, of waking up hard and lonely and alone.

He missed her with a deep, physical ache. Telling himself that he'd done the right thing for both of them didn't ease the pain.

But Allison deserved the chance to live her life without the burden of someone else's baggage. In time, she'd thank him. She'd find another man. A younger man.

Some nameless, faceless fuck with a shiny future and an uncluttered past who was free to follow his heart. Who could help her follow her dreams.

Matt took a deep breath, his hands clenched on the table.

He heard a sound, a scrape, and looked up. Taylor was standing right outside the kitchen door, her face obscured by the screen.

"Hey, kid." He dredged up a smile from somewhere, deliberately relaxed his grip. "How long have you been there?"

"I won't go."

He dragged his mind back from the depths. "What?"

"To Grandma Jolene's. I won't go back."

"Whoa, there. Hang on."

"If you try to make me, I'll run away."

Oh, Christ. "I said, *hang on*. Nobody's making you do anything."

"I *heard* you. Talking. My . . . Luke said Grandma Jo wants custody. That means I have to go live with them again."

"It doesn't mean anything. Nobody's going anywhere yet." Matt looked at her through the screen, four feet tall, strung so tight she vibrated like a fishing line from a screaming reel. He gentled his tone. "Come here."

She shifted her weight on the doorstep.

"Come on. I'm not talking to you through the door."

Taylor slipped inside.

Thank God. He pushed out the chair beside him with one foot. She sat with a wary glance at him.

Matt scrubbed his face with one hand, choosing his words, arranging his thoughts. He'd always been careful not to criticize Kimberly to their son. He didn't want to turn Taylor away from her grandparents, either.

"Here's the deal," he said. "The Simpsons—your grandparents—love you. And yeah, they want you to live with them. But your mom, she wanted you to live with your dad. And he asked us to take care of you while he's away."

"Grandma Tess said I could stay."

"She wants you to stay. And I want you to stay. We all do. We love you," Matt said firmly, so there could be no doubt. "So I'm asking. What do you want?"

Taylor's gaze was flat and too adult. "I'm a kid. It doesn't matter what I want."

Recognition jolted through Matt. *I don't get what I want*, he'd said to Allison.

That is the saddest thing I've ever heard.

"It matters," he said. "To me, to Grandma Tess and Grandpa Tom, maybe even to a judge. But you have to tell us what it is."

"I want to stay," she whispered.

Matt nodded once, short and decisive. "Then you'll stay."

Her eyes met his, glistening with hope and a desperate longing to believe. "They won't listen to me."

He swallowed the lump in his own throat. "We'll make them listen. We'll get our own lawyer. We'll do whatever it takes."

Taylor's lower lip quivered. The hope welled and spilled over as tears. Turning in her chair, she buried her face against Matt's arm and let out one quick sob.

The breath Matt had been holding whistled out. He put his arm carefully, gently around her and held her as she cried.

And she did not turn away.

MATT FORCED HIS constricted throat muscles to swallow. "You look good," he told his mother.

Tess smiled at him affectionately from her bed in the intensive care step-down unit. "Liar."

She looked gray and thin and frail, her color leached by the fluorescent lights and the god-awful blue and white hospital gown. A clear, narrow tube still provided her with oxygen.

Tom reached through the metal rails of the bed to hold his wife's hand, the one that wasn't hooked up to monitors. "Last time he saw you, you were breathing through a machine and covered in plaster. You look great, babe."

Matt came to her bedside, leaning in awkwardly to kiss her cheek. She smelled different, an astringent, hospital smell.

But her eyes were the same, warm, searching. "How are you, Matt?"

Miserable. There was a sick hollow inside him that no amount of work could fill, a restlessness the ocean could not calm, an emptiness that would not go away.

"I'm fine," he said. "You're the one we're all worried about. How are you doing?"

Tess's brow puckered. "I'm bored with me. Is it the kids? Are they all right?"

"Everybody's fine." He made himself smile, forced himself to focus on the stuff that mattered, the things he could do something about. "Josh drove your new car up here."

Tess's smile bloomed. "Josh came with you?"

"Josh and Taylor. They're in the waiting room. The nurse okayed her to come on back, but I wanted to see you myself first."

"I don't want to scare her," Tess said.

"She'll be more worried if she doesn't get to see you," Matt said.

"Is she still having nightmares?"

"Mom, I told you, the kids are fine. Both of them."

"Is Allison with them?"

Matt tensed. *Hell.* His mother liked Allison, liked the thought of him paired up and moving on with his life. He did not want to upset his mother. *Visits should be brief, quiet, and pleasant*, the guidelines for visitors said.

"No." He cleared his throat, prepared to lie. "She couldn't get away. Her parents paid her a surprise visit this weekend."

"That must be nice," Tess said, still watching his face. Whatever else had broken in the crash, her mother's instincts had clearly survived without a scratch. "You be sure to thank her for the books. And the lovely card."

Allison had sent his mom books?

Of course she did. She was thoughtful that way, generous in body and heart.

"I'll tell her," he said.

It's over, he'd said. That didn't mean he'd never see her again. That she wouldn't speak to him. Did it?

"Did you get a chance to meet them?" Tess asked.

"Who?"

"Her parents."

They were checking out tomorrow. He could hardly wait.

"Babe," Tom said. "The kids are waiting."

"Oh." Tess blinked, looking momentarily lost. Confused. Old, Matt thought, his heart lurching.

"I'll get them," he said.

"No." Tess's voice strengthened. "I don't want to be in bed when they see me."

"Mom, it's okay. They know you're . . ."

"Recovering," Tess said firmly. "Which will be a lot easier for them to accept if I'm sitting in a chair like a normal person."

Tom scowled. "The doctor told you not to overdo it."

"The doctor also said I am making wonderful progress, and that the more I move around the less chance I have of developing blood clots. So." She pinned him with the *Don't-mess-with-me-mister* look that had kept them all in line for as long as Matt could remember. "You better call a nurse and get me to a chair."

Matt watched, helpless, as his father and the nurse maneuvered, braced, and supported Tess in stages from lying to sitting to standing.

She froze, rigid with pain and effort.

Tom held out his arms and smiled into her eyes. "You and me, babe," his father said. "Like dancing."

Matt's eyes stung.

He remembered once—he must have been seven or eight—watching his parents get ready to leave for some function on the base, his dad, tall and formal in his dress blues, his mom, unfamiliar in a dress that glittered and clung. The look of pride on his father's face, the secret shining in his mother's eyes. The same look they wore now, as if they were the only two people in the room, in the world. Matt had felt, well, weird seeing them that way for the first time, two grown-ups, two strangers, two characters in a story, as if he and his sister and brother were only spectators, minor participants in their parents' fairy tale.

It still felt weird. Weird and good.

"Thatta girl," his father said. "I've got you."

And his mother stepped forward.

Matt's muscles clenched in sympathy as she battled her way across the linoleum, one step, two.

"Easy," said the nurse.

Three steps. Four.

By the time Tess lowered, panting, onto her chair, a trickle of sweat ran down the small of Matt's back. She closed her eyes.

"Good job," Tom said.

"Oh, please," Tess said. But she was smiling.

"NICE CAR," TOM said as he and Matt stood in the parking lot. The kids were in the lobby, grabbing snacks from the vending machines for the long ride home. "You done good, son."

Matt moved his shoulders, unaccustomed to his father's praise. "No problem. I changed the oil and the fluids, checked the belts and tires. She's good to go."

"Polished her up some, too," Tom said. "You must have been up all night."

Another shrug. The truth was, Matt had slept less in the past three nights than when he'd been dividing his time between two beds. He'd jerk awake at two in the morning, craving the curve of her neck, the small of her back, the smell of her hair. Or lie, stiff and lonely, in the dark, waiting for his alarm to go off.

Better to stay up with the car, to do something physical, tangible, right.

"How's Allison?" Tom asked.

Matt set his jaw. "She's fine."

They stood together, shoulder to shoulder, staring at the white and glass façade of the hospital.

"Appreciate you bringing the car," Tom said.

"Maybe now you've got your own transportation, you'll actually grab some sleep at the motel."

Tom grunted. "I don't like to leave her alone. You think I'd be used to it, all those years overseas. But I don't sleep so well without your mother."

Right there with you, Dad.

"How much longer is she in for?"

"Barring complications, the doctor says maybe a couple of weeks. They've got a rehab program here to teach her how to get on."

"Weeks," Matt repeated. They stretched ahead of him, echoing and empty. "That's a long time to be away from home."

Tom grunted. "I am home."

Matt glanced at him sideways.

Tom's eyes twinkled. "It's okay, son. I'm not losing it. You know she grew up in Chicago. Your mother. All the Saltonis, all in one neighborhood, the same church, the same schools, the same friends. Then she marries me, and we're moving all over, living on bases in enlisted housing, never a place to call her own."

"I remember," Matt said.

"I know you do. Your sister, Meg, she loved it, a new school, a fresh start every year. Luke, he doesn't remember much about it. He was eight when we bought Pirates' Rest. But you and your mother, you liked to put down roots. The moving was harder for you. I said to her once early on I was sorry I couldn't give her a home like she had growing up.

"And your mother, she says to me . . ." Tom blinked. Cleared his throat. "Your mother says, 'Wherever you are is home, Tom. Anything else is just a house to put it in.'"

Matt squinted at the hospital building because, Jesus, if he looked at his dad he'd start bawling like a baby. "Mom's going to be okay," he said. "Everything's going to be okay."

Tom sniffed mightily. "Isn't that what I've just been telling you? Your mother's been looking after us all her life. Me. You kids. It's time for me to take care of her now, that's all. As long as I've got her, everything else will work itself out."

"Thanks, Dad," Matt said.

He remembered the way he'd felt with Allison, the way she made everything better at the end of the day.

As long as I've got her . . .

Except he didn't have her anymore. And that was his own damn fault.

TAYLOR SAT ON the curb outside the high school building after school on Monday, waiting for Josh.

She was totally old enough to walk home by herself. But when Uncle Matt decided he was right about something, he was stubborner than a donkey, as Mom would say.

Taylor swallowed the familiar lump in her throat when she thought of Mom. Things were better now that she knew she could stay on the island. Uncle Matt said so—*Whatever it takes*, he'd said—and she believed him. She didn't want to go back to Grandma Jolene's. But she missed her school and she missed her friends and even though Fezzik was the best dog ever, she still missed Snowball. It sucked being the new kid, especially at a school where everybody had known everybody else since forever. And this weekend had felt all mixed up, no Allison and no Aunt Meg and talking or not really talking to her dad—to Luke—on the computer and then crying all over Uncle Matt before they piled into the truck and drove to the hospital to see Grandma.

Taylor stared at her sneakers until the laces blurred, feeling tears behind her eyes. That had been the worst, seeing Grandma Tess in the hospital.

Like Mom.

What if Grandma died like Mom?

Taylor swallowed again, hard, but it didn't stop the tears from burning the back of her throat. It was like once she started leaking she couldn't stop.

Some of the girls from Taylor's class came by, Rachel Wilson and Madison Lodge, walking with Rachel's big brother, Ethan. Josh's friend.

Taylor tugged down the brim of her hat so they wouldn't see her sniveling.

Madison was okay. Her mom had helped out at the inn this weekend. Mrs. Lodge's cookies weren't very good and the way she tied up her shirt to show her stomach when she thought Uncle Matt might be looking was kind of gross. *Call me Cynthie*, she said. As if Taylor would. But she wasn't mean. Madison wasn't mean, either.

Rachel was mean.

"Hey, Taylor," Madison said as they walked along the curb.

Rachel sniffed. "Why are you talking to her? She's a stupid dingbatter."

Taylor raised her head. "Fuck off, Rachel."

Ethan laughed.

Rachel's eyes widened. "You can't talk to me that way. Nice girls don't talk that way."

"Guess you talk like that all the time, then," Taylor said. There was a certain wretched satisfaction in baiting Rachel, who was pretty and popular with long, dark hair that her mother French-braided every morning. "Since you're not nice."

"At least I'm a girl." Rachel smiled, going in for the kill. "At least I don't dress like a boy in a stupid baseball jersey and a stupid army hat."

Red hazed Taylor's vision. She jumped to her feet, fists bunching at her sides. "Take it back."

Rachel tossed her head, the French braid switching from side to side. "Why should I? You do dress like a boy. Everybody says so."

"Hey, Rache, take it easy," said her brother.

"Does everybody say you're a bitch, too?" Taylor asked.

"At least I'm not a boy," Rachel said.

Taylor couldn't stand it. She couldn't breathe. Rage and misery balled together in her chest, squeezing her lungs.

"Come on, Rachel, leave the kid alone. Maybe she doesn't dress like a girl because she lost her mom."

Rachel sneered. "She probably died of shame."

It was the last straw.

With a howl of grief and fury, Taylor flung herself at Rachel.

Only Rachel's brother stepped in the way, and she tripped over his feet. She went down, pain exploding in her knees, ripping across her palms.

Rachel tittered as Taylor swayed on hands and knees on the ground.

"Shit," Ethan muttered. "Chill, would you? Both of you."

He tripped her. Taylor lurched to her feet in a welter of blood and snot and tears and punched him as hard as she could in the stomach.

His breath whooshed out. *"Oof."*

Rachel screamed.

"Hey." Warm, strong hands. Warm, calm voice. *Joshua*, grabbing her shoulders, pulling her back. "Knock it off."

Taylor almost sobbed in relief.

Madison hopped from foot to foot. "Here comes Miz Nelson."

The vice principal.

"Shit," Ethan said again.

"I'm gonna tell," Rachel said.

Joshua threw her a hard look. "What? That your brother got beat up by a little girl?"

Josh's scorn withered Rachel as nothing else could have done. Josh was one of the lucky few, the golden ones who sauntered through the halls of Virginia Dare a head taller than their other, lesser, pimpled peers. Taylor clutched his arm, clinging to his protection, her head spinning, the pain in her knees almost blinding.

"Okay, man?" Josh asked Ethan.

Ethan nodded, red-faced and admiring. "Sure, Josh."

"Cool. Come on," Josh said to Taylor. "We got to get you outta here."

Nineteen

ALLISON DROVE TO the Pirates' Rest to say good-bye to her parents. They were leaving.

And not a moment too soon, Allison told herself. If her parents hadn't shown up, she would still be with Matt. She wouldn't even be thinking of updating her resume, considering another move.

She passed through the center of town, charmed as always by the mix of new and old, bright kayaks standing up beside lichened gravestones, flower planters spilling under stunted oaks, pleasure boats floating as sleek and white as gulls on the timeless waters of the harbor. Like the Outer Banks themselves, the population of the island was shifting. Renewing itself.

Was she really considering moving on? *Running away.*

She didn't know if she belonged here, but she wanted to find out. She wanted to stay. With or without her parents' blessing. With or without Matt.

It was her life. Her choice.

Two figures trudged along the sandy shoulder of the road, one tall and broad-shouldered, one short with an uneven gait. Allison slowed the car, her heart thumping as she recognized the tall one's tawny mop, the Marine cap tugged over the short one's head. Joshua and Taylor.

Allison frowned. Was Taylor limping?

She steered wide and pulled in front of them, coasting to a stop by the side of the road. Unrolling her window, she leaned out. "Are you guys all right?"

Taylor raised her head.

Tears, Allison thought. She got out of the car.

"It's okay, Miss Carter." Josh dropped a hand on Taylor's shoulder, supporting or restraining her. "We're fine."

Allison looked at Taylor. *Oh, God, her knees.*

"It is not okay. She's not fine." Allison crouched to inspect the damage, a fierce maternal instinct roaring to life inside her. Taylor's jeans were split across, her knees crusted with dirt and blood. "Oh, sweetie."

Taylor's chin wobbled.

Allison turned over the girl's palms. Scraped and raw. "Okay, that's it." Allison stood. "Get in the car."

Josh hesitated. "We're pretty dirty."

Bloody.

"Don't worry. Leather cleans," Allison said briskly. "In the car. Now."

She expected Josh to call shotgun, but he settled in to the backseat with Taylor. She watched the girl nudge him with her shoulder, saw his big hand drop casually on her head, giving her a quick rub like a dog.

She lost another little piece of her heart to both of them.

"So what happened?" she asked as she pulled on to the road.

She saw the quick glance they exchanged in the rearview mirror, and her Teacher's Spidey Sense went on alert.

"She tripped," Joshua said.

"Really. Who tripped her?"

They drew a little closer together in the backseat, a united wall of Fletcher silence.

Allison sighed. Did she really want to interfere with that lovely family bond? "You do know fighting is against school rules."

"So's bullying," Josh said.

Allison was shocked at her rush of protective anger. "Did somebody bully you?" she asked Taylor.

"It's cool," Josh said. "We handled it."

Allison sought Taylor's gaze in the mirror. "Taylor?"

A stiff nod.

"Okay. Well, if you need help hiding the bodies let me know," Allison said, deliberately teasing, carefully light, and was rewarded when Taylor smiled.

HER PARENTS' CAR was still parked in front of the inn. Matt's truck was missing from its usual spot out back.

"Where's your dad?" Allison asked.

"I think he had a charter," Josh said.

Allison tried hard to feel relieved instead of disappointed. She wanted to see Matt, but she wasn't sure she could face him. She didn't need him to thank her for taking care of Taylor.

She focused on Taylor. After the girl had changed into a pair of basketball shorts—carefully, because of her scrapes—Allison sat her down at the kitchen table and gently sponged the embedded dirt and gravel from her knees.

Taylor hissed.

Fezzik whined and thrust his head against her hand.

"You're doing great," Allison said.

The dog's ears perked as sounds penetrated from the hall. *Scrape thump, scrape thump* down the stairs.

"Really, I don't understand why these people don't put in an elevator," Marilyn's voice complained.

Her parents. Allison stiffened. She'd completely forgotten them.

"You don't put an elevator in an old Craftsman house like this," Richard said. "A competent bellboy would do."

Josh stood. "I'll go help them."

"They're fine." Allison raised her voice. "Mom, Dad? I'm in the kitchen."

"Allison!" Her mother came through the doorway, radiating Chanel and disapproval. "What are you doing here?"

"I told you I'd stop by."

"Not here at the inn. Here." Her mother waved her hand. "In the kitchen. Working."

"I'm not working, Mom. Taylor had a little accident."

Her mother stepped forward to squint at Taylor's knees. "Good heavens." Marilyn turned pale. "Is she all right?"

Allison gave Taylor's foot a reassuring squeeze. "She's going to be fine."

"Well, put a Band-Aid on her or something. You don't want that to get infected."

Allison smiled. "Thanks. I'll take care of it."

"Good." Her mother blinked. "Why are you the one taking care of her? Where is her father?"

"He's in Afghanistan," Taylor said.

"She means Dad," Josh said.

"Mom, we're fine. I've got this."

Marilyn's brow puckered despite the Botox. "The children are his responsibility, not yours. We just don't want to see you taken advantage of."

"It's okay. I want to help."

Richard stared at her broodingly. "That's what you always say. One of these days, little girl, you'll learn you can't solve the whole world's problems."

Allison regarded her parents with love and exasperation.

All of her life, she'd told herself that they weren't bad

people. A little selfish, a little self-absorbed, a little controlling, maybe, but not bad.

But for the first time, she understood them. Because when she was with Josh and Taylor, she felt the same need to intervene, to manage, to protect.

The difference was she wasn't a little girl anymore.

"Joshua," she said quietly, "take my parents' bags to their car, will you? They have a plane to catch."

"You could come with us," Marilyn said. "Just for a drink at the airport. There's time."

"Thanks, but I don't think so. I'm needed here."

"You're only doing this for that man," her mother said. Josh stopped dead in the doorway. Oblivious, Marilyn continued, "When you come to your senses—"

"I'm doing this for me," Allison said. "I love you, Mom and Dad, but this is my life now. My choice. My home."

As soon as she said the words, she felt an incredible lightness, as if a burden had evaporated from her shoulders. The sudden relief made her dizzy.

Buoyed by the rightness of her decision, she got to her feet. Kissed her parents' cheeks. "Have a safe trip. Call me when you get to Philadelphia."

Marilyn wavered. "Well, really, I . . ."

"Come on, Marilyn." Richard surprised Allison with a brief, hard hug. "Allison's right. We'll miss our flight."

They left.

Allison nodded to Josh. He went into the hall to grab her mother's bag. She heard the front door open and close, open and close, and Josh's footsteps returning in the hall. When he came back into the kitchen, she was almost finished bandaging Taylor's knees.

"Thanks, Miss Carter."

"Yeah, thanks."

"It's Allison," she told them. She patted Taylor's shoulder as she rose again to her feet and then, unable to help herself, kissed the top of her head. "Why didn't you guys come to find me in the first place? Back at school."

Josh shrugged.

"We're not supposed to bother you," Taylor said.

Something lit inside Allison, a flare of indignation, a burning coal of resolve. "You are not a bother. You come get me anytime. You can call me anytime."

Josh nodded, unimpressed.

"What if you're not there?" Taylor asked.

Allison looked at Joshua, narrowing her eyes.

"Dad said you might be leaving," he said, his voice flat, his face expressionless.

The way his mother had left.

And Taylor's.

Allison sucked in her breath. Her head pounded. Her tongue felt weighted. This was important; she had to get this right. She couldn't overstep or lead them on. She had no official connection to these children other than her role as Joshua's teacher. All she could offer them was her love. And her honesty.

"I don't want to leave. And I'd never go without telling you."

Lame, she thought. They deserved better.

She tried again. "I'm here now. For as long as you need me." The back door opened behind her, but in her struggle to do the right thing, to say the right words, she barely noticed. "Even if you don't need me, I'm here."

Josh's gaze flicked beyond her. His eyes widened.

"We need you," Matt said quietly.

She whirled, her heart leaping into her throat.

Matt stood in the open kitchen door, shaved and showered and holding a giant pot in foiled paper, spilling pink ruffled blooms and glossy dark leaves.

She swallowed hard. "How much did you hear?"

"Not enough." He strolled forward, a warm, deep glow

in his dark blue eyes. "That's okay. I have some things I need to say to you first."

Josh grinned. "Come on," he said to Taylor. "They don't need us."

Matt didn't take his eyes from Allison. "Yeah, we do. Just not at the moment. I have things to say," he repeated.

But when the kids were gone, he didn't seem in any hurry to speak.

She waited, trembling on the edge of hope. Afraid to jump.

He set the pot on the kitchen counter.

"That's beautiful," she said to fill the silence. "For your mother?"

"It's a camellia. For you."

She melted. "Oh."

"I didn't want to give you cut flowers." He raked his fingers through his hair. Shoved both hands in his pockets. "Because of the poem."

It was so *not* what she was expecting him to say that she gaped. "What poem?"

"The tattoo one. I looked it up online."

The sunlight slanting through the kitchen windows fired the yellow hearts of the flowers to flame. Understanding unfurled in her heart. Not flowers that had been picked, but living blooms.

Tough, terse, taciturn fisherman Matt Fletcher had bought her a plant. Was Googling poetry. Because of her.

She beamed. "That is quite possibly the most romantic thing I ever heard."

"I can do better. I want to do better. For you." He cleared his throat. "In the poem, that guy's up on the hill alone. But at the end of the day, he looks down and sees the lights go on."

She trembled, overcome that he'd read and remembered. "Matt . . ."

"He sees the light," Matt repeated, looking directly into her eyes. "And that's how he finds his way home. You are my light, Allison. My reason to come off the mountain. My home."

A flood of joy rose inside her, lifting her to the summit. She couldn't speak or breathe.

He took her hands between both of his. Strong, steady hands. Working man's hands. "I gave you the plant to . . . hell, to ask you to put down roots, I guess. To stay with us. To grow with me."

"Yes," she said.

Matt drew back to study her face. "Yes?"

"Yes, I love you. Yes, I'll marry you." She closed her eyes. "Please tell me that's what you were asking."

His laughter shook them both. He swept her into his arms, his mouth finding and taking hers. "*Yes*. Marry me, Allison."

They kissed a long time.

"I can't leave Dare Island," he told her eventually. "Not now, maybe not for a couple of years. I have responsibilities here, the kids, my parents. I don't know if it's fair to ask you to wait that long, to take me on, to take all of us on. But God knows I love you. I need you. As long as I've got you, we can work everything else out."

Her life was changing around her, full of light and life and joy. Her future stretched before her, bright and limitless as the sea.

"I want to stay," she said honestly. "I love my job, I love the island. I love you, Matt. I want to make my home with you, wherever you are."

He looked back at her, his lazy smile lighting his eyes with love. "You are my home," he said. "My parents taught me that. Everything else is just a house."

Turn the page for a special preview of

Carolina Girl

Meg Fletcher returns to Dare Island
and faces her past—as well as her future.

Coming in 2013 from Berkley Sensation

AT THIRTY-FOUR, MEGAN Fletcher was determined not to turn into her mother.

She settled behind her desk on the forty-seventh floor, stowing her Louis Vuitton bag away in the bottom right-hand drawer. Aside from her piled inbox, the gleaming surface was almost bare, every file in order, every pen in place. She rubbed absently at a fingerprint. Maybe she had inherited Tess Fletcher's compulsive tidiness, Meg admitted to herself. But image was important. An uncluttered workspace was a sign of an organized mind.

She set her BlackBerry within reach. She'd deliberately kept her schedule free to deal with the long to-do list that had accumulated in her absence.

Her mother made lists, too, stuck on the refrigerator or scrawled by the phone. But while her mother spent her days making beds and baking cookies, readying guest rooms and running errands, Meg oversaw a department of thirty people and an advertising budget of seventy-four million dollars.

Meg slipped off her Vera Wang snakeskin pumps, surreptitiously wiggling her toes under her desk.

It was good to be back.

She surveyed her domain with satisfaction: the tasteful artwork chosen by a design firm, the waxy green plants watered and replaced as needed by a plant service, the sliver of Manhattan skyline visible through her window. Her private conference room, accessible through glass pocket doors.

Back in charge. Back in control.

Four weeks ago, her brother had called with the devastating news that their mother had been badly injured in a car accident.

Their dad had retired from the Marines twenty years ago, but in a crisis, the Fletchers still functioned as a military family. *Back to back to back.*

Despite Franklin Life's recent acquisition of Parnassus Insurance—making this absolutely the *worst* time for Meg to be away, Derek had pointed out—Meg had dropped everything to rush home to North Carolina. She'd thrown herself into the details of her mother's care, quizzing doctors, advocating with nurses, spending nights at the hospital so their father could snatch a few hours' sleep at a nearby motel.

Thank God for Derek. Derek Chapman, the company's tall, blond, ambitious chief financial officer, had kept Meg in the loop. He wasn't only a member of the transition team; he was the man Meg loved. She believed him when he told her this acquisition was good for the company and good for them. A larger organization meant more responsibilities, more opportunities, and more money.

But even from six hundred miles away, Meg had felt the tremors of the merger move through the company like aftershocks. From her mother's hospital room, with its lousy cell phone coverage and crappy internet connection, she'd done her best to cope with press inquiries and her staff's jitters.

Now that she was back, it was her job to handle the necessary layoffs as humanely and discreetly as possible, out of view of the media.

Friday afternoon, she thought, docking her laptop. Any announcements of future personnel cuts should go out at the end of the week, the end of the news cycle.

She powered up her Keurig and her laptop at the same time, intending to review the latest joint press release from her counterpart at Parnassus while her coffee brewed. But when she attempted to log on to the company network, an error message popped onscreen. Incorrect password.

Irritation flickered. Her password had worked fine all weekend. And this morning.

Frowning, she tried again. Same result. It just figured that on her first day back the system would go wonky.

She picked up her phone. Dead.

Dammit. She didn't have time for this crap.

Barefoot, she padded across her office and stuck her head out the door. "Tracy, can you please give IS a call? My computer and my phone are all screwed up."

"Will do," her assistant said cheerfully. "And Stan just called. He wants to see you."

Stanley Parks, the chief operating officer. Meg's boss. "What time?" she asked.

"As soon as you're free, he said. He's in the conference room now. He sounded really stressed out."

Meg's adrenaline surged. Another crisis brewing. Another opportunity to shine. This is what she did, what she lived for.

She slipped on her pumps and strode down the hall like a batter approaching the plate, muscles loose, brain focused. It felt good to be back in the game.

* * *

FIRED.

Meg stared blindly out the cab window at the gray blur of Manhattan rumbling by, her personal possessions in a cardboard box on the seat beside her.

"Forced to let you go," Stan had said, not quite meeting her eyes. The familiar, falsely reassuring phrases thumped into her like stones.

Until an hour ago, when she'd still held the power of hiring and firing, before she'd been escorted to the street and deposited on the curb like so much garbage, she'd been the one to use those same words herself. *"Eliminating redundant positions across the board,"* she'd written in press releases. *"Human Resources will assist you with the transition process,"* she'd said kindly, passing the tissue box across her desk.

She had always prided herself on handling such situations compassionately and professionally. *"I understand you feel that way,"* she had murmured, secure in her job, her record, her stringent standards of performance.

Betrayal seared her throat like bile. She hadn't understood at all.

The words didn't matter. The tone didn't change a thing.

She'd been dumped. Sacked. Axed.

She wanted to throw up.

Tomorrow she would make a list. Make a plan. But now she wanted to crawl off like a wounded animal, to curl into a fetal ball in the closet and suck her kneecaps. Maybe huddled in the dark beside her untouched golf clubs and unused tennis racket, she could begin to sort through the hot mess of her emotions. The ruins of her career.

She had worked for Franklin Insurance since her graduation from Harvard, earning her MBA from Columbia at night, steadily rising through the ranks, every grade, every performance review, every promotion another rung on her personal ladder of success. *Never look down, never look back.*

Until she'd walked into that conference room and saw Judi Green from HR sitting with a stone-faced Stan, Meg had never suspected that her own job could be in jeopardy.

That she could be considered replaceable. Dispensable.

"This acquisition shook things up for all of us." Stan had frowned down at the folder open in front of him. *"Your absence at such a critical time for the organization was . . . noticed."*

The unfairness of it hit her like a slap. Heat whipped her face. *"Stan, my mother was in the hospital. I was in touch with you every day. You told me to go. You told me everything would be fine."*

Derek had told her everything would be fine, too.

Derek.

The smell of the cab assaulted her nostrils. Her stomach churned.

He must not know. He would have stopped this. Despite his position on the transition team, the other officers must have kept it from him. And if Derek wasn't in the loop . . .

She moistened her lips, sick at heart, frightened for him. What if Derek had been blindsided, too?

For the past six years, their corporate fortunes had been hitched together. *"We make a good team,"* he'd said the first time he asked her out at a company retreat in Arizona.

She'd been flattered. Derek was perfect for her new life; intelligent, ambitious, career-focused.

After they returned to the city, it had become routine for them to spend Wednesday and Saturday nights together. With Derek, she never had to make excuses for working late or explain why she was too tired for sex. Soon she had a toothbrush at his place, closet space, a drawer. She had measured the progress of their relationship the same way she'd tracked the rise of her career. In increments.

Two years after Derek had been named chief financial

officer, three months after Meg's promotion to vice president of marketing, Derek had suggested they buy the condo together.

What would they do now, if they both lost their jobs?

She needed to know that he was all right. That *they* were all right. Instinctively, she reached for her BlackBerry.

It was gone.

She stared at the empty pocket, a pit opening in the center of her chest. Her electronic lifeline had been stripped from her along with her company laptop and corporate credit card, her ID badge and office key. She clenched her empty hand into a fist.

"Fifteen dollars and seventy cents," the taxi driver said.

She looked up. The cab was double-parked outside the discreet limestone façade of her Central Park West address.

She fumbled for a bill—a twenty—and thrust it through the glass divider. Almost a thirty percent tip. Now that she was unemployed, she ought to curtail her expenses, she thought with the part of her brain that continued to function. Set a budget. Live within her means.

She climbed out of the cab, dragging the box across the seat. All the years of working, of scraping, of getting by, rose like a bad smell from the gutter to haunt her.

She took a deep breath, willing her stomach to settle.

She was hardly destitute. Her severance package included a year's salary and health insurance. But the down payment on the condo—an investment in her future with Derek, she'd told herself at the time—had taken most of her savings. She could be out of a job for months.

The doorman sprang forward to take the cardboard carton from her arms.

Meg clutched the box tighter, all she had left of twelve years with the company; her two framed diplomas and a photograph of her family, her makeup bag, an extra pair of shoes.

No pictures of Derek. Their relationship didn't violate

company protocol. She reported to Stan, not Derek. But even though they were generally acknowledged as a couple, Derek didn't feel it was appropriate to advertise their liaison at the office.

"I've got it. Thanks, Luis."

The doorman frowned, a solid, graying man in his sixties, round in the middle like a whiskey barrel. Luis had been at the building longer than she had. He might have to put up with rain and rude residents, but at least he had job security. "Let me give you a hand to your apartment."

She forced her numb lips to curve into a smile. "No, no, I'm okay."

His warm brown eyes narrowed in concern. "You sure? No offense, but you don't look so good."

A remark like that to another tenant could have gotten him in trouble. But Luis knew Meg, knew she had worked her way through college waiting tables and scrubbing toilets.

"*You don't need to share all the details of your personal life with the doorman, darling,*" Derek had chided.

But Luis had a grandson, Meg had a brother, in Afghanistan. It made a bond.

She opened her mouth and felt, to her horror, tears clog her throat.

"You sick?" Luis asked. "That why you came home early?"

"Yes." Shame flushed her face like a fever. But what else could she say? Oh, God, what would she tell her family? "Yes, I had to . . . leave work."

"I'll get the elevator for you," Luis said.

She was too exhausted to argue. She followed him down the hall to the elevators.

The third-floor, two-bedroom apartment she shared with Derek didn't provide the Central Park view he had wanted. But the space had still cost more than Meg could comfortably afford. Despite Derek's larger salary, she had insisted on their splitting expenses right down the middle.

Her parents had not approved of the condo or, she sometimes thought, of Derek. They could not understand why, after six years together, she and Derek didn't simply get married.

Meg had dismissed her family's concerns. She didn't need a ring to establish her worth or validate her relationship. The joint investment in the condo was another step, another sign that her life and career were proceeding according to plan.

She swallowed hard. Or they had been until an hour ago.

She let herself into the empty apartment. Leaning back against the closed door, she closed her eyes. The living room had the chilled hush of a funeral parlor. The surrounding units were quiet, everyone at work. No scraping furniture penetrated into the apartment, no footsteps, no chattering TVs, only the muted sounds of traffic drifting from the street.

What was she supposed to do with herself in the middle of the day? What was she going to do?

She took off her shoes, her jacket, her earrings, divesting herself of her corporate armor piece by piece. Without it she felt naked. Vulnerable.

She wandered through the apartment like a sleepwalker, her limbs weighted by lethargy, her body infected by an odd, internal restlessness.

She couldn't eat. Couldn't text or call or go online. They'd never bothered to pay for a landline or personal computer. Why should they? The company provided everything. Now, even if she'd had her BlackBerry, her phone and email contacts, her personal network, were all wiped out when IS had disabled her account.

No wonder her password had failed that morning.

She stopped at the window, staring down at people flowing by like twigs pushed along by a current: envoys from office buildings moving purposefully along the sidewalks, mothers pushing strollers on their way to the park, tourists wandering arm-in-arm, stopping to point or to kiss. Everyone had somewhere to go, someone to be with, while she stood alone, apart, removed from all of them.

Where was Derek?

He didn't come at lunchtime. She was relieved. As long as he was at the office, he still had a job.

But he wasn't home at five o'clock.

Or at six.

Or at seven.

She understood why he didn't call. She didn't have a phone. She didn't want to leave the apartment to buy one. What if Derek showed up while she was out? She didn't know any of their neighbors well enough to go knocking on doors. What could she say? *"Hi, I've lost my job and I can't reach my boyfriend, may I use your phone?"* She shuddered. That would be a hell of an introduction.

She paced the thick, mushroom-colored carpet. Her inactivity, her isolation, her helplessness drove her crazy. How could Derek do this to her? He must know she was waiting. He must have heard that she'd been . . . Her mind recoiled from the word *fired*. She'd been let go.

She didn't get it.

She'd worked hard to make herself indispensable. Admired. She was everybody's pick for classroom games, college study groups, task forces at work. Even Derek had asked her out. Everybody wanted her.

Her mind flashed back eighteen years. *Almost everybody.*

She bit her lip. She didn't think about that anymore. She didn't care about that anymore. About him.

But it was discouraging to realize how quickly she'd tumbled to the needy, weepy teen she had once been. She flung herself onto the couch.

By eight o'clock, she was shaking with fear and a hot, defensive anger. Derek still wasn't home. What if something had happened to him? Her mother, after all, had recently been the victim of a drunk driver. Didn't he care about her feelings at all?

At nine o'clock, a key scraped in the lock.

She jumped to her feet, bubbling over with worry, relief, and resentment. "Where have you been?"

Derek stopped inside the door, his blond hair shining in the yellow light of the hall, his face shadowed. "Putting out fires."

He sounded tired.

She crossed her arms against her chest. "With what? Scotch?"

"I had to go out with the team after work. You know how it is." He stretched his neck, rolled his shoulders. "Christ, what a day."

She did know. He was under stress, too, she reminded herself. "Are you all right?"

He slid out of his jacket. Shot her a look. "What do you think?"

She didn't know what to think. He hadn't told her anything yet. "I was worried about you."

He nodded as he crossed to the dry bar, accepting her concern as his due.

She waited for him to reciprocate with questions. Sympathy. She didn't expect him to coddle her. That wasn't their way. But surely he would say something. When he didn't, she prompted him. "I suppose you heard about my day."

He poured himself two fingers of Laphroaig. A calculated amount, suggesting restraint and appreciation at the same time. He would have had the same at the bar. Derek never did anything—even drink—without calculating its effect. "Hell, yes. That's all anybody wanted to talk about. I had a bitch of a time getting them to focus on the significant aspects of the acquisition."

Ice trickled down her spine. Frosted her voice. "You don't consider my firing significant?"

The bottle cracked against the rim of his glass. "Of

course it's significant. I just meant I had a lot on my plate this afternoon." He set the bottle down and crossed the room, cupping her jaw in his capable, familiar hands. "It was hell for me, not being able to talk to you."

His breath was warm against her face. Meg closed her eyes. It was hell for her, too.

Derek's scent enveloped her, his wilted shirt, the smokiness of Scotch, the cool, expensive tang of his cologne. "I wish you had come home," she said, hating the admission, detesting the needy, uncertain tone of her voice.

"I wanted to," he said. "I thought you'd appreciate some time to yourself."

She opened her eyes. "Twelve hours?"

He released her face. "It wasn't that long."

She wasn't going to argue over minutes. "You said we were partners, Derek. We're a team. I needed you to have my back today, and you weren't here."

His brows twitched together in annoyance. "I have your back."

"I just got fired!" With an effort, she modulated her voice. She was going to be reasonable if it killed her. "You're on the transition team. You could have fought for me. You at least could have warned me."

"You know I couldn't do that. I can't show any favoritism. I have to act in the best interests of the company."

"What about my interests? Or don't they matter anymore?"

"Of course you matter. Have you considered that this could be the best thing that could happen to you? To us."

Meg gritted her teeth. "What the hell are you talking about?"

"Look, there was always going to be a certain awkwardness as long as we were with the same company. Now there's nothing holding us back. Personally or professionally." He smiled at her, charming for a finance guy, and unease moved in her bones.

"Nothing except *I'm out of a job.*"

His lips tightened. "There's no need to raise your voice, Meg. People are losing their jobs all over. It's this economy."

"The economy didn't fire me."

"My point is, you can find another job. This could be the opportunity we need to figure out what we really want. Where we're going."

"We know where we're going. Or I thought I did." One rung, one step at a time. *Never look down, never look back.* "I thought we were getting there together."

"We are together. All the time. All we ever talk about is work. This is our chance to expand our horizons. Examine our priorities."

Easy for him to say. He had a job.

"Forgive me if I don't feel very high on your list of priorities at the moment." She sounded bitter. Well, she felt bitter. *Twelve hours.*

He examined her face. Set down his drink. "I know this is hard for you. This transition has been a strain on both of us. But I'm up to my ears right now. I can't afford to get caught up in some personal drama. I have to keep my head in the game."

She drew back, stung. "I'm not asking you to stay home and hold my hand all day. I'm just saying I could use a little emotional support."

He drew in his breath, the way he did when she was being difficult. "Maybe you should think about getting away for a while. Going home."

She stared at him in disbelief. She *was* home. "I just got back. I need to stay." *I need to fight.* "I need to look for another job."

"Sure," Derek said. "But it wouldn't hurt for you to step back and get a little perspective first."

She had to work to keep her voice even. "Are you saying you don't want me around?"

"Of course not." His breath escaped in a long-suffering sigh. "My job's on the line, too, you know. You can't get upset because I don't have the luxury of giving you the attention you deserve right now."

Her jaw ached. Probably because she was clenching it so hard.

"Fine." She would not cling. She refused to whine. Even at sixteen, she'd had too much pride to beg. She took a deep breath and said, "My mother's in rehab." *Relearning to walk and stand and dress herself.* "Maybe I'll go back down for a couple of weeks to help out. That would certainly provide us with perspective," Meg added, unable to keep the bitterness from creeping back into her voice.

She waited, her blood drumming in her ears, for Derek to ask her to reconsider. To plead with her to stay.

He smiled, clearly relieved. "That's a great idea. I know how close you are to your family."

It went against her nature to bite her tongue. But she was no longer the heartbroken, weepy, deluded adolescent she'd been in high school. She didn't need Derek to fix her problems. She didn't want his pity. She wanted him to . . . What?

Hold her. Want her, she supposed.

Which was ridiculous. Of course he wanted her. They'd just bought a condo together.

So she forced herself to nod and listen as he told her about his day. As if a recitation of his schedule could somehow fill the void inside her chest.

First thing in the morning she was buying a computer to check airfares to North Carolina.

THE BAGGAGE CAROUSEL clacked in time to the headache pulsing behind Meg's eyeballs.

Her flight from LaGuardia had been delayed forty-seven minutes, making her miss her connection, stranding her in Charlotte for almost two hours.

She stood in the Jacksonville baggage claim, watching

the same six damn suitcases sidle through the rubber curtain and circle the conveyor belt. *Clack, clack, clack.*

None of them was hers.

She adjusted her stance, arches aching in her three-inch heels, and dug for her new phone. With one eye on the moving belt, she checked the display screen.

Nothing.

Her stomach dropped. Maybe Matt was on his way. Or maybe her brother hadn't gotten her text explaining she was late. But then wouldn't he be here, waiting for her? Wouldn't he have called?

Unless he hadn't noticed the change in her phone number. She hadn't confided in him about her firing over the phone. It was still too recent. Too raw. Maybe her brother was leaving messages on her defunct office voice mail.

She winced. If Matt didn't turn up, if he didn't call back soon, she'd have to rent a car to drive the hour and a half from the airport to Dare Island.

The carousel wheezed. Bags and machinery thumped. The passengers around her pressed forward as the first bags from her flight rattled into sight and toppled onto the belt. A young mother in jeans and flip-flops retrieved an infant seat. A Marine hoisted his duffel bag. A sleek red Tumi suitcase slid through the curtain, looking as out of place in this one-runway town as Meg felt.

At last.

Meg stooped for her bag, only to be easily shouldered aside by a large, warm, male someone at her back.

A long arm reached around her. A strong hand—tanned, long fingered—grasped the handle of her suitcase.

She recognized his hand before she saw his face.

Knew his voice in the pit of her stomach, in the telltale leap of her stupid heart, before she registered his words.

"I've got this," Sam Grady said, and plucked her bag from the belt.